Phoebe was at th   upper shelf, presumably to get one of the large serving bowls. She'd pulled up a small step stool to compensate for her short stature and was currently balanced precariously atop it on her tiptoes. A disaster waiting to happen if he ever saw one.

"Here, let me get that," he said, crossing the room quickly.

She started at the sound of his voice and turned her head toward him. It overset her balance, and she frantically waved her arms in an attempt to maintain her footing.

Sprinting the last few feet, Seth was able to get to her in time. Grasping her by the waist he steadied her and then set her feet on the floor. "Are you okay?"

She looked up at him, her gold-flecked brown eyes wide, her lips parted in surprise. Then she answered his question with a nod.

"*Gut.*" He released her and reached up to the top shelf, where he pointed to a large blue bowl. "Is this what you were trying to get?"

Again Phoebe nodded.

Why did she look so stricken? Had she been startled so deeply? Perhaps he'd spoken more harshly than he'd intended.

Seth handed her the bowl and she seemed to finally recover some of her composure.

"*Danke.*" Then she lifted her chin. "I wasn't clumsy, you know. You just startled me." There was a note of defensiveness in her tone.

"My apologies. And I never said you were clumsy."

Her cheeks pinkened. "*Nee*, of course not."

An Amish Christmas Match

Winnie Griggs

FOREVER
New York   Boston

Copyright © 2024 by Winnie Griggs

Cover design by Daniela Medina. Cover illustration by Kriss Keller. Cover copyright © 2024 by Hachette Book Group, Inc.

Forever
Hachette Book Group
1290 Avenue of the Americas, New York, NY 10104
read-forever.com
@readforeverpub

First Edition: September 2024

Forever is an imprint of Grand Central Publishing. The Forever name and logo are registered trademarks of Hachette Book Group, Inc.

The publisher is not responsible for websites (or their content) that are not owned by the publisher.

The Hachette Speakers Bureau provides a wide range of authors for speaking events. To find out more, go to hachettespeakersbureau.com or email HachetteSpeakers@hbgusa.com.

Forever books may be purchased in bulk for business, educational, or promotional use. For information, please contact your local bookseller or the Hachette Book Group Special Markets Department at special.markets@hbgusa.com.

Library of Congress Cataloging-in-Publication Data
Names: Griggs, Winnie, author.
Title: An Amish Christmas match / Winnie Griggs.
Description: First Edition. | New York : Forever, 2024.
Identifiers: LCCN 2024005264 | ISBN 9781538766378 (mass market) | ISBN 9781538766385 (ebook)
Subjects: LCSH: Amish—Fiction. | LCGFT: Christian fiction. | Romance fiction. | Novels.
Classification: LCC PS3607.R55264 A84 2024 | DDC 813/.6—dc23/eng/20240207
LC record available at https://lccn.loc.gov/2024005264

ISBNs: 9781538766378 (mass market), 9781538766385 (ebook)

Printed in the United States of America

BVGM

10 9 8 7 6 5 4 3 2

To my husband, who is my very best friend and biggest supporter—thank you for your patience and belief in me.

To Connor and Renee—thank you for always being there to answer my calls for brainstorming help and for being squarely in my corner, no matter what.

You all make my life richer in more ways than you will ever know.

An Amish
Christmas
Match

Chapter 1

Phoebe Kropf rubbed the sleep from her eyes and yawned, feeling the crisp air from this last day of November seeping through the windows of her small bedroom. It was still dark outside, but she could tell by glancing at the clock that she'd overslept. *Mamm* and Rhoda would already be up and busy in the kitchen. With a determined sigh, she swung her legs out of bed and stretched.

She crossed the room to fetch her clothes, ignoring the chill from the cool floorboards on her bare feet. As she dressed, Phoebe whispered a little prayer.

Gotte, *I know I for sure and for certain messed up on Thanksgiving Day, making a mess when I dropped* Mamm's *sweet potato and marshmallow casserole all over the floor. But I haven't spilled or broken anything in the days since then—and for that I am truly grateful. Please help me to remember to move with deliberation, to not anticipate or improvise, to always follow* Mamm's *and* Rhoda's *lead. And to not get jealous or rattled when I see*

Mamm *share the handwritten recipes, some from her own* mamm, *with Rhoda. I want to be helpful the way a woman of twenty-one should be and to please my* eldre.

As she adjusted the strings on her *kapp*, Phoebe smiled at her latest origami creation sitting on her dresser. The prancing horse with one leg slightly raised and the knee bent was the picture of grace and strength. If only she could be like that.

Shaking off those thoughts and ready to face whatever the day would bring, Phoebe made her way downstairs, smiling at the familiar creak of the third and eighth treads. When she nearly lost her footing on the bottom stair, though, she reminded herself of her earlier vow to move with deliberation rather than haste.

She entered the kitchen to find *Mamm* and Rhoda already bustling about, preparing breakfast. Inhaling the comforting aroma of freshly brewed coffee, she allowed the warmth from the oven and stovetop to chase the chill from her bones.

"*Gut matin*," she greeted as she grabbed a worn apron from the hook near the door. "I'm sorry I overslept."

Mamm's face softened in an indulgent smile. "It's all right, *liebchen*, Rhoda and I are taking care of getting breakfast ready."

It had been two weeks since the wedding and Phoebe was becoming accustomed to seeing Rhoda as a member of the household. What was harder to get used to was how much *Mamm* had come to rely on Paul's new wife and how well the two of them worked together.

It was wrong to be jealous, and she was working hard to overcome those feelings. It should have been easy since she and Rhoda had been scholars together for eight years. But somehow it wasn't.

Determinedly pushing away those thoughts, she offered a bright smile. "I'm here now so I can help. I see the eggs aren't out. I'll fetch them and get to whisking."

As she finished tying the apron around her waist Phoebe noted the look that passed between her *mamm* and Rhoda. Was it because she was late or because they didn't trust her with the eggs?

"I was just about to ask Rhoda to take care of that," *Mamm* said. "Why don't you set the table instead?"

Rhoda cast her a look that was a strange mix of apology and sympathy as she wiped her hands on her apron and moved toward the refrigerator.

She supposed that answered her question—*Mamm* clearly didn't trust her to handle the eggs and Rhoda didn't entirely disagree. Sure, she'd tripped in the chicken yard a week ago and dropped an entire pail of eggs. But it wasn't her fault a hen had gotten underfoot. And *Mamm* knew it was only when she was in a hurry, or nervous or excited, that she was so clumsy.

Deciding she would remain positive, Phoebe nodded and moved to the sideboard to collect the dishes and silverware.

Counting out five plates, she placed them on the table without incident, then did the same with the flatware and glasses. That done, Phoebe pulled out the butter, blackberry jam and apple butter and put them on the center of the table.

There. She'd accomplished her assigned task without mishap. What else could she do?

Phoebe looked around the kitchen and noted the fresh-baked loaf of bread sitting on the counter. Since *Mamm* and Rhoda seemed to have their hands full she'd just take care of slicing it herself. Humming, Phoebe grabbed a large knife and began cutting the bread into nice thick slices, just like her *daed* and *bruder* liked.

"Phoebe!" Her *mamm's* sharp cry startled Phoebe and her hand slipped, tracing a thin red line on the side of her hand.

Mamm rushed over and took Phoebe's bleeding hand in her own. "*Ach du lieva.* What were you thinking? I've told you to let me or Rhoda handle the sharp knives."

She wanted to shout that she wasn't a child and that she wouldn't have cut herself if she hadn't been startled. But that wouldn't prove to anyone that she was an adult—only actions could do that. "I'm sorry. It was just a bread knife."

Mamm tsked. "There's no 'just' when you talk about sharp implements." Then her expression softened. "You know I only want to keep you safe, don't you?"

"*Jah.*" But why did it always feel like she was being punished? True, she was somewhat accident-prone, and she'd had trouble with her studies all through her schooling and still could barely read. But why couldn't *Mamm* see she wasn't a *kinner* anymore? In fact, she was old enough to have a *mann* and home of her own. Rhoda was proof of that.

Perhaps it was having Rhoda take her place in their home. Perhaps it was just restlessness. But lately she'd begun to chafe more and more under the way she was always treated as if she needed help with all but the most basic of tasks.

Mamm finished examining the cut and patted Phoebe's hand. "It looks like a shallow cut, and it's already stopped bleeding. Run a little water on it and let me and Rhoda finish getting breakfast ready."

Phoebe nodded, noting that Rhoda had already quietly stepped in and finished slicing the bread.

Just then, the kitchen door swung open and her *daed* entered, fresh from the barn, closely followed by her *bruder* Paul, Rhoda's husband. As the pair shed their coats and boots, setting them by the door, *Daed* inhaled appreciatively. "*Ach*, these smells alone are enough to warm a man's insides." Then he spotted Phoebe and his expression drew down in concern. "*Dochder*, have you hurt yourself?"

He didn't say *again*, but the word hung on the air, as if it were understood.

"It's nothing." Phoebe forced a cheerful tone. "Just a shallow cut."

Daed crossed the room and placed a gentle hand on Phoebe's shoulder. "We know you're trying, Phoebe. Just remember, everyone has their strengths. Yours may lie elsewhere."

Phoebe nodded, appreciating his words of encouragement. But why couldn't she be more like *Mamm* and Rhoda?

Like every other girl of her acquaintance?

She saw the warm smile exchanged between Rhoda and Paul across the room and felt an ache deep inside. Would she ever find that for herself?

As *Daed* and Paul washed their hands, Phoebe couldn't shake the feelings of inadequacy and frustration that gnawed at her. Would she ever be able to prove to her family that they didn't have to treat her like a *kinner*?

Her family loved her, of that she had no doubt. Her four *brieder* had always been protective and were indulgent, even when they teased her. Part of that was because she was the only girl. But it was also because she was the *boppli* of the family. It had been thought that after Paul, her mother couldn't have any additional children, so Phoebe's appearance five years later was a welcome surprise.

She just wished she could have lived up to their expectations for her.

When everyone was finally seated and they bowed their heads for a moment of silent prayer, she again asked for the patience to be deliberate in her actions and accepting of the role her family—and *Gotte*—expected her to play.

The talk around the table centered mostly on Honey, one of the cows who might or might not be slowing down her milk production, and the possible causes.

After the meal, Phoebe pushed away from the table. "I believe it's my turn to wash the dishes."

Mamm tapped her chin. "But your hand. Perhaps you should let me—"

"My hand is fine, and you and Rhoda took care of preparing breakfast. I can take care of the dishes." She saw the startled looks on the faces around the table and winced. She'd not only spoken firmly but she'd also interrupted her *mamm*.

Before she could offer an apology, though, *Mamm* nodded. "Very well, you wash the dishes. I'll dry and Rhoda can clear the table."

Happy with the small victory, Phoebe went to the counter to fill the sink.

She enjoyed working side by side with *Mamm*, making small talk about the day's chores, the neighbors' new *boppli* and what they would cook for lunch. She didn't even mind that *Mamm* was ready to grab each dish almost before she could rinse it.

Just as they finished, Paul reentered the kitchen headed for the basement. Then he paused for a moment. "Phoebe, I almost forgot, Edna called a little while ago. She says she needs to speak to you and will call back at nine o'clock."

Daed and Paul operated a harness repair business from the farm so they had a phone in the work shed for business purposes.

Phoebe stiffened. Was something wrong? Though Edna always seemed spry and full of life, she was older than *Mamm* and *Daed*. And she was like a *grossmammi* to her. "Did she say what it was about?"

"*Nee.*" He shrugged. "But she didn't seem upset so I don't think it's bad news."

Phoebe relaxed.

Still, what could have prompted Edna to call her?

* * *

Phoebe was in the workshop, standing by the phone, a full ten minutes before nine o'clock just in case Edna called early. She paced back and forth in front of the work-table where the phone rested. The familiar earthy smell of leather and the musky scent of mink oil tickled her nose. *Daed* and Paul were on the other side of the workshop, giving her enough distance for a bit of privacy. But she could feel the occasional sideways glances they were giving her. No doubt they were as curious about her phone call as she was.

Four years ago she'd moved in with Edna and her husband, Ivan, for a few months to help out as Ivan lay on his sickbed, preparing for the end of his time on earth. She and Edna had grown very close that summer, sharing hopes, dreams and fears through those long, hushed days of vigil.

Edna had never made Phoebe feel inadequate or clumsy, not then and not at any time since. Truth to tell, she'd had Phoebe take care of many housekeeping and cooking tasks on her own. She'd made it clear that she didn't believe Phoebe's difficulties with reading and writing meant she was simple-minded, especially since, by Edna's reckoning at least, she seemed competent in other aspects of her life. And strangely enough, Phoebe never felt particularly slow-witted when she was in Edna's company.

Edna had left Bergamot three weeks ago for an extended visit to family she had in Sweetbrier Creek, a community about ninety miles away, and Phoebe missed her dearly.

When the phone finally rang Phoebe jumped and then pounced, almost knocking the phone from the table. The heat climbed in her cheeks as she caught the raised-brow look *Daed* sent her way.

"Hello?" Her voice sounded breathless even to her own ears.

"Phoebe, it's so *gut* to hear your voice."

"And yours too." And it was. Edna's voice was familiar, warm and comforting, just like a soft-from-use quilt on a chilly winter's day. "How are you enjoying the visit with your *shveshtra*?"

"It's been *gut* seeing everyone and catching up with what's happened in their lives. But I'm actually staying in the *dawdi haus* of one of my niece's sons. There are six Beiler *brieder*, ages twelve to twenty-nine, living alone without parents or any womenfolk to help them, so I've been keeping house for them for the past few weeks."

Phoebe smiled. She imagined with Edna's no-nonsense approach she'd gotten that household of untamed menfolk in order in no time at all.

"That's actually why I've called you."

Phoebe's smile faded. "I don't understand."

"I had a little accident last *nacht*." At Phoebe's excla-mation she hurried to explain. "It's nothing serious, but I won't be able to use my right hand for five or six weeks and these boys truly need someone to help them out."

What did that have to do with her? But before she could ask, Edna answered her unspoken question. "I think you would be the perfect person to take on the job."

Chapter 2

Phoebe straightened. Surely she hadn't heard that right. "Me? But there must be some family member, or at least someone who lives closer, who would be better."

"There are no cousins or close relatives available right now without placing a burden on them, and *nee*, I actually don't think there would be anyone who would be a better fit."

That seemed a strange thing to say. "Still, I imagine there are any number of girls who could serve as housekeeper, especially under your supervision."

"True. But these *brieder* need more than a housekeeper. They need someone who knows how to care for them in other ways. Seth, the oldest, has his hands full keeping the farm running, working on his side business, and trying to be a *daed* to the others. The next two *brieder* live at home but have jobs outside the farm. The middle boy is on *rumspringa* and is apprenticing with a local furniture maker. The two youngest are still in school."

"Sounds like a busy household. But I still don't understand—"

"Seth is doing the best job he can, but these *brieder*, especially the younger ones, need someone to mother them, they need someone who'll understand how much to discipline, how much to teach and how much to let them be boys. And you are perfect for that."

Phoebe wasn't sure she agreed with her friend on that point—she couldn't even convince her own *mamm* that she was capable. But rather than argue the point she moved on. "Even so, Sweetbrier Creek is a long way from Bergamot and Christmas will be here soon. I don't see how I could go."

"*Ach*, think of it as an adventure. I know what your life is like. How would you like to spend some time in a place where no one knows anything about you and has no set expectations?"

That gave Phoebe pause. What *would* that be like?

"Besides," Edna added, "it would give us a chance to spend some time together. The *dawdi haus* has an extra bedroom."

Phoebe was beginning to warm up to the idea. "I'd like some time to think about it if that's okay. And I'd need to discuss it with *Mamm* and *Daed*."

"Of course. Is one day enough? I can call you tomorrow at the same time."

"We're celebrating my *bruder* Michael's birthday at his home tomorrow. Monday would be better."

"Then Monday it will be. But Phoebe, remember this. Of course you have a duty to respect and honor your *eldre*, but you are a young woman of twenty-one with a *gut* head on your shoulders, and you can make decisions for yourself." And before Phoebe could argue the point with her, Edna hung up.

Phoebe slowly lowered the handset of the phone, her mind whirling with thoughts of Edna's unexpected request. Should she do it?

"Is Edna well?"

Daed's question interrupted her thoughts. "*Jah.*" Then she caught herself. "I mean, *nee.* She hurt her arm yesterday. But she said it's not serious."

"And for that she had to make a phone call to you?"

"Actually, she asked me to help her with something. But I'd like to talk to both you and *Mamm* about it together."

Daed's brow drew down in question, but he merely nodded. "Then we will speak of it at the lunch table today." And with that he went back to work.

Phoebe appreciated that he didn't press her. She donned her coat and left the work shed, but didn't return to the house immediately. Instead she headed down the drive to fetch the mail, one of her regular tasks. As she walked, she felt a little spark of excitement. The thought of being part of a new household where no one knew her or her history stirred a sense of adventure within her. Should she do it? *Could* she do it?

She'd reached the mailbox by then and gathered up what appeared to be two sales flyers, a magazine of some sort, and four white envelopes. Without bothering to study the pieces closer she turned and headed back toward the house.

What would her *eldre* think about her accepting a job so far away?

* * *

Phoebe scooped up a small portion of mashed potatoes and then passed the bowl to Paul, seated on her left. The knot in her stomach had pulled too tight for her to be able to eat much.

Unbidden, a memory from her childhood returned to her. At the end of her first-grade year she'd been frustrated and upset seeing her classmates begin to read and yet the words on the page made no sense to her. When this continued into second grade *Mamm* had insisted that she was such a clever girl, all she needed to do was focus. She'd worked with her every evening, but the more *Mamm* worked with her and the more she'd desperately tried to please *Mamm*, the more the words and letters twisted and danced on the page, mocking her efforts to make sense of them. She could still recall with absolute clarity the moment her *mamm's* demeanor had changed from determination to defeat, from teacher to acceptance that her *dochder* would likely never be able to read. When *Mamm* had told her they didn't need to work on her reading any longer, that instead she would focus on teaching her how to be a *gut* homemaker, Phoebe had understood just what that meant. She'd cried herself to sleep that *nacht*.

Daed spoke again, pulling her thoughts back to the present. "So *dochder*, what did Edna ask of you that you need to discuss with me and your *mamm*?"

Phoebe took a deep breath. "A few weeks ago Edna took on the job of housekeeper for some relatives, a group of young men, the six Beiler *brieder* who apparently need a lot of help."

"*Ach*, I knew Edna couldn't just sit back and visit for very long." *Mamm* had an indulgent smile on her face.

Phoebe smiled back, then continued. "Edna hurt her arm yesterday and won't be able to keep house for them very well for the next several weeks."

"*Ach*, poor dear. I hope she's not in much pain."

"She says she feels fine, she just can't do much with only her left hand. Which is where I come in." Again, Phoebe breathed deeply. "She'd like me to go to Sweetbrier Creek and help out until she's able to resume her work."

Mamm paused with her fork halfway to her lips, her brow raised almost to her hairline. "What? That's ridiculous. You told her you couldn't go, didn't you?"

Why was it ridiculous? "I told her I'd need to think about it and also talk to you both before I decide."

Mamm's unbending posture softened ever so slightly. Was that an element of concern beneath her stern refusal? Would *Mamm* ever see her as a capable adult rather than a child to be cosseted?

"A wise response." *Daed's* words brought her attention back to him. "What is it you want to do?" His tone and expression were measured, giving little of his thoughts away.

"Turn her down, of course," was *Mamm's* quick, predictable response. There was no doubt about the concern in her expression now.

"Actually, I think I'd like to go. Edna needs the help or she wouldn't have asked." She shot a quick look *Mamm's* way. "And she'll be there so it's not as if I'd be entirely on my own."

"And where would you live while you're there?" *Daed* had set his utensils down and was stroking his beard, something he did when he was thinking through a problem of some sort.

"Edna lives in the Beilers' *dawdi haus* and she says there's room for me to move in there with her. It would only be for five or six weeks."

"But that means you'd be gone over Christmas." *Mamm's* lips remained set in a stubborn line but again

Phoebe thought she detected a note of pleading underlying her tone. "I think it best you tell Edna to find someone else."

Was that really the reason? Or did *Mamm* think she couldn't handle such a responsibility? "I can always make it a condition that I come back home for a couple of days at Christmas."

"But—"

"I think that's a reasonable compromise."

At the interruption, *Mamm's* gaze turned to meet *Daed's* and Phoebe watched as something unspoken passed between them. Then *Mamm* sat back and focused on her plate, her expression unreadable. Paul and Rhoda wisely kept silent but they also exchanged glances.

Daed turned back to her. "Tell me about these six *brieder.*"

Did that mean he wasn't going to try to talk her out of it? "The two youngest are still in school. The oldest has been trying to care for all of them himself." She lifted her chin. "I don't know much more but I trust Edna when she says I can do what is needed to help them."

Phoebe focused on her *daed*, but from the corner of her eye she saw *Mamm's* hand tighten on her fork.

To her relief, *Daed* nodded. "Edna has a sensible head on her shoulders."

Afraid to get her hopes up just yet, Phoebe turned to her *mamm* and braced herself.

But to her surprise *Mamm* nodded. "If this is really something you want to do, then of course you should give it a try." Then she met Phoebe's gaze. "But remember, if you feel the need to return home before the time is up, then I'm sure Edna will understand."

Daed cleared his throat, reclaiming Phoebe's attention.

"If you feel called to help this *familye* of *brieder*, then you may go with our blessings." He pointed his spoon at her. "And this could be a *wunderbaar* opportunity for you. A chance to see if you're ready for a home of your own."

A home of her own. Phoebe sat up straighter as her resolve strengthened. "I think so too." She would do this and when she returned they could no longer treat her like a *kinner* but rather as the full-grown woman she was.

Daed was right about it being an opportunity but perhaps not in the way he meant. It was a chance to break free from the low expectations of her *familye* and friends and to embark on an adventure in a new setting with people who didn't know anything about her difficulty with the basic skills of reading and writing, not to mention the clumsiness that plagued her whenever she got nervous or flustered.

Later, as Phoebe helped clear the table, not even the seamless way Rhoda and *Mamm* worked around her could steal her smile. Accepting Edna's offer to join her in Sweetbrier Creek felt like something big, something that would mark a milestone in her life and maybe, just maybe, give her a chance to find her own path.

Chapter 3

Seth Beiler quickened his pace as he headed toward the house from the equipment shed. He was late for breakfast but since Mark was in charge of cooking their morning meal he didn't feel particularly eager. He usually cooked breakfast during those times when there was no house-keeper available, but Edna had encouraged him to let his *brieder* take more responsibility, under her supervision. He'd only agreed because he was behind on the orders for his side business, making hand-carved chess sets. And after the problems they'd had with last year's crops his *familye* could really use the extra income these brought in.

Edna's injury was most definitely a setback for them. He'd thought he'd have until after Christmas before he needed to find a more permanent solution to their need for a housekeeper, and by then he'd have the bulk of his orders for chess sets fulfilled.

They'd had the worst luck keeping housekeepers the past few years. Two had gotten married and moved away.

A third had decided to move in with her newly widowed *shveshtah* and help with the *kinner*.

And now this.

Despite not particularly looking forward to whatever meal Mark had prepared, Seth picked up the pace. He'd always been insistent that he and his *brieder* have breakfast together, and as the oldest it was his place to set a good example.

He grimaced at that thought. Sometimes he hated being the oldest, the responsible one, the surrogate *daed* to his *brieder*. But it was the role circumstances and *Gotte* had assigned him, and who was he to complain?

Even before Seth opened the side door he could hear the sounds of horseplay inside. Edna, *Mamm's shveshtah* who was serving as their housekeeper for the time being and was living in the *dawdi haus*, had told him she would rest and not to expect to see her for a day or two. After yesterday's disaster with the near-fire Levi had caused in the kitchen he hoped she would be ready to rejoin them soon. Even if she couldn't actually work with her injured hand, at least she could instruct and keep an eye on them and their efforts.

In the three weeks she'd been here she'd done so much to bring some measure of orderliness to their household. He hadn't realized just how far things had slipped, how his *brieder's* rowdiness had grown more and more common around here lately.

Seth stepped inside the kitchen and halted as he was hit in the forehead with a hard object. All motion ceased as the five occupants froze and stared at him with expressions that ran the scale from guilt to apprehension to barely suppressed amusement.

Glancing down at the floor, Seth realized two things. One, he'd been hit by a nearly black biscuit. And two, it hadn't been the only biscuit used as a missile. He could see at least nine other hockey-puck-like items scattered about the floor and table. He also saw a cup of coffee and a glass of milk that had fallen victim to whatever had been going on in here this morning.

Where was Edna? So much for things being done under her supervision.

Jesse, who'd obviously been responsible for throwing the biscuit that had hit him, spoke first. "I'm sorry, Seth. I was aiming for Daniel but he ducked."

As if that excused him.

"I see you all took my talk about trying to be more orderly to heart."

"*Ach*, Seth, don't be so stuffy." Levi picked up the two biscuits that were near his feet. "We were just having a bit of fun."

Fun. When was the last time he himself had enjoyed a bit of fun? He waved a hand, encompassing the room. "We'll just have store-bought bread this morning. Clean up this mess and get the table set."

His *brieder* went to work while Seth peeled out of his jacket and boots.

In the meantime Edna entered with a jar of what looked like preserves. Apparently she'd been down in the basement. She took one look at the cleanup going on and met Seth's gaze with a shrug. Then she crossed the room and placed the jar on the counter.

"I see there's been a bit of a ruckus since I left the room. But you seem to be doing a *gut* job of cleaning everything up." She adjusted her sling. "I think I'll go back to my rooms and have a cup of tea and then lie back down for a bit. Please don't wait on me for your breakfast." And with that she made her exit.

What had that been all about?

She was usually a stickler for getting things cleaned up. Perhaps her wrist was paining her more than she'd let on. He'd have to see about getting some help, at least part-time, so she didn't feel the need to help out so much.

In short order they had taken their places around the table.

After the pause for a time of silent prayers, the Beilers dug into the food with gusto.

"I hope *Aenti* Edna is better soon," Levi said. "Her cooking is worlds better than yours."

Mark merely shrugged. "If you think you can do better the job's all yours." Then he turned to Seth. "How long do you think it'll be before she can use her hand again?"

Seth gave Mark a stern look as he forked up some only slightly overcooked eggs. "For as long as it takes to heal. And we are very grateful for all she has done for us so far, ain't so?"

There were some guilty looks amid a chorus of agreement around the table.

"We've been on our own before," Seth reminded them. "There are six of us—we can handle this."

"Still," Daniel said, "she plans to go back to Bergamot eventually. What if she decides to do it now since she's hurt?"

Seth met Daniel's gaze with a lift of his brow before focusing back on his meal. "Same as now. We do our own housework."

His words were immediately greeted with groans and protests from around the table.

"You can't expect us to do laundry," Mark said indignantly.

"Or scrub floors," Kish added.

Seth didn't look up. "That and more is exactly what

we'll all be doing for the next several weeks. We will follow the task list I've posted, no complaints. After all, *Aenti* Edna has said she'll lend a hand where she can so we won't be entirely on our own." But after seeing how she handled things this morning he wasn't sure just how much help she was going to be.

Before he could say anything more Levi shoved scrambled eggs and a couple of strips of bacon between two slices of bread and pushed away from the table.

Seth frowned. "Where are you going?"

Levi grabbed his dishes and headed for the sink. "I need to head out. *Onkel* Uri asked us to arrive at the pickup point thirty minutes early today."

"You should have said something last night." Seth tried to keep the annoyance from his voice. "We could have adjusted our schedule so you didn't have to eat on the go."

Levi was already at the counter, giving his breakfast dishes a suspiciously quick wash. They had a standing rule that everyone carried their dishes to the counter. And on days when they were without a housekeeper everyone did their own dishes. Whoever cooked cleaned the pots and serving pieces.

"No point in making everyone adjust their schedule for me." Levi grabbed the lunch pail he'd apparently filled earlier. "See you all this evening." And without further explanation he was out the door.

The rest of his *brieder* powered through their breakfasts with more haste than manners.

In no time at all, Jesse and Kish had headed out to school, Daniel had headed to his job at their neighbor John Fretz's orchard, and Mark had left for Calvin Detweiler's woodworking shop, where he apprenticed for four and a half hours a day.

Which left Seth standing in the kitchen alone. Since Mark had been in a hurry to get to work, Seth had volunteered to wash the pans and serving dishes, and he tackled that now. Sometimes he felt more like a housekeeper than a *bruder* in this place.

Then he gave his head a mental shake. In truth he was a surrogate parent and this was all part of that role. He should consider it hands-on training for when he had *kinner* of his own.

Then he grimaced. He hadn't considered having *kinner* to be a priority, not even when he'd married Dinah. After all, he had five half *brieder* to raise. But they were getting older now—and so was he—and he sometimes wondered what it might be like.

Chapter 4

Later that morning, Seth wiped his hands on a rag as he studied the patched water trough. So far so good. Hopefully it would hold this time.

He removed his hat and wiped his forehead with the back of his hand. This particular chore hadn't been on his list when he got up this morning, but few days went just the way he planned them lately.

The sound of approaching footsteps caught his attention. He squinted against the morning sun then replaced his hat. It was Edna—did that mean she was feeling better? Then he frowned. She was coming up the drive rather than from the direction of the *dawdi haus*. Had she been out for a walk? Perhaps she was suffering from cabin fever—even at sixty-nine and with an injury he knew she didn't like being inactive.

He stood, remaining where he was, waiting for her to draw near.

"*Gut matin*," he said. "I hope this means you're feeling better."

She nodded but didn't waste time on pleasantries. "There's something I need to speak to you about."

"It sounds serious." Seth's chest tightened. She was going to quit and return to her *shveshtah's* home or back to her own in Bergamot, he could feel it.

The older woman nodded without smiling. "It is. Do you mind if we go to the house where we can sit?"

"Of course." He swept a hand in the general direction of the house. "After you."

He and his *brieder* would have to shoulder the household chores full-time. He didn't look forward to having to tell them. And beyond that, he was going to miss having her around—they all would. She'd been more than a housekeeper, she was *familye*.

As they moved past the *dawdi haus*, Seth's thoughts scrambled for ways to handle this latest setback. Could he talk Edna into staying another week to train them on the proper way to do laundry and some of the other tasks? Their play-it-by-ear approach hadn't always provided the best results.

Once inside, he waved her toward a seat at the table then sat across from her and folded his arms. Best not to draw this out with small talk. "I take it you're leaving us."

She smiled for the first time since she'd come up the drive. "*Nee.* I told you I'd help out as long as I was in Sweetbrier Creek and I'm a woman of my word."

Some of the tension that had built inside Seth uncoiled. "Then what is it?"

"I've been wondering, it's been nearly five years since Dinah passed. Why haven't you found a new *fraa*?"

He stiffened again. "Forgive me, but I can't see where that's something we should be discussing."

"Just humor your nosy old *aenti*. You can obviously use

a helpmeet here, someone who's more than a housekeeper with a life of her own elsewhere." She gave him a direct look. "While I've enjoyed working with you and your *brieder*, I'll have to return to my home in Bergamot eventually. A *fraa* seems like the obvious solution."

Why was she pursuing this? "And one day I'm sure I will find someone."

She studied him a moment. "Are you still mourning Dinah after all this time?"

"*Nee*. I mean, *jah*, I miss her. And my *brieder* do, too, I'm sure. She was with us for four years and we were all better when she was around."

"I see. Given that you just said you and your *brieder* were better when you had a *fraa* in the house, what's holding you back?"

How could she possibly think this was any of her business? "Courting takes time and effort and I have little to spare of either."

Edna waved her *gut* hand dismissively. "If you wait for the perfect time it will never come. I think it's something you should really think about."

He was ready to put an end to this very uncomfortable discussion. "I will. Now, if there's nothing else, I need to get back to work." Why would she have called him in to discuss so personal a topic?

"There was one other thing."

Smothering a sigh, he settled back down in his seat.

"I have a *gut* friend back in Bergamot, Phoebe Kropf."

She'd come here to discuss a friend? Then he sat up straighter. Could this friend of Edna's be a potential housekeeper he could hire? He hadn't thought of looking outside the community but that was actually a *gut* idea. Someone with a fresh perspective might be just the thing.

"Phoebe's family is related to my Ivan so I've known her for a long time. Phoebe was wonderful kind to me and Ivan when he got so sick. She spent many hours sitting by his bedside with me, providing comfort and support."

"She sounds like a *gut* friend." He would prefer a younger person but the woman's nurturing skills would come in handy with his *brieder*.

Edna nodded. "She is. And she will be a *gut* person to take care of you and your *brieder* until my hand is healed."

He raised a brow. "You mean take care of our house, don't you?" Then he nodded. "Whatever the case, if you'll vouch for her, then that's *gut* enough for me."

His response seemed to startle her. "It is?"

"*Jah.*" He spread his hands. "Of course I'll need to discuss wages with her, but I'm sure we can reach a decision we can both live with."

"*Gut.* Because I just spoke to her and she plans to arrive tomorrow morning."

So she'd been coming back from the phone shanty when he spotted her. Edna leaned back in her chair, and her expression took on a pleased-with-herself air. He crossed his arms. "Not that I'm ungrateful, but that was a bit presumptuous, don't you think? What would you have done if I'd said I preferred someone I know?"

She shrugged without any sign of repentance. "What's done is done. I didn't think you would turn down the help and I wanted to make sure Phoebe was willing before I got your hopes up."

Recognizing that Edna was a force unto herself, he decided not to let her I-know-best attitude irritate him. Instead he'd just be glad she'd found a solution to their current problem so quickly.

"Of course she'll stay in the *dawdi haus* with me," Edna

continued. "And I can show her around and explain what she needs to know here so you won't need to worry about the time it'll take to get her familiar with everything."

"Sounds as if you have it all figured out. Is there anything I need to know about this friend of yours?"

"As I said earlier, Phoebe is kind and supportive. She's also a bit unconventional, which in my estimation is a *gut* thing. As for the rest, I think I'll let you discover it on your own."

"Unconventional? You do understand that I prefer to have someone who'll bring a sense of order to our home. My *brieder* need structure, not more chaos."

"Don't you worry, Phoebe will bring just what's needed to this household."

He had a feeling there was something she wasn't telling him. "Do you mind if I ask why she would come all this way to help someone she doesn't know, and during the Christmas season at that? Doesn't she have *familye* of her own?"

"Of course. In fact she's agreed to come here with the understanding that she'll need to return home for two or three days around Christmas."

He nodded. "That shouldn't be a problem."

"*Gut.*" Edna stood. "Now I'll let you get back to your work and I'll get to mine, what little I can do anyway."

Was she trying to avoid any more questions he might have? Seth stood and moved to the door. Then he remembered tomorrow was Tuesday. "I'll make my weekly trip to town today so I'll be here when she arrives tomorrow. Let me know if you need anything from the market."

Edna nodded, then her eyes widened. "*Ach*, I almost forgot."

Seth turned back to see her removing something from her sling.

"I fetched the mail while I was at the phone shanty. Looks like you have a couple of new orders."

Seth smothered a groan as he moved to take the mail from her. New orders were a *gut* thing. The money he made on the chess sets he handcrafted went a long way toward supplementing their income. But he'd gotten a whole lot more orders this year than he'd expected and everyone wanted them delivered in time for Christmas. He'd just have to find a way to work faster and put in additional hours between now and Christmas.

As he headed toward his workshop Seth mulled over what Edna had told him. It was *gut* that they had a new housekeeper coming. He wondered if Edna's friend would be at all like Edna herself. Hopefully she'd have his *aenti's* energy if not her personality. And it would be *gut* for Edna to have a friend living here with her. It probably hadn't been easy for her to be on her own in this all-male household.

His only concern was that, unlike Edna, she'd be too soft, too sympathetic to be able to keep up with his *brieder*.

Then his thoughts turned to what else she'd discussed with him. Much as he hated to admit it, she was probably right about him needing to consider marrying again. His *brieder* might be getting older, but the two youngest could definitely do with a woman who could fill the role of *mamm* in their lives. His and Dinah's marriage had certainly not been a love match, but they'd been *gut* friends and each understood their roles. She'd genuinely loved his *brieder* as if they had been her own *kinner*, and his load had certainly been lighter when she'd been around.

He mulled the idea over the rest of the morning while he ran his errands in town.

When he returned and went inside to grab a sandwich for lunch, he spotted Edna reading her Bible in the living room.

"*Aenti*, I've been thinking over what you said earlier about me needing a *fraa* and perhaps you're right. Life was certainly easier and calmer when Dinah was still alive."

Edna set her Bible in her lap. "Easier and calmer—is that what you're looking for?"

She said that as if it was the wrong answer. "Of course. After all, that's what's needed here."

"I notice you didn't mention anything about love."

He spread his hands. "Naturally I would want someone who is loving and *Gotte* fearing, someone who can offer friendship and mutual respect." He shrugged. "Other than that, I'd like to find someone just like Dinah—organized, confident, efficient."

"And do you know of someone like that?"

He rubbed the back of his neck. "I've been thinking on that since we spoke this morning and no one comes to mind. Perhaps I need to look outside of Sweetbrier Creek to find such a woman. Would you know of anyone in Bergamot who fits that description?"

Edna nodded. "Let me think on it. I might be able to find just the girl for you."

"*Danke.*"

In the meantime, perhaps he'd ask his cousin Caleb in Sugarcreek and his cousin Zilla in Franklin if they could recommend anyone. Actually, he'd go ahead and get letters out to them today.

With any luck he might be doing some long-distance courting by the time Edna's friend was ready to return home. In fact, he might even be engaged before Edna herself left them.

This promised to be the answer to his problems—with a woman moving in as his *fraa*, what need would he have for a housekeeper?

Chapter 5

We're almost there. It should be the next lane."

At the driver's words, Phoebe leaned slightly forward on the seat, eager to catch a glimpse of the place she'd call home for the next several weeks.

For the first thirty minutes of the ride she and Sandra, the driver, had carried on a lively conversation, helping Phoebe keep her nervousness at bay. But the conversation had eventually tapered off and Phoebe had been left to her own thoughts.

Now that she'd committed to taking on this task she was having second thoughts. This was the first time she'd been so far from home and, other than that summer she'd spent with Edna, it was the first time she'd spent time away from her *eldre*.

And no matter how much she told herself that she'd be able to run a household, with a bit of direction from Edna of course, a small part of her wondered if *Mamm* was right to doubt her.

But it was too late to turn back now—she'd told Edna she would do this, so do this she would.

The first thing Phoebe spotted after Sandra's heads-up was a phone shanty. Just past that was a gravel drive. And though the sky was blue, everything was wet and glistening, an indication that the rain they'd passed through about twenty minutes ago had come from this direction.

Once they'd turned onto the drive, Phoebe leaned forward to study the buildings up ahead. There was a large, two-story white clapboard house, not very different from the type of homes peppering the landscape back in Bergamot. It was skirted with a wide wraparound porch that held a pair of rocking chairs on one end and a bench and three ladderback chairs on the other. She could also see a pair of clotheslines that stretched from the side of the house to the barn's loft.

A paddock near the barn contained a pair of buggy horses who had tromped a muddy path around the inside of the fence. Before she could take in much more, Sandra had pulled the car to a stop near the porch.

Phoebe climbed out of the car onto the wet gravel and arched her back. It felt so *gut* to stand after sitting for so long.

Immediately the door to the house was flung open and the familiar figure of a woman with a ramrod-straight spine and a commanding bearing, her five-foot-two height and arm in a sling notwithstanding, stepped out on the porch.

Phoebe's mood brightened and a little bubble of joy expanded in her chest.

Edna hurried to her with her free arm outstretched for a hug. "*Wilkom, wilkom.* I'm so glad you decided to come," the woman said as the two of them embraced. Then she pulled away. "And the Beiler *brieder* will be happy to see you too."

Phoebe looked around the place again. "Where are they?"

"Levi, Daniel and Mark are at work. Kish and Jesse are at school. Seth is in his workshop." Then she waved a hand. "*Ach*, there he is now."

Phoebe turned and studied the man approaching them. He appeared to be a little taller than Michael, the biggest of her *brieder*. His hair and beard were both a light brown, similar to a warm oak color. His easy, confident walk seemed unhurried yet ate up the distance with surprising speed.

The eldest *brieder* was more handsome than she'd expected, which made her uncomfortably aware of her own plain features. Then she frowned. He had a beard? She turned to Edna. "He's married?"

"Widowed."

Phoebe immediately felt a rush of sympathy for the man. She also had questions. What had happened to his *fraa*? How long had they been married? How long had she been gone?

But now was not the time to ask such questions.

When he was still a little distance away he stopped and she saw his eyes narrow. Then he looked from her to Edna, who had a suspiciously bland look on her face.

Whatever his thoughts or conclusions, however, they remained his alone—she couldn't tell anything from his expression.

His eyes captured her attention as he drew closer. They were a grayish blue that reminded her of the soft denim of a well-worn pair of overalls. But there was nothing soft about the light reflected there. They were assessing, weighing, studying her with the same curiosity with which she was studying him.

A moment later he was moving again, only stopping when he was a few feet from her.

"Phoebe?" The voice was rich, deep.

She nodded, feeling suddenly tongue-tied.

"I'm Seth. Thank you for agreeing to come."

Phoebe finally found her voice. "I'm happy to be here." Then she touched her throat. "*Ach*, I almost forgot." She spun around and leaned back into the car. "I baked some snickerdoodles last night for you and your *brieder*." She backed out, holding the basket she'd carefully packed the cookies in.

Phoebe wasn't sure exactly what happened next, but one minute she was turning to show him and Edna her gift and the next the basket was upended on the wet ground with cookies scattered all around it.

For a moment no one said anything, Phoebe wasn't even sure she took a breath. All she could do was stare down at the cookies and think what a terrible first impression she was making.

Finally she broke the silence. "I'm so sorry. I'll make some more when I get settled in properly."

He waved a hand. "It's all right. We're not used to having sweets around here anyway."

What did he mean by that? Didn't they like sweets? Had she made a misstep already? She finally looked up and met his gaze. But she couldn't tell anything more from his expression than she had from his tone. It was unnerving not to have any idea at all what he was thinking.

"And speaking of getting properly settled in," Seth moved to the open trunk of the car where Sandra was unobtrusively waiting, "I'll take your bags to the *dawdi haus*. Edna can help you get settled in."

Edna nodded and waved her toward the house. "*Kum, kum.* I'll put on a kettle so we can warm you up with a nice hot cup of tea."

Up until now Phoebe hadn't really felt the cold but suddenly that was all she could think of. Drawing her coat closer around her, she walked beside her friend, eager to see the place that would be her home for the next several weeks. Despite the accident with the cookies, she still had a chance to make a *gut* impression here. It would be the start of an adventure, a chance to see how she could prove herself away from her *familye* and friends.

Edna led her down the drive as it paralleled the house and after a moment Phoebe could see that the *dawdi haus* was attached to the main house via the shared back porch.

Once inside she found the *dawdi haus* to be very snug and cozy. The whole front interior of the house was an open area with a kitchen and dining table taking up about a third of the space and the living room the rest. There was a hallway leading off the middle of the room, which apparently led to the bedrooms and washroom.

Before Phoebe could take in much more Seth entered with her bags.

"Shall I set these in your room?"

"*Danke*, but I can take them from here."

"Then I'll leave you to get settled in." And with that he turned and made his exit.

"Your room is the one on the left." Edna gestured toward the hallway as she put a kettle on the stove. "Put away your things. I'll have the tea ready by the time you get back."

Ten minutes later Phoebe was sitting across the small table from Edna, a cup of tea in hand. "*Danke*. This tea is wonderful *gut*."

Her friend nodded acknowledgment. "Are you ready to take on this job?"

"For sure and for certain." Then she grimaced. "Though I don't think I made the best of impressions with Seth."

Edna waved her *gut* hand. "*Ach*, don't let that worry you. And it was a wonderful sweet gesture for you to bring the cookies in the first place."

Phoebe decided to change the subject. "I take it Seth is the only one of the *brieder* at home right now?"

"*Jah*." Edna took a sip and then set her cup down. "You can look for Mark to get home shortly after lunch, and the two scholars will be home once school lets out. Levi's and Daniel's hours are a little less predictable, though they are usually home in time for supper. But for now it's just Seth."

"You said earlier that he was in his workshop. Does he work at something besides the farm?"

"*Jah*. He's very talented. He makes hand-carved chess sets that are sought after, especially this time of year."

Chess sets—how intriguing. "I'd like to see some of his work."

"I'm sure he'll be happy to show it to you if you ask him."

Phoebe took a sip of her tea, deciding she'd get to know the eldest Beiler before she asked.

* * *

Seth settled on the chair at his worktable, picked up a bolt of red velvet and measured a piece to fit the tray where the game pieces would be stored. Lining the drawers, creating the painstaking nests for each game piece, was his least favorite part of the job but it had to be done. As he worked, he thought about the newcomer.

To say Phoebe wasn't what he'd expected was an

understatement. For one thing she wasn't anywhere near Edna's age, in fact from all appearances she was much younger than even him. Thinking back on his conversation with Edna yesterday, though, she hadn't mentioned Phoebe's age, only that she was a friend. He'd just figured that that meant she was someone close to Edna's own age. But he suspected she'd known exactly the assumption he'd made and had done nothing to correct it. Sometimes he thought Edna had an odd sense of humor. If she'd wanted to throw him off balance, she'd certainly accomplished that.

But none of that was Phoebe's fault so it wouldn't be fair to hold his *aenti's* bit of mischief against her. As far as appearances went, Phoebe was slightly built and couldn't be any taller than five foot four, but Edna was proof that stature shouldn't affect her ability to care for the house. And she was pretty enough he supposed, but not such a beauty that she would be a distraction to his *brieder.*

The incident with the cookies seemed to have unsettled her, which was understandable. She was no doubt nervous to be coming to an unfamiliar household full of menfolk.

What did concern him was that he'd sensed a fragility about her. And it wasn't just her small stature. Rather it seemed a frailty of temperament.

Phoebe seemed to lack the spirit and strength of purpose he felt she would need if she planned to manage his household and keep his *brieder* in line. Edna had assured him her friend was up to the task but now that he'd met the girl for himself he wasn't so sure.

To be fair, it might just be that she was tired from her trip, and she might even be feeling some concern over what awaited her here. Perhaps she'd show more determination and mettle once she'd settled in.

Last night Seth had informed his *brieder* that Edna had found them a new housekeeper, and the news had been met with relief and jubilation.

How would they react when they saw how young Phoebe was? She couldn't be much older than Levi and Daniel, if that.

Could this young woman possibly have the presence to command the attention of his active, independent-minded *brieder*?

Chapter 6

Phoebe stood and carried her teacup to the sink, then rinsed it. "It's nearing lunchtime," she said as she dried the cup. "Perhaps I should get lunch ready for the three of us."

Edna raised a brow. "Seth usually just eats a sandwich. And he claims to prefer to eat alone."

"Then I'll see that he has a wonderful *gut* sandwich and maybe something extra to go with it." She paused, considering. "And since this is my first day, I'm sure he'll be all right if we join him for lunch, just so he and I can get to know each other better."

Edna seemed amused by her statement but merely said, "Then *kum*, I'll show you the kitchen."

Since the *dawdi haus* shared a porch with the main house, Edna led her out the door, across the porch and into the kitchen.

As soon as she stepped inside Phoebe looked around, noting the similarities to and differences from *Mamm's* kitchen. This kitchen was larger with more cabinets. But there was no sign of a stairway to the basement so it must be located elsewhere. The stove seemed similar, which was *gut*, she wouldn't have to learn something new.

But the biggest difference was the feeling it evoked. *Mamm's* kitchen had a large calendar with pictures of landscapes on it and a clock with a brass pendulum that ticked loud enough to provide a backdrop for the other sounds. There was also a string of birthday cards hung over the window. The cards were changed out as more recent ones came in, but it was always crowded. All together it gave the kitchen a cozy, welcoming look.

This kitchen was stark. The only thing on the wall was a plain wooden perpetual calendar that hadn't been updated in several months. The mudroom, which was easily visible from the kitchen, had wall hooks for hats and coats and a corkboard with notes pinned on it. That was it. Perhaps they saved the more decorative items for the living room.

Edna took a seat at the large wooden table. "Why don't you go through the pantry and cabinets to get familiar with what and where things are here?"

Conscious of the fact that Seth would be arriving soon for lunch, Phoebe opened doors and gave the various contents a cursory once-over.

Then she turned back to Edna. "I saw some sliced ham in the refrigerator. I assume that's what Seth likes on his sandwich."

"*Jah*. He also adds pickles and mustard."

"And what do you like on yours?"

"Mayonnaise and lettuce."

Phoebe grabbed two plates from the sideboard and placed several thick slices of the ham on one of them. She set it on the table then fetched the lettuce, jar of pickles and condiments. The pickles and condiments joined the platter of ham on the table, and she took the lettuce to the counter. She peeled off a few leaves of lettuce, prepped them and returned the rest to the refrigerator.

She placed the loaf of bread next to the plates. A fork for the pickles and couple of spreaders for the condiments completed the picture.

Then she stood back and studied the result of her effort with a finger on her chin. "It needs a side of some sort. I wish I hadn't been so clumsy and dropped those cookies."

"I won't have you calling yourself names," Edna said firmly. "That was an accident. And you're here for a fresh start, ain't so?"

Phoebe nodded, then suddenly brightened. "I saw some boiled eggs and relish in the refrigerator. I can easily prepare an egg salad."

Edna's frown melted away. "An excellent idea."

Phoebe spun around and quickly moved to the refrigerator. Then she paused. *Move with deliberation. One food-dropping accident today is already one too many.*

Proceeding on, she gathered up the ingredients she needed and whipped up the egg salad without incident. She'd just finished when she heard the outer door open.

After shedding his jacket and boots in the mudroom, Seth moved into the kitchen and then paused at the unexpected sight that greeted him. He studied the contents of the table and then the two women. *"Was ist das?"*

"Edna tells me you usually have a sandwich for lunch and eat by yourself," Phoebe said brightly. "I thought I'd get everything set out and we could all eat together today."

She was smiling like she'd done something *wunderbaar.* "That really wasn't necessary."

Apparently she didn't pick up on his tone because she was still smiling as she carried a bowl of something to the table. "It was no trouble. And my *mamm* always says that a meal tastes better when it's shared with friends."

Seth was used to making his own sandwich and eating alone most days. Which was how he liked it. He'd actually been looking forward to relaxing with the new farm magazine he'd received yesterday while he ate his sandwich.

But Phoebe had obviously done this to please him and it would be churlish to tell her he'd rather eat this one meal of the day alone. So he swallowed his annoyance and nodded acknowledgment. "*Danke.*" He moved to the mudroom sink to wash his hands.

When he took his seat at the table he found that glasses of milk had been poured up and a bowl of egg salad was on the table beside the sandwich fixings. Phoebe apparently didn't understand the simple pleasure of a well-made sandwich on its own. But again he merely smiled and once the prayer time had ended resignedly served himself a portion of the salad.

"How was your trip?" he asked, trying to make polite conversation as he thought fondly of the farm journal waiting for him beside his recliner.

"It was pleasant. Sandra, my driver, is quite a talker and she made the time pass quickly. Other than a heavy rain shower during the middle of our drive it was uneventful."

"Bergamot is about a two-hour drive, ain't so?"

"*Jah.* But from what I could see the countryside here is very similar to what I left behind." Then she gave him a shy smile. "It's the first time I've been so far from home."

Her wistful expression made her look particularly young. Had she even spent much time outside her *eldre's* home? She must be younger than he'd first thought.

He decided to change the subject. "Has Edna showed you around yet?"

"We started but didn't get further than the kitchen. I wanted to make sure your meal was ready when you came in for lunch."

"That was thoughtful of you but you don't need to go to all this trouble in the future. I'm perfectly happy with a plain sandwich on its own."

"It wasn't any trouble. And it is why I'm here, after all."

He certainly couldn't argue with that, at least not without saying something he'd regret. "Well, once you've seen the rest of the house, feel free to explore the property."

"*Danke*, I would enjoy that."

"It'll be *gut* for you to be familiar with where everything is if you're going to work here."

Her smile faltered a moment, but she nodded. "Of course." Then she asked a question of her own. "What sort of livestock do you have?"

"Two cows and a calf, about twenty chickens, three buggy horses, and one team of draft horses."

"And that's enough to take care of the needs of your *familye*?"

"It is, but there isn't much left over at the end of the day."

"I'm *gut* with animals, even my *daed* says so. I can help you tend to them if you like."

"*Danke*, but I think you'll have more than enough work to do with keeping house."

Why would that bring a disappointed expression to her face? He'd just told her he wouldn't add extra to her workload. He glanced Edna's way, but she was focused on her sandwich, apparently content to let the two younger people carry the discussion.

Phoebe bounced back quickly, though. She certainly seemed resilient enough.

"Do you have a winter garden I should tend to?"

Apparently he was going to keep disappointing her. "Unfortunately, we haven't been able to focus any time on trying to keep a kitchen garden going."

"Perhaps I can help with that."

This time he didn't refuse her. "That would be greatly appreciated. But only if you have enough time, taking care of the house and my *brieder* comes first."

She nodded, then changed the subject. "Is there anything I should know about you and your *brieder's* eating habits? Any food preferences or things to stay away from?"

He shook his head. Then he straightened. "On the subject of eating habits, Levi, the second oldest of my *brieder*, works with our *onkel's* construction company so he's sometimes late for supper, depending on what job they're working and how far away it is." He shrugged. "Other than that, there aren't any special requirements. We all just eat whatever is put in front of us." He loaded his fork with a second bite of her egg salad.

She smiled. "You sound like my *brieder*."

So she had *brieder* too. "Tell me about your *familye*."

"I have four *brieder*—Paul, Michael, Adam and Peter. They're all married and Paul and his wife, Rhoda, live with us in my *eldre's* home. I'm the youngest of the bunch and the only girl."

"So you're used to dealing with a houseful of men?"

"For sure and for certain." Then she smiled. "You

needn't have any worries that I'll be intimidated when dealing with your *brieder*."

He was beginning to see a little spark of that spirit he'd looked for earlier.

And this egg salad actually went quite well with his ham sandwich.

Chapter 7

Once lunch was over, Seth headed for his recliner and read for a while. He could hear the sound of the women chatting as they worked, though he couldn't make out any of the actual conversation.

Not that he was trying to eavesdrop.

He wondered how many more of his routines Phoebe was going to disrupt. He supposed he should start putting his foot down, to let her know his preferences, the way he thought things should be done to make the household flow smoothly. But not on her first day. He'd let her get settled in and meet his *brieder*, then he'd gradually introduce her to the routines and order he had in place for keeping their busy household functioning as it should.

Fifteen minutes later he realized he'd been looking at the same page in his magazine and hadn't read anything. He set the magazine down and stood. He might as well be doing something productive.

He passed through the kitchen and noticed Edna was

alone. Where was Phoebe? All signs of their recent lunch were gone—the table had been cleared and cleaned, the dishes were done and the dishrags hung neatly to dry. Order—he could appreciate that.

"Is your young protégée taking a nap?"

Edna gave him a stern look, obviously not amused. "She just left for the phone shanty. She promised her *mamm* and *daed* she would call once she got settled in."

Seth frowned, not liking this feeling of being on the defensive. "The phone is supposed to be for business or emergency use only."

"She's obeying the request of her *eldre*. Certainly you can't fault her for that." This time Edna's tone was positively acerbic. "It's not something she'll do often."

Not knowing how to respond to that he merely nodded, then made to leave.

But Edna wasn't done with him. "Before you go, I'd like to know what you think of Phoebe so far."

He crossed his arms. "You didn't tell me she was so young," he said sternly.

"You never asked." Her tone was more amused than repentant.

"She looks younger than Daniel."

"Phoebe is twenty-one, so she's actually the same age as Daniel."

It was obvious he wasn't going to get her to admit to any deception.

"But you haven't answered my question yet—what do you think of her?"

What *did* he think? The new housekeeper still seemed to have one foot in childhood and appeared a bit too eager to please. "It's too early to form an opinion—she's only been here a few hours. Let's wait and see how she deals with my *brieder*."

Edna raised an eyebrow. "That's still not an answer but I suppose we'll leave it at that for now. At least you're not rushing to judgment." Then her eyes narrowed slightly. "Let me just say that Phoebe is special and she's wonderful dear to me. If you give her a chance and treat her kindly, she will go above and beyond for you."

Seth saw the earnestness in her demeanor. "I'll keep that in mind. Now, was there anything else you needed?"

"*Nee*. Phoebe will be back soon and I should give her that tour I promised her."

"While you're at it, you can go over the household work schedule I posted on the corkboard." It was what he used when assigning household tasks among his *brieder* during those times when they didn't have a housekeeper. He'd also gone over it with each of their housekeepers to use as a guideline. "I find it helps maintain an orderly household if everyone knows when things will get done."

Edna nodded with a smile. "That's a *gut* way to approach things."

Seth was nearly to the workshop when it occurred to him that she hadn't actually agreed to go over the schedule with Phoebe.

* * *

Phoebe hung up the phone and slowly walked back up the drive toward the house. She'd been able to speak to both *Mamm* and *Daed*—unexpected since *Mamm* didn't like to speak on the phone. *Daed* had just wanted to make sure she had arrived safely. *Mamm*, on the other hand, spoke to her as if she'd been gone for days instead of having left just this morning. Her questions came one on top of the other, not giving Phoebe time to answer.

"Do you feel comfortable there? Are they treating you all right, not demanding too much? You're not feeling overwhelmed, are you?"

Phoebe had finally just cut in. "Don't worry, *Mamm*, I'm settling in fine. The *dawdi haus* is nice. The only Beiler I've met so far is Seth, the oldest, and he has treated me well. I've learned how to run a household by watching you, and Edna is here to help me if needed so there's no need for you to worry."

"That is *gut* to hear." *Mamm* hadn't sounded like she believed Phoebe's claims that all was well. "Just remember, you can return home before your time is up if you need to."

Phoebe was glad *Mamm* hadn't been able to see her roll her eyes. "I'll remember. But I need to go now, Edna is waiting for me. *Gutentag.*"

Would *Mamm* ever see her as anything but her little girl who needed constant supervision?

As she neared the house she saw Seth walking toward his workshop. He must be a skilled wood-carver indeed to be able to make chess sets *gut* enough to market. It was tempting to follow him and ask to see his work. But for now she would keep to the house.

She entered through the mudroom door and let Edna know she was ready for a tour. As her friend took her through the Beiler home, Phoebe looked closely at everything, trying to gain some understanding of the Beiler *familye* from their environment.

The living room had the same stark feel as the kitchen, though there were some periodicals by one of the recliners and an unfinished puzzle on a card table that had been pushed into one corner of the room.

She discovered that the door to the basement stairs was

located at the front end of the hall. Edna paused only long enough to point it out but led her past it.

There were two bedrooms on this floor. Seth, as man of the house, occupied the larger. The one next to the basement stairs had been turned into an office. Both rooms were neat and orderly, with nothing out of place. In the bedroom, the bed was perfectly made and everything in the room was precisely placed or put away. There was a windup clock and a Bible on his bedside table. The large braided rug on the floor beside his bed was mostly shades of brown with a little navy blue scattered in. There were no feminine touches in the room to indicate he'd ever shared this room with a *fraa*. How long had he been a widower?

In the office the papers on the desk were in neat piles and a stapler was precisely lined up with the edge of the desk. A calendar hung on the wall, and this one reflected the actual date. Next to the calendar was a nondescript wall clock. An extra chair was placed directly in front of the desk and a four-drawer file cabinet stood behind it. Again there was nothing present that didn't serve a practical purpose.

Seeing these two rooms told her a lot about the man who inhabited them.

Next Edna led her up to the second floor. There were five bedrooms up there. The rooms were fairly similar with only a few decorative touches such as the arrangement of the beds, the colors of the quilts and the items on the dresser to differentiate them.

Edna pointed to a doorway on the far end of the landing. "That's a set of stairs that leads to the attic. You shouldn't have a need to go up there while you're here." She headed back toward the stairs. "*Kum*, I'll show you the basement now."

When they finally finished the tour and made it back to the main floor, Phoebe could hear the sound of someone moving about in the kitchen. Had Seth returned for something?

She immediately headed in that direction then stopped when she realized it wasn't Seth but a younger male—one of Seth's siblings she guessed.

Edna stepped forward to make the introductions. "Phoebe, this is Mark, one of Seth's *brieder*. Mark, this is my friend Phoebe who's going to be helping out here for a few weeks until my arm heals."

So this was the *bruder* who was doing an apprenticeship with a furniture maker. She could see some resemblance to Seth. The same light-colored hair, though Mark's tended toward sandy rather than the warmer oak of Seth's. He was also more compactly built than Seth but he was still taller than her.

Mark's eyes had widened. "But you're young."

Phoebe frowned at the unexpected reaction. "I'm twenty-one," she said indignantly. Was this *youngie* questioning her ability to take care of their household?

A blotchy red crept up his neck into his cheeks. "I'm sorry. It's just that, well, Seth said you were Edna's age."

Phoebe cast a quick look Edna's way.

The older woman merely shrugged. "It sounds like a misunderstanding to me. I merely said you were my friend—we didn't discuss your age."

Phoebe had a feeling Edna was enjoying the mix-up. Giving her friend a stern look, she turned back to Mark. "Well, whatever the case, I hope you're not too disappointed."

"*Nee*. And welcome to our home."

"*Danke*. So you're the one who's apprenticed to a

woodworker and also on *rumspringa*, is that right?" She noticed he hadn't yet removed his coat.

"*Jah*." His head tilted slightly. "You know a lot about me."

"I asked Edna about all of you. But I don't really *know* you. For instance, what's your favorite food and what's your least favorite, what do you like to do and what don't you like to do."

The boy grinned. "Those are easy. My favorite food is pancakes and syrup, my least favorite is Daniel's version of chicken stew. The thing I most like to do is play volleyball with the others in my *rumspringa* group and my least favorite thing to do is take care of laundry." He wrinkled his nose. "It's what Seth put me in charge of before Edna came."

Phoebe hid a grin. "Well, that's quite a list. And I feel like I know you better already."

Mark poured up a glass of water and took several deep swallows. Then he moved to the corkboard, studied the notes there and snagged one of them. He held it up for Phoebe to see. "I'm off to take care of some chores. I look forward to seeing you again at supper." Then his grin turned mischievous. "Your cooking has got to be better than my *brieder's*." And with that he was out the door.

Phoebe turned around to face Edna. "Speaking of supper, I should get busy with that."

Edna raised an eyebrow. "Do you have any idea of what you want to cook?"

Phoebe paused at that. She'd never been in charge of planning a meal before, she'd merely helped prepare some of the ingredients while *Mamm*, and lately Rhoda, did the planning and directing. She mentally went over what she'd seen in the pantry and refrigerator.

Her mind went blank for a moment and she met Edna's gaze. "Any suggestions?"

Edna shrugged. "You're in charge."

She was in charge. Words she'd never heard before. What now?

Chapter 8

Phoebe straightened and went to the pantry. She saw a box of noodles there and it gave her a glimmer of an idea. She quickly moved to the freezer where she found some chicken and the refrigerator where there was a large block of cheese. "I think I'll make *Mamm's* cheesy noodle and chicken casserole." It was something she'd watched *Mamm* prepare dozens of times and was one of the few recipes she felt she could handle from memory with perhaps just a little help from Edna.

"That sounds wonderful *gut*. What about dessert?"

Phoebe chewed her lip while she considered her options. Cookies she could handle, but she didn't think a batch of snickerdoodles was a proper dessert for six men and growing boys. When it came to cakes and pies, however, she was a total klutz. Anytime she'd tried to bake one on her own she'd met with less-than-successful, sometimes disastrous, results. "I'm afraid I'm not so *gut* with dessert," she finally admitted. "And I don't do well with following written recipes." It was always mortifying to own up to her limited reading skills. But Edna was already familiar with this particular failing.

"I can talk you through it." Edna gave her an encouraging smile. "I think we should make a peach cobbler tonight. Why don't you go down to the basement and fetch a couple of jars of canned peaches so we'll have them when it comes time?"

As Phoebe descended the basement stairs she felt some of her confidence return. That was one of the things she liked about Edna. The widow might have a somewhat tart personality but she had a *gut* heart. When Phoebe had trouble with something, Edna never looked at her like she was slow-witted, never told her whatever the task was should be easy or that she only had to try harder. Edna just calmly offered to help, which usually meant talking Phoebe through it without being condescending or pushing her aside to do it herself.

When Phoebe returned to the first floor, she heard the sound of voices. She paused outside the kitchen doorway and just as she'd suspected, what appeared to be the two youngest of Seth's *brieder* were in the mudroom, noisily shedding their coats and boots. The boy she suspected was Kish was recounting a story about how someone named Annabeth had been smiling at him during recess.

Jesse, the younger of the two, was grinning but otherwise not participating in the discussion.

"Where is your friend?" Kish asked. "Is she here yet? Will she be cooking our supper so we don't have to eat Daniel's cooking again?"

Phoebe stepped into the kitchen. "*Jah*, I'm here. And *jah*, I plan to cook your supper."

The boys whirled around to face her.

She smiled at them both. "*Gutentag.* I'm Phoebe and

I'll be working here with Edna for a while." Then, before either of them could comment, "And *jah*, I'm younger than what you expected but I promise I'll still be able to do the work required."

While the boys digested her words she took a moment to study them. Kish was broader, with wider shoulders and more muscular arms than his younger *bruder*. He also carried himself with more self-assurance.

Jesse had more of a not-yet-filled-out boyishness about him and seemed more restrained. The boy pushed his glasses higher on his nose with one finger and studied her with an earnestness that seemed beyond his years.

When she asked them about their favorite and least favorite things to do, instead of pointing to team sports and chores, Jesse said his favorite thing was working on puzzles and playing board games, and his least favorite was hunting.

Phoebe felt an immediate connection to the boy.

Then she remembered how it was when her *brieder* came in from school and later from the fields. *Mamm* always had something on hand for them to eat, telling Phoebe that growing boys needed lots of fuel. Again she kicked herself for dropping those cookies.

"Are you boys hungry? I haven't had time to prepare any proper snacks, but I saw some crackers in the pantry and some cheese in the refrigerator. How does that sound for a quick snack?"

The boys immediately signaled their approval.

Phoebe set the jars of peaches on the counter and went to work pulling the impromptu snack together.

She saw a pitcher of apple juice in the refrigerator and decided that was just the thing to go with their snack.

She was going to be able to do this after all.

* * *

Seth studied the now-complete chessboard with a critical eye. The grid lines were straight and the board level. Each square seemed exactly the same size. The color of the wood was rich and deep. But it might have looked better if the dark squares were just a touch darker for better contrast. He'd tinker with the stain again before he made the next one.

This one was ready to send out to his customer. Tomorrow he'd start all over again on another set.

He always felt a slight sense of letdown at the end of a project like this. It was as if he put a part of himself into the construction of these chess sets and yet didn't have the opportunity to enjoy them himself. None of his *brieder* liked the game the way he did so he rarely had a chance to play, even on his own set.

Putting away that unproductive thought, he stood and stretched. He reached for one of the sturdy packing boxes he kept on hand then stopped. Perhaps he'd deal with the packaging tomorrow. He had some paperwork and bills in his office to take care of. And he was curious to see how Phoebe was doing. She'd no doubt met the three youngest of his *brieder* by now. How was she faring? Had she been able to hold her own against their rambunctiousness?

Once inside the mudroom, Seth wiped his boots on the mat and removed his jacket. He could smell an appetizing aroma wafting from the kitchen—that was a *gut* sign.

As he stepped into the kitchen proper he spotted Edna sitting at the table. Phoebe was at the sideboard, trying to reach the upper shelf, presumably to get one of the large serving bowls. She'd pulled up a small step stool to compensate for her short stature and was currently balanced precariously atop it on her tiptoes. A disaster waiting to happen if he ever saw one.

"Here, let me get that," he said, crossing the room quickly.

She started at the sound of his voice and turned her head toward him. It overset her balance, and she frantically waved her arms in an attempt to maintain her footing.

Sprinting the last few feet, Seth was able to get to her in time. Grasping her by the waist he steadied her and then set her feet on the floor. "Are you okay?"

She looked up at him, her gold-flecked brown eyes wide, her lips parted in surprise. Then she answered his question with a nod.

"*Gut.*" He released her and reached up to the top shelf, where he pointed to a large blue bowl. "Is this what you were trying to get?"

Again Phoebe nodded.

Why did she look so stricken? Had she been startled so deeply? Perhaps he'd spoken more harshly than he'd intended.

Seth handed her the bowl and she seemed to finally recover some of her composure.

"*Danke.*" Then she lifted her chin. "I wasn't clumsy, you know. You just startled me." There was a note of defensiveness in her tone.

"My apologies. And I never said you were clumsy."

Her cheeks pinkened. "*Nee*, of course not." Her gaze slid from his and she turned and carried the bowl to the counter near the stove.

Something about her pose as she stood there with her back to him made him feel the need to comfort her. He decided to ignore the impulse—she had work to do and so did he. But instead of turning toward his office, he found himself saying, "Whatever it is you're cooking smells wonderful *gut*."

She turned at that and gave him a grateful smile. "*Danke*. It's something my *mamm* taught me to cook."

"I look forward to tasting it." Satisfied he'd done what he could, he turned and headed down the hall.

Chapter 9

Once Seth left the room, Phoebe took a deep breath. Had she made a fool of herself with that thoughtlessly blurted comment about not being clumsy? Seth seemed to be a wonderful kind man. And very strong. He'd lifted her from the stool and set her down with very little effort.

"Isn't it time to get your casserole from the oven and put in the cobbler?"

Edna's question brought Phoebe's thoughts back to the present. She grabbed a couple of pot holders and pulled the cheesy, bubbling dish from the oven and replaced it with the dish holding the cobbler Edna had talked her through preparing earlier.

She liked Edna's way of instructing. Rather than using measuring cups and spoons, Edna showed her how to approximate measures in the palm of her hand, or with a coffee cup for larger quantities, and then mix by hand and "feel" when it was right.

As for side dishes, she'd decided to make green beans

and copper pennies, a carrot recipe she was able to prepare with just a little help from Edna.

As she worked at the stove, Phoebe hummed. She felt a sense of satisfaction in what she was accomplishing. This was the first time she'd actually planned and cooked an entire meal herself. True, she'd had some help from Edna, but it had been instruction, not hands-on. And she'd carefully tasted each dish, just to make sure, and they were *gut*. Maybe not as *gut* as if *Mamm* had prepared them, but more than passing *gut*. It was a meal she was looking forward to serving the Beilers.

She just hoped it would make a *gut* enough impression to make up for her earlier mishaps.

* * *

At the sound of a knock, Seth looked up from his desk. Mark poked his head inside with a quick "Supper's ready," then disappeared, leaving the door open a crack.

Seth finished making a note in his invoice ledger then stood.

He hadn't gotten quite as much work done as he'd intended. He blamed it on the break in his routine—having a new person in their household always took a little getting used to.

And the encounter in the kitchen earlier had left him on edge. Because of her strange reaction of course—it had nothing to do with the feel of her trim waist in his grasp.

Why had she immediately felt called upon to explain that she wasn't clumsy when the thought hadn't entered his mind? Was it because she'd dropped the cookies when she arrived this morning? He hoped she wasn't someone who needed constant reassurances.

Seth stepped into the kitchen a few moments later to find that Daniel had arrived home while he was in his office. And apparently he'd been introduced to Phoebe because he was already talking her ear off about his work on the Fretz apple orchard, including how he was trying to convince John Fretz to try some new grafting techniques.

Seth decided to rescue her. "Daniel, why don't you let Phoebe set the table while you get the milk out."

Phoebe gave him a smile then moved to the sideboard. "Your *brieder* tell me you don't normally wait very long for Levi to arrive."

"That's right. Levi knows what time we eat. When he has to work late we just make sure to put a serving aside for him."

"I'll do that right now." And she grabbed a tin pie plate and scooped up a generous serving of each dish, then covered it with foil and set it in the still-warm oven.

Seth took his place at the head of the table. Two chairs to his right were open. The one next to him was where Edna normally sat and the one to her right was Levi's place.

He caught Phoebe's gaze and waved to the second chair. "You can just take Levi's seat since he's not here. I'll pull up an extra chair before breakfast."

Phoebe nodded and moved to the chair he'd indicated, but before she could sit, Edna slipped over and took that seat instead.

"You take that one on the end," she said as she settled in more comfortably. "It'll be easier since you're left-handed."

Seth saw the pink bloom in Phoebe's cheeks. Was she self-conscious about being left-handed? Truth to tell, he hadn't noticed it until Edna pointed it out.

As soon as she settled in her seat they bent their heads

for prayer. When Seth looked up again he turned to Phoebe. "So what have you prepared for our meal?"

The new housekeeper smiled. "There's a cheesy chicken and macaroni casserole, green beans with bacon, and copper penny carrots."

Copper pennies! Seth tried to maintain his smile while his stomach rebelled. He'd had a bad reaction to that particular dish several years ago and hadn't been able to stomach them since. There were a couple of snickers around the table—all of his *brieder* knew about his feelings on the dish.

"Well, that all sounds delicious," Daniel said, coming to his rescue. "I'll dish up the macaroni casserole since it's here by me and too large to send around. You all just pass your plates this way."

Edna dished herself some green beans and passed the bowl, while Kish did the same with the carrots.

Seth kept his eyes on the bowl of carrots as it came closer and closer to him. When the bowl made it to Mark, who sat to his left, he thrust his plate at Daniel, asking for a generous portion of the casserole. When Mark passed him the carrots, his stomach rolled over and he quickly passed it along to Phoebe.

"But you didn't get any for yourself," Phoebe protested as she accepted the bowl.

He waved to his plate, still in Daniel's hand. "No need to wait on me. Go ahead and pass it along."

She gave him a searching look, then nodded, serving herself and passing the bowl on to Edna.

Seth was careful to get a large serving of green beans when that bowl made it to him.

As they dug into their meal, Kish piped up from across the table. "Hey, Seth, I see you missed getting carrots. Want me to pass the bowl back your way?"

There was a snicker in the boy's voice and he saw several other of his *brieder* hiding smirks. It wasn't often they were able to get the best of him, and it seemed they were enjoying this.

"*Nee*. I believe that this delicious casserole and these green beans will be enough to fill me up."

He resisted the urge to glance Phoebe's way, instead giving Kish the full force of his glare.

This was normally one of his favorite times of the day. When all his *brieder* were gathered together—well, almost all—and they were talking about how their day had gone. It kept him feeling connected to them, made him feel like all was as it should be in his home.

But this evening he was worried about having insulted Phoebe, which for some reason made him irritated with her.

The moment of awkwardness was broken when Edna spoke up. "That just leaves more for the rest of us." She pointed her fork at Seth's plate. "Unlike the green beans, which seem to be going fast."

After that the conversation moved on to other topics and no further mention was made of the copper pennies.

* * *

Phoebe pushed her chair back from the table. "Is everyone ready for some peach cobbler?"

Her question was greeted with a chorus of *jahs*, but before she could actually stand, Edna put a hand on her skirt, stopping her. "Daniel, the cobbler is rather heavy, would you mind getting it?"

"Of course."

While Daniel did as Edna asked, Phoebe removed the bowl of carrots from the table to make some room and fetched the saucers and spoons. She hadn't missed the looks that passed between Seth and his *brieder* whenever the carrots were mentioned tonight. Apparently there was a story there, one they, or Seth at least, was trying to keep from her. She promised herself to get to the bottom of it soon.

Just as Phoebe took her seat again, a young man entered. This must be Levi.

"I should have known," Mark said. "You're here just in time for dessert."

"I've always had great timing," Levi responded, but his gaze never left Phoebe. "Who do we have here?"

Phoebe offered him a smile. "I'm Phoebe, Edna's friend and your new housekeeper."

"Edna, I do like your taste in friends." Then he returned Phoebe's smile. "I'm Levi."

Phoebe was already up and halfway to the stove. "I have a plate all prepared for you. And there's more if that's not enough."

"*Danke.* It's been a long time since lunch and I could eat a steer." He grabbed a pot holder and took the plate from her. As soon as he spied the contents he shot Seth an amused glance, then turned back to her. "You cooked copper pennies, I see. It's my favorite way to eat carrots but for some reason we don't get it around here very often."

So it seemed it wasn't carrots in general that Seth had a problem with, but copper pennies in particular. *Gut* to know. She made a mental note to scratch that particular recipe from her menus going forward.

But for now she nodded Levi's way. "I'm wonderful glad I could serve you something you enjoy. Please, take my chair, I'm done eating."

"Don't be silly, you haven't had your dessert." He set his

plate on the table next to hers. "It won't take me but a minute to fetch another chair." When he returned a moment later with another chair, he managed to slide her chair closer to the head of the table and then effortlessly slide his between hers and Edna's.

As soon as he was settled he forked up a hearty bite of the casserole and his eyes lit up as he chewed. "Mmmm, delicious." He turned and gave her a smile. "Pretty as a springtime flower and a *gut* cook as well. You're certainly going to improve our lives around here."

Phoebe felt the heat climb in her cheeks. She wasn't used to getting this kind of attention. She reached for her glass but overreached and ended up knocking it over. Luckily the glass was two-thirds empty and Seth grabbed it before very much of the contents escaped.

There was a moment of awkward silence as she dabbed at the spill. Then Edna spoke up.

"I don't know about the rest of you but I'm ready for my serving of cobbler. Daniel, you're the closest, start serving it up."

That provided enough of a distraction to give Phoebe time to regain her composure so that by the time she'd finished cleaning up the spilled milk and had taken her seat again, the heat of her flush had ebbed considerably.

"Tell us something about yourself," Levi asked as she settled into her chair. "Are your *familye* farmers?"

She shook her head. "*Nee.* Well, two of my *brieder* do have a small farm that they work together. But my *daed* and youngest *bruder* operate a harness repair business."

"And do you only have the three *brieder*?"

Levi was certainly asking a lot of questions. Was he really interested or was he just trying to smooth over her earlier clumsiness? Either way she was grateful. "*Nee.*

There are four of them. Michael has a bicycle shop in town."

His brows went up. "Bicycles—do you ride?"

Seth listened to the easy way Levi talked to Phoebe, drawing her out, flattering her, making her smile. Levi had always had a certain charm about him that females found fascinating. He would have to get his *bruder* alone soon and warn him off Phoebe. It wasn't fair to her since nothing was likely to come of it and she'd be returning to Bergamot soon.

Once everyone finished their dessert Seth pushed back his chair, signaling that the meal had come to an end. "That was a wonderful *gut* supper, Phoebe. *Danke* for preparing and serving it."

As they'd been taught, each of his *brieder* carried his own dishes to the counter before leaving the kitchen. Seth frowned when he realized Levi wasn't heading into the living room afterward but instead sat back down at the table.

He'd definitely have to have that talk with his *bruder* soon.

Chapter 10

Levi offered to dry the dishes while Phoebe washed. The other Beilers had disappeared into the living room and Edna sat at the table reading. Did her friend feel the need to chaperone or did she want to stay close in case Phoebe needed help?

Levi kept up an entertaining conversation as they worked, asking lots of questions about her, but also telling entertaining stories about himself and his *brieder*. It was from his storytelling that she learned Seth was a half *bruder* to the others, having had a different *daed*.

This one of Seth's younger *brieder* was charming and amusing, making her smile often, but just as often making her want to roll her eyes. She'd known a few boys like him, observing as they interacted with the others in their youth group. They always wore a smile and knew how to put smiles on others' lips. They seemed to breeze through life, never letting worries slow them down. But this was the first time she'd found herself the focus of one, which made this experience a little different.

She knew better than to make too much of the attention
Levi was showing her, though. She was well aware that to
him she was a novelty, a new member of the household,
someone close to his own age who he could try to win over
with his charm—that was all this was.

That being said, she'd come here to experience new
things and to see if she could fare well on her own. So she
would enjoy this for what it was—a diversion.

At one point Phoebe could hear a ruckus of some sort
coming from the living room. Before she could decide
whether to check on it or not, Levi spoke up.

"Seth must be in his room or his office." He met her
gaze and smiled. "Don't worry, their games get a little
rowdy sometimes is all." He placed the drying cloth on the
counter. "I'll go check it out."

As Phoebe finished with the dishes she wondered about
his statement that Seth must be in his office. Did Seth never
relax with his *brieder* and join in their fun? She wiped her
hands on the drying cloth, then hung it on the hook over the
sink. Then she turned and looked around the kitchen, making sure everything was in its place and that the table, stove
and counters were spotless. The fact that they were gave her
an unexpected sense of pleasure.

Edna closed her book and stood. "I think you've had
a successful first day. I imagine you must be ready to
turn in."

Phoebe wasn't sure exactly how successful it had
been—she'd dropped a box of cookies at Seth's feet, had
all but fallen into his arms and then spilled a glass of milk
at supper. But she smiled at her friend. "I made it through,
for sure and for certain." She waved a hand toward the
living room. "But before returning to the *dawdi haus*, I
want to check in and see if there's anything Seth expects

from me either before I turn in or when I fix breakfast in the morning."

Edna nodded. "Well, these old bones are ready to call it a day." She gave Phoebe a raised-brow look. "I trust you can get settled in for the night on your own."

"Of course."

With a nod, Edna turned and headed for the back porch exit.

Phoebe smoothed her skirt, then moved to the living room, pausing on the threshold as she took in the scene.

The boys had pulled out a cornhole board and were having a rousing game with Kish and Daniel on one side and Levi and Mark on the other. Jesse seemed to be keeping score. And it appeared that several tosses had gone way off course if the items littering the floor were any indication.

Conspicuously absent from the room was Seth. Had Levi been right, was the oldest Beiler in his office?

Levi looked up and spotted her. "Want to join us?" He held out a blue beanbag. "You can take my turn."

Phoebe was tempted. She felt it was important that she build a relationship with the family outside of her role as housekeeper. But would that be overstepping?

Before she could decide she heard someone coming down the hall.

A moment later Seth showed up. The mood of the room immediately sobered. Seth looked around and she saw his gaze taking in every fallen and misplaced item. For a minute no one said anything.

Then Phoebe spoke up. "This is *gut*. Seth is here so now the teams are even again." She met his gaze. "You can join one team and Jesse the other. I'll keep score."

There was a moment of complete silence where it felt

like his younger *brieder* were all holding their breaths. Was it so unheard of for Seth to be playful?

Phoebe's invitation caught Seth completely off guard. The boys had quit inviting him to join them in their games years ago, and he told himself that was how he preferred it. He'd stood as *daed* to them for so long it was difficult to see himself as anything else. Those days when he was just one of the Beiler boys were so far in the past that he could no longer remember what that had felt like.

But as he was held by Phoebe's gaze, he saw the innocent expectation in her expression and found himself nodding in spite of himself. And when he was rewarded by a dazzling smile he couldn't find it in himself to regret it.

"I suppose I can play a game or two."

"Jesse's with us," Levi said immediately.

Seth smiled at Daniel and Kish. "Looks like I'm on your team."

His *brieder* smiled a welcome.

Seth hadn't played cornhole toss—or anything else—in a while but as they progressed he found he was enjoying himself. The camaraderie and good humor filled a hole inside him he hadn't realized was there. And watching Phoebe, the way she laughed with them and how she cheered for everyone, regardless of whose team scored, was a delight to watch.

But then knowledge of the work he had to do niggled at him and he reluctantly straightened. "The morning will come soon enough. I think we should start winding down for the night."

There was a bit of mumbled grumbling but the boys began to fold away the cornhole board, a portable set, into a compact unit.

Phoebe moved to pick up some of the items that had been knocked off a side table earlier but Seth stopped her. "We'll take care of straightening the room. You've had a long first day, I'm sure you're ready to turn in."

She smiled. "*Danke*. If you're sure you don't need me, I'll say *gut nacht*."

He nodded. "We'll see you in the morning."

"Sweet dreams," Levi added.

Seth cut his *bruder* an exasperated look but Levi just grinned.

As Seth helped his *brieder* put the room to rights he thought about the new housekeeper. In some ways Phoebe was like his *brieder*—she was young, she had a childlike side to her and she seemed eager to please. And she'd handled the meals and cleanup well. It wasn't her fault she didn't know about his aversion to copper pennies.

Had she noticed?

Of course she had—after the way his *brieder* had acted she'd have to be blind and deaf not to. But she'd handled it with *gut* grace.

Her tendency to spill things was another matter. For now he'd put it down to first-day jitters. But he would keep an eye on her to see if it would be a problem.

* * *

As Phoebe made her way to the *dawdi haus* she thought of the almost boyish way Seth had competed in their cornhole game. She got the impression he didn't usually join the others in their good-natured fun, which was a shame. He should strive to do more of it, because it looked like he was having a *gut* time, as did his *brieder*.

Then her thoughts turned to how her day had gone. All

things considered she'd had a *gut* day. Managing a house full of men and boys was going to be a challenge, but she rather enjoyed the idea of being kept on her toes.

And Seth seemed willing to let her take charge of things around the house, which was an entirely new experience for her. It gave her hope that, given the chance, she could prove she was a capable woman after all.

* * *

Phoebe was in the kitchen just before dawn the next morning. But even though the sun hadn't come up, there were signs she wasn't the first one in the household to greet the day—the light had been turned on, the coffee had been brewed and there was an empty coffee cup in the sink.

She looked out the window and sure enough there was the glow of a light shining softly from the barn. Someone—and she was sure it would be Seth—was apparently milking the cows. Taking a deep breath, Phoebe turned from the window and went to work getting what she hoped would be a *gut* breakfast ready.

The Beilers were all hardworking men and boys and they would need something hearty. She checked the contents of the pantry and refrigerator again and decided on potatoes, eggs, sausage and biscuits. Since she would need Edna's help for the biscuits and the woman hadn't made an appearance yet, she'd start on the other items.

She washed and peeled the potatoes then cut them up and placed them in a bowl of cool water and set them aside to soak just as she'd seen *Mamm* do.

Then she fried up the sausage and put it in a shallow bowl lined with paper towels and set it on the back of the stove to stay warm.

Where was Edna? It wasn't like her to oversleep.

She'd just seasoned the potatoes and dumped them in the skillet that still held some of the sausage drippings when Seth walked in with two milk pails full of the frothy white liquid.

"*Gut matin*," she greeted him.

He nodded acknowledgment as he set the pails on the counter.

Phoebe wiped her hands on her apron and went to the pantry. "I'll get the milk strained and into jars right away. Edna showed me where everything was stored yesterday." She backed out of the pantry with a cheesecloth and several large glass jars.

Seth didn't step away. Instead he picked up one of the pails. "Here, let me help. These are heavy."

So while Phoebe held the cheesecloth-draped funnel over the mouth of the jars, Seth poured the milk from the pails. When the pails were empty and the jars were safely in the refrigerator without incident, Phoebe breathed a little sigh of relief. Then she realized the potatoes had been left unattended a little too long and rushed to the stove.

In her haste she forgot to use a pot holder as she grabbed the handle of the skillet and let out a yelp of pain.

Seth moved with surprising speed for a man of his size and deliberation. "*Was is letz?*"

Before she could answer he saw her hand and his brow drew down in concern. "We need to tend to that right away."

"But the potatoes—"

With an irritated frown he swiftly turned the stove off and moved the skillet to a cold burner. Then he ushered her to the sink where he ran cool water over her hand. Despite the fact that he still wore that stern expression his touch was oddly gentle and comforting.

"There," he said after a few minutes of holding her hand under the water, "that should have cooled it down. How does it feel?"

He looked up then and met her gaze. Bent over her hand as he was, their faces were almost level. Up close, those smoky-blue eyes of his were even more captivating than they were from a distance, especially when they were focused entirely on her.

"Gut matin."

Phoebe's head jerked up as if she'd been caught doing something she shouldn't.

Edna came farther into the room and then frowned. "What happened? Are you hurt?"

Phoebe rushed to reassure her. "It's nothing serious. Just a little burn."

Edna grimaced. "I'm sorry I overslept. I should have been here to help you."

"Nonsense. You know that I'm perfectly capable of having one of these little accidents no matter who happens to be around." Then she cut a quick, guilty look Seth's way. What did he think of her remark?

But he'd already turned to fetch something from a small cabinet where they stored medical supplies. "Here," he said as he returned. "A little of this salve and a loose bandage for a day or two and you should be fine." He paused for a moment and then nodded as if coming to a decision. "It'll be easier if I do it for you." And without waiting for her response he opened the tin of salve and gently spread a generous dab on the reddened skin. Then he took the gauze and wrapped it around her palm.

Afterward, when he'd turned to put away the medical supplies, Phoebe gazed at the stove. "I can finish the potatoes and scramble the eggs, but I'd need to be able to get both my hands in the dough to make the biscuits. I guess we'll have to do without today."

She had the impression Seth wanted to respond to that, but Levi entered the kitchen just then. And he'd obviously overheard part of their conversation, because the first words out of his mouth were, "I've been known to bake a passable pan of biscuits before. I'll be glad to give it a try, especially if our charming housekeeper will guide me."

"Offer accepted." Phoebe gave him her sweetest smile. "But Edna is better with biscuits than I am so I'm sure she'll be happy to oversee your efforts while I get the rest of our breakfast prepared."

Levi gave her a look that said her smile hadn't fooled him, but he turned to Edna and put a hand over his heart. "*Aenti*, I would be truly honored if you would lend me your expertise."

Unmoved by his theatrics, Edna inhaled on an exasperated note and shook her head. "Actually, I'm afraid trying to bake biscuits now would take too long."

Phoebe raised a brow in challenge. "Not if we do fried biscuits."

This did manage to draw a smile from Edna. "*Gut* idea."

Levi looked from one to the other of them. "What are fried biscuits?"

"Something Phoebe's *mamm* sometimes cooks. They're quite *gut*." She turned to Phoebe. "You get the cooking oil ready while Levi and I prepare the dough."

Phoebe moved to do as she'd been told but as she looked for the right frying pan, she found that Seth had quietly stepped up beside her.

"Which one?" he asked.

She met his gaze in surprise, then waved a hand toward the frying pan she thought would work best. He fetched it, set it on the stove then grabbed the oil. "How much?"

She answered, still not sure what she thought of his help. Was it purely because he was being considerate of her burn? Or was he concerned how she would do with one hand after messing up so many times with two?

By this time the other *brieder* were drifting in. Phoebe fielded their questions about her bandaged hand and then put them to work—setting the table, fetching whatever jams, syrups and butter they wanted to spread on their biscuits, pouring up glasses of milk.

Meanwhile she went to the refrigerator to grab the eggs but found Seth there at her elbow again. "Tell me what you need."

Deciding to just be grateful for his help and not overthink it, Phoebe gave him a smile. "A dozen eggs, some of that sour cream and the stick of butter I put in the freezer earlier."

His brow went up as she named off her ingredients but he did as she requested without comment. Under her direction he cracked the eggs into a large bowl and then whisked them until they were nice and fluffy.

She nodded in approval. "That looks *gut*."

His lips quirked at that. "I have scrambled eggs before," he said drily.

She grinned. It felt kind of strange to be the one giving directions rather than the one taking them. "Now add a nice dollop of sour cream to the eggs while I get the grater."

He frowned. "Dollop? How much is that exactly?"

She paused with her burn-free hand on the cabinet door. "You know, a dollop."

"*Nee*, I don't know or I wouldn't have asked. In fact I don't believe there is any such measurement." His expression and tone had grown testy.

She knew she should quietly agree and then restate the measurement to something more precise, but her burn was throbbing painfully and something inside her balked at meekly appeasing him. "Of course there is. It's about the same as a heaping tablespoon."

"Then you should say a heaping tablespoon." His frown deepened. "Although that doesn't sound very exact either."

Phoebe rolled her eyes. "*Ach*, it doesn't need to be exact." And with that she marched back across the room, grabbed a spoon, scooped up some sour cream and dumped it into the bowl with the eggs. "There. Now if you don't mind whisking that in, I'll have the butter ready to add to the bowl in just a moment."

For a heartbeat Seth just stood there with his mouth slightly agape. Phoebe spotted the broad grin on Levi's face before he turned around. She also caught the sound of a quickly muffled snicker from one of the younger boys. *Ach*, she'd forgotten they had an audience. Had she embarrassed the man of the house in front of his *brieder*?

Chapter 11

Seth couldn't believe she'd just treated him like an obstinate schoolboy. He'd only been trying to make sure the eggs were prepared correctly. Proper measurements were important and her lax attitude toward that concept didn't bode well for the results that would end up on their plates.

This was very different from the way Dinah had cooked. His former *fraa* had been very precise, using measuring cups and spoons and following recipes without deviation. It hadn't been in her nature to be spontaneous or experimental with food. Or anything else for that matter.

Which had served her well in maintaining their household.

As he continued with his whisking, perhaps using a bit more energy than required, he told himself that they were lucky to have Phoebe as a fill-in housekeeper. He could live with anything for the five or so weeks until Edna was healed well enough to take back over.

Phoebe returned to his side, drawing his thoughts back

to the present. Her conciliatory expression said she was ready to move on from their disagreement and he supposed he should do the same.

She held up the grater she'd retrieved from the cabinet. "Now we just need to grate the frozen butter into the eggs," she said, "and once it's stirred in we'll be ready to cook them up."

That didn't sound right. "Don't you cook the eggs *in* the butter?"

"We'll add a little butter to the skillet, of course. But adding it in the eggs this way makes them fluffier." Her tone and expression were now those of a *mamm* gently teaching her child. But he gritted his teeth and nodded. Taking the grater and the butter from her, he went to work. "Whatever you say, you're the cook."

He was glad he hadn't argued when he saw her smile and stand straighter.

Continuing to grate the butter, he watched her from the corner of his eye as she moved to the stove. She added a little butter to the skillet that was already there and turned on the burner under it.

Studying her, he noted that she didn't move with the same confidence and purpose that Dinah had, but there was a certain gawky grace about her.

"The skillet is ready whenever you are," she said a moment later.

With a nod he moved to the stove to pour the eggs in.

And it seemed Levi was ready to fry the biscuits at the same time.

This would be interesting—his *bruder* had a competitive streak in him. The two of them working side by side would no doubt bring that out again.

A few moments later Seth held a spatula in hand. He

absently turned and stirred the eggs as they cooked to make sure he didn't over- or undercook any sections—a technique he'd learned from watching Dinah cook. Phoebe was across the room, discussing something with Jesse, and both of them were smiling. She certainly had a knack for that—making his *brieder* smile.

He did appreciate that she trusted him enough with the task not to hover.

"Phoebe's a *gut* influence on you." Levi's unexpected statement caught him off guard. Had something of his thoughts shown on his face?

But then his *bruder* gave him a suspiciously innocent look as he nodded toward the skillet. "Those look a whole lot better than the last eggs you cooked for us."

Seth merely glared at him and turned the burner off.

Levi grinned and did the same.

After the two of them had moved away from the stove, Phoebe moved forward and bent to open the oven door. Seth remembered that she'd put the sausage and potatoes there earlier and moved to her side and put a hand lightly on her shoulder to stop her. "You shouldn't be carrying these heavy platters with that fresh burn on your hand. Go take your seat and I'll get the food on the table."

His offer was met with a smile that made her face go all soft and warm.

"*Gut* idea," Levi interjected. "I'll help."

Phoebe turned her smile on him as well, and then with a "*Danke*" that included both of them, she turned and took her seat at the table.

Before he could stop himself, Seth frowned Levi's way. But his *bruder* merely grinned and carried the bowl containing the biscuits to the table.

Once silent prayers were done and everyone had been

served, Phoebe started getting compliments on the food, just as she had at supper yesterday.

"This fried biscuit is *gut*."

She smiled. "That was Levi and Edna's doing. And I agree, they did a *gut* job."

"I never had scrambled eggs like this before. I like them."

Again she passed on the compliment. "That was mostly Seth."

"You did something different to the bacon, didn't you?"

"*Jah*. I added some brown sugar and a little bit of mustard to the pan when I cooked them."

Mustard and brown sugar? Was that something her *mamm* had taught her as well?

"Despite what you just said," Levi pointed a forkful of eggs her way, "you're responsible for this meal."

As the meal continued, Seth noticed how Levi focused more and more of his usual teasing and charming banter on Phoebe.

He should definitely have a word with his *bruder* this morning before he left for work.

To be honest, though, Phoebe wasn't paying any more attention to Levi than she was to any of his other *brieder*. She chatted with all of them as she ate, even trying to draw out the normally quiet Jesse. And he was impressed that she didn't make an issue of her burn, which must be painful if for no other reason than where it was. Edna had certainly done well in her selection of Phoebe to help them out.

As usual after breakfast his *brieder* scattered to their various jobs or schoolings. He tried to pull Levi aside for a talk but Levi said he had to get to his job early, so Seth had to let him go. He was determined to handle it this evening, though.

He didn't immediately get back to his chores. Instead he helped Phoebe carry the last of the dishes from the table. "You shouldn't get that bandage of yours wet," he said matter-of-factly. "I'll wash and you can dry."

Her eyes widened slightly but she merely nodded.

A few moments later, as he handed her the first dish for drying, he said as casually as he could, "You know, you don't have to go to so much trouble for our breakfast. Me and my *brieder* would be just as happy with a hearty bowl of oatmeal."

"Oh." The word was infused with disappointment.

Had he said something wrong?

"I can fix oatmeal occasionally, of course." She seemed to be carefully picking her words. "But I think a little variety is a *gut* thing, so I'll cook other things as well so no one gets bored with their meals." She raised her chin as she accepted a clean platter from him. "Unless you object?"

"*Nee*, of course not. The menus are entirely up to you." He'd only meant to save her some work, not insult her. Too bad he didn't have Levi's way with words.

She nodded, her expression one of satisfaction. Then she changed the subject, cutting him a sideways glance. "Speaking of menus, I take it copper pennies are not a favorite of yours."

Seth tried not to grimace. "*Nee*. I had an unfortunate experience the first time I ate them and have not been able to make myself eat them ever since. I hope you're not offended."

"Of course not." She gave him a mischievous grin as she took a plate from him. "I feel the same way about brussels sprouts so you won't see any of those included in the meals I prepare while I'm here."

He returned her grin. "I think I can live with that."

"So tell me about your farm," she said as she stacked the now-dry dish on the counter with the others. "What crops do you raise here?"

"Corn and soybeans."

"My *daed* and younger *bruder* grow corn, but as I said last night, just a few acres' worth. Their harness repair shop is their main business and keeps them pretty busy."

Curious about her home life, he asked a few questions of his own. In the process he learned that she loved animals, she had a buggy horse named Primrose and she liked to sneak treats out to Scooter, the barn cat back home. He imagined that as the youngest of her siblings and the only girl she'd been the darling of her *familye*, though she didn't show signs of having been spoiled. Her youngest *bruder*, Paul, was the only one still living at home and he was recently married.

Seth wondered if she knew how much of her feelings she revealed as she spoke. She loved her *familye*, for sure and for certain. But there was something about Paul's new wife joining their home that bothered her. And when he mentioned Thanksgiving, she gave a vaguely worded response and quickly changed the subject.

Now, what had happened to generate that reaction? But he didn't press.

When the dishes were done, he hung his rag on the hook over the sink and rolled his sleeves back down.

"By the way," Phoebe said before he could move away, "I noticed your *brieder* were scrambling to get their lunches prepared before they headed out. I can take that on for them—have their lunches prepared and ready to go so it's one less thing for them to worry about as they're rushing to leave. I just need to find out what they like to have in their lunch pails."

Seth leaned back against the counter. "I can tell you that. Everyone has sandwiches with either a piece of fruit or a chunk of cheese. Kish and Mark like peanut butter and jelly, Jesse likes just peanut butter. Levi and Daniel like ham, but Daniel likes just meat and Levi likes mustard on his."

She put away the last of the dried dishes. "You know their likes well."

He shrugged. "After *Mamm* passed I was the one in charge of preparing everyone's lunch. At least until I married Dinah and she took over." He rubbed the back of his neck. "When she passed, my *brieder* were old enough to take care of it themselves." He gave her a pointed look. "And they can still take care of it themselves—you have enough other work to do."

"I don't mind. And it really won't interfere with my other chores."

He shrugged. "Then I will leave it to you to decide. I'll write down what I just told you so you'll have it handy."

"That's not necessary, I'll remember."

"It'll be no trouble." Then he changed the subject, waving a hand toward his *aenti*, who sat at the table sipping on a cup of coffee. "Did Edna go over the work schedule with you?"

"Work schedule?" Her gaze flew to Edna's.

Edna merely shrugged.

Seth let out an exasperated sigh. It seemed Edna did whatever Edna wanted to do. "Here, let me show you." He moved to the corkboard and pulled the pushpin from a neatly penned and stapled document. He moved to the table, waving Phoebe over to a spot on the opposite end from where Edna sat.

Why did Phoebe look so apprehensive? Surely she'd expected to have some assignments laid out for her.

Chapter 12

Phoebe took her seat, her hands clasped tightly in her lap as he set the daunting-looking list on the table between them. Would he expect her to read it?

"Dinah developed this when we were first married," he began. "I've updated it a few times since."

This was the second time he'd mentioned his former *fraa's* name. What had she been like?

"It's a *gut* blueprint to use to keep all of the work organized and to make sure everything gets done. It also makes it easier to allocate the tasks fairly when my *brieder* and I are between housekeepers." He slid the paper in front of her. "I've gone over it with every housekeeper we've had since."

Every housekeeper? "How many housekeepers have you had?"

He frowned. "Four in the five years since Dinah's been gone."

Was it a touchy subject?

But he'd returned to the original topic. "As you can see, the tasks are listed based on the frequency that they should be carried out. At the top are the ones that need to be done every day—cooking, sweeping, dishes, tending the livestock, collecting the eggs and such. Next are the tasks that should be done weekly—laundry, cleaning baseboards, mending and such—and each is allocated to be done on a particular day. For instance today is the day to do the mending. Edna can show you where the basket is." Then he glanced at her bandage. "Of course if you don't feel up to it today I suppose it could be skipped this week."

She brushed that particular worry aside. "It shouldn't be a problem." She was much more concerned with how regimented this was.

"*Gut*." He turned back to his list. "Then there's a checklist of chores that need less frequent attention, to be done as time allows or as need arises." He leaned back. "Any questions?"

"*Jah*. How important is it that these chores get done on these specific days?"

His forehead wrinkled. "What do you mean?"

"I mean if I feel like doing tomorrow's tasks today and push today's off until tomorrow, is that a problem?"

"Why would you want to switch them like that?"

She chose her words carefully. "I don't know. Maybe my eyes are feeling strained the day mending is on the list and I don't want to have to focus on delicate work. Or maybe there's something else I feel is needed more."

He stroked his beard. "You're in charge of the housework so I suppose, as long as it all gets done within a week's time, it doesn't have to be done in a specific order."

"*Gut*. And I will for sure and for certain get it all done."

He stood and cast a quick, exasperated look Edna's way,

before turning back to Phoebe. "I'll put this back on the corkboard so you can find it when you need it. And I'll be in the equipment shed for the next hour or so and then in my workshop if you should need me for anything."

"Actually, I do have one more question."

Seth paused in front of the corkboard, a wary look on his face. "And that is?"

"How do you want me to handle the shopping when there are groceries or supplies I need for the house?"

He pinned the list back in place. "I go to town most Tuesdays to pick up supplies and ship packages when I have product to go out—it's on this list. You can accompany me to do your shopping then."

Today was Wednesday so it seemed she'd have to wait nearly a week.

He must have read something in her expression. "Is there anything you need that can't wait until Tuesday?"

"*Nee*. That sounds *gut*. And between now and then I'll check with your *brieder* and look through the pantry to see what's needed."

He pointed to a notebook on one end of the counter. "No need. There's a running list we keep in there that we all add to when we think of something we're running low on or need. You can just add anything there you need from town as well."

Him and his lists. But Phoebe nodded. She could have Edna help her read the list when the time came so she could memorize what was there.

Once he'd donned his coat and headed out Edna met her gaze. "So you survived your first morning and got everyone out the door on time."

Phoebe straightened. "Did you doubt that I would?"

"*Nee*, but I think perhaps you did."

Phoebe grimaced. "I forget how well you know me." Then she drew her shoulders back. "How do you think I did?"

"Phoebe Kropf, you know it's wrong to fish for compliments."

Feeling properly chastised, Phoebe stood and fetched the broom from the mudroom. Just as she reached for the wooden handle, Edna spoke again without looking up.

"That being said, I believe more than ever that I was right about you being *gut* for this *familye*."

Phoebe smiled and found herself pushing the broom across the floor with a lighter step.

Later that morning, she headed to the chicken yard to collect the eggs.

First she scattered the chicken feed to encourage the chickens to leave the nesting boxes. There appeared to be nineteen or twenty hens. It was hard to get an accurate count when they were moving so much. That seemed like a large flock compared with the dozen at home but she supposed they needed that many to keep up with a household comprised of six energetic menfolk. Once she'd scattered enough feed she went to the coop and moved from nesting box to nesting box to collect the eggs. She carefully placed each egg she found in a straw-filled basket. She also checked around on the floor of the coop, making sure none of the hens had decided to make her own nest. While she worked she thought about Seth and his lists. She'd never met anyone so determined to manage the world around him.

What had made him that way? Was it just his nature? Or had something happened to change him? From something he'd said it seemed Dinah had been that way too. Was that the kind of woman he was attracted to?

Not that that was any of her concern.

This morning she'd watched Seth and Levi work side by side at the stove. The two Beilers had such different personalities. She guessed Levi wouldn't have so much as blinked at her use of *dollop* as a measurement. And he would have entertained her with his attention and nonsensical small talk while they worked, doing his best to make her smile.

Seth on the other hand was all business and liked things to be done a certain way. Still, he'd offered to help her cook breakfast without drawing attention to himself. Other than his pushback at the word *dollop* he'd allowed her to take the lead. And he'd also helped with the dishes.

She was coming to see that there was a kindness in Seth, a genuine caring for those around him, that wasn't readily evident on the surface. Like when she'd burned her hand earlier—he hadn't made her feel clumsy or incapable. He'd just treated it like an accident, made sure she was okay and moved on.

And last night, when they'd played cornhole toss, she'd seen yet another side of him, a more playful side.

And she'd for sure and for certain like to see more of *that* Seth.

When she'd finished checking all the possible spots where the hens might have laid their eggs she had seventeen of their offerings safely tucked in her basket. Pleased that she'd managed to perform the task without breaking any of the eggs, she exited the chicken yard, carefully latching the gate behind her.

She'd only taken a few steps when seemingly out of nowhere a dog raced toward her, barking loudly. Startled, Phoebe let out a yelp and dropped her basket.

"Checkers, down!" At the sharply uttered command,

the dog immediately quieted but continued to watch Phoebe suspiciously.

Seth got between her and the dog and studied her in concern. "I'm sorry. Did he hurt you?"

She bent down to retrieve her basket, keeping a wary eye on the dog. "*Nee*, but I'm afraid I dropped the eggs." She studied the contents in dismay. "It looks like about half of them are broken." Two careless accidents and it wasn't even noon yet.

"I'm sorry Checkers startled you. He's rather protective of the place and doesn't trust strangers."

She studied the animal warily. "How did I miss meeting him yesterday?"

"Checkers tangled with a coyote a few days ago and got scratched up pretty bad. We penned him up so we could tend to his injuries. Mark must have let him out this morning." He scratched the dog's ears. "It seems he's feeling a lot better now."

Looking closer, Phoebe could see several scratches and scars. It also appeared the animal had a bit of golden retriever in him.

"Poor boy. I'm glad he recovered okay."

Seth straightened. "Hold your hand out and let him sniff it. Once he realizes you belong here the two of you will be friends in no time."

Phoebe carefully set the basket down, but before she could do as he'd instructed, Seth placed his hand lightly on her shoulder.

"To show him we're friends," he explained matter-of-factly when she shot her gaze his way.

Phoebe nodded, but even when he removed his hand she was very aware of his touch.

She tried to push that aside as she resolutely faced

Checkers and did as Seth had instructed. She liked animals and hoped the golden-retriever-looking dog would sense she wasn't a threat.

Sure enough, after a few moments the dog's tail started wagging and he was treating her as he would an old friend.

"Looks like you've won him over."

"He just needed to see me as a member of the *familye*." She straightened. "Edna tells me you make chess sets. Is that what you were working on?"

"*Jah.*"

"That sounds like wonderful creative work."

He smiled. "I'm not sure about that, but it's something I enjoy doing."

"I'd like to see one of your sets sometime if that's okay with you?" She hoped that hadn't been too forward of her.

But he didn't appear to mind. "Of course." He nodded toward the workshop. "I have one in my shop I'm working on now if you'd like to see it."

"*Jah*, I'd like that very much."

He picked up the basket of eggs and allowed her to lead the way.

As Phoebe walked in she caught a whiff of wood shavings accented with the almost sweet smell of the stains and glue. Then as her eyes adjusted to the workspace she saw small blocks of wood front and center on the table. A closer look showed that he'd begun working with one of them, as the figure of a horse—a knight—was taking shape.

"There's a finished set over here," he said as he moved to a smaller table under one of the windows.

She immediately crossed the room to study his handiwork. The board was obviously made by a skilled craftsman. She reached down to touch it, then paused and glanced at Seth. "May I?"

At his nod, she stroked the board and discovered that the squares were each inlaid separately. He'd let the natural color and grain of the wood show through with the contrasting squares getting their color from the different types of wood they were constructed from. She looked back at him. "This is beautifully done."

"*Danke*. There's also a drawer underneath for storing the pieces."

She looked closer at the raised base and sure enough there was a drawer built onto the underside. She pulled it open to see spaces designed to hold individual chess pieces and rows of checkers. There were two rows of checkers arranged vertically and between them the individual chess pieces were carefully arranged horizontally against a bed of blue velvet.

She carefully lifted the dark king and stroked its smooth surface, studied the remarkable detail in the crown, admired the rich color. "Seth, this is truly *wunderbaar*. The pieces are so rich and detailed."

"*Danke*." Then he asked almost too casually, "Do you play?"

"*Jah*. I used to watch my *daed* and my *grossdaadi* play when I was a *kinner* and the game fascinated me. My *grossdaadi* eventually taught me. He was very patient and did his best to teach me the finer points. When he passed I started playing with my *daed* because none of my *brieder* were interested in learning."

"That sounds like my *brieder*—the not-being-interested part. They much prefer checkers." Then he touched his beard. "You say you know how to play, but do you actually enjoy the game?"

She nodded. "It's something my *daed* and I can do together, a special connection for us."

He met her gaze with a smile. "Then how would you like to play a game after lunch today?"

"Oh, that would be wonderful fun. But I haven't played in a while."

"Don't worry, I'll go easy on you."

She seemed amused by that. "That's kind of you, but please don't feel you have to. Once I learned the basics of the game, *Grossdaadi* never played other than his best. He said it was the only way for me to learn to play well."

"Sounds like your *grossdaadi* was a wise man."

"*Jah*, he was. Because he also said letting someone other than a beginner win out of sympathy is treating them as if they have no ability to either win or accept defeat graciously."

* * *

When Seth walked into the kitchen later he found Phoebe had prepared another lunch for three. But this time, in addition to sandwiches, she'd made some sweet potato fries instead of egg salad. An interesting choice. Hadn't she heard what he'd told her yesterday about keeping it simple?

Edna must have stepped out for a minute—she wasn't anywhere in sight. Phoebe hadn't spotted him yet and he could hear her singing softly and slightly off key as she worked.

Not wanting to be accused of spying on her he cleared his throat.

The singing stopped abruptly and her head swiveled around to face him. But there was no apology, just surprise.

"Sorry if I startled you. How's your hand feeling?"

"It's fine. Except for having to wear this bandage it hardly gets in my way."

"*Gut* to hear."

Edna came in from the living room just then. "*Gut*, we can eat now." Her eyebrows were furrowed and her lips were pursed in something that was part frown, part pout. "I'm hungry but Phoebe insisted we wait for you."

He turned back to Phoebe with a frown. "That wasn't necessary. I sometimes get caught up in my work and may be up to an hour late for lunch."

"I'll keep that in mind in the future." She gave Edna an exasperated look. "But it's only a few minutes past noon so you're not late today. And Edna knows there are other things she can snack on."

With a tilted chin and an inelegant *humpf* Edna took her seat at the table.

Seth saw Phoebe grin indulgently as she turned to get something from the refrigerator.

After their plates were served they dug into their meal.

"These sweet potato fries were certainly worth the wait." Edna wagged one of the fries Phoebe's way. "I'd never have thought to cook such a thing. But it's much better than having just a plain sandwich, don't you think?" The woman gave Seth a pointed look.

"*Jah*, they're quite tasty."

"If there's something else you'd prefer to have with your sandwich in the future, just let me know and I'll be happy to fix it for you."

"As I mentioned yesterday, there's really no need for you to go to any trouble. Just a plain sandwich is fine with me."

Her chin came up and he could see a little pink bloom in her cheeks. Had he said something wrong again?

"Perhaps I'm doing this for me and Edna. You certainly

don't have to eat it if you don't want to. You can just treat it like you do copper pennies."

It seemed he *had* said something wrong. "*Nee*, it's quite *gut*. I just didn't want to make extra work for you."

She nodded but didn't say anything.

Had he just made matters worse?

Chapter 13

There was an awkward silence, which was finally broken when Edna asked Seth about fixing a loose floorboard in the *dawdi haus*. After that the rest of the conversation was polite small talk.

When the meal was finally over, Phoebe carried the dishes to the sink. "If you want to go ahead and set up the chessboard for our game," she told Seth as she worked, "it shouldn't take me long to wash these few dishes."

Relieved she was still in the mood to play, Seth moved to the sink. "You're still wearing that bandage so I'll wash, you dry."

"Danke."

Edna carried her plate one-handed. "The two of you are playing chess?"

"Jah."

"Then I think I'll get out of your way and go to the living room to do some reading."

They took care of the dishes in relative silence, but much of the earlier tension was gone.

As Phoebe dried the last few dishes, Seth headed down the hall. He returned a few minutes later with a wooden chessboard, which he placed on the table and quickly set up.

Phoebe hung up her drying rag and then took her place across from him. He watched as she studied the board. What was she thinking?

She looked up and met his gaze. "This set is similar to the one you showed me earlier. Did you make this set too?"

"*Jah*. It was one of the first ones I made. As you can see, it's a little less polished than the ones I make now."

"But it has the wear and warm look of loving use. In some ways I like it more than the ones in your workshop."

Her response surprised him. "I made it as a gift for my *daed*."

"He liked to play?"

Seth nodded. "We played often, right here at this table. He's the one who taught me how." Then he waved a hand. "You have the first move."

Four moves into their game Seth could see that she knew the basic moves of chess but wondered if she understood the strategy part. There didn't seem to be any rhyme or reason to her moves. Seven moves in he realized he was in serious trouble.

He eventually won the game but he had to work for it and he still wasn't sure what kind of strategy she'd used.

"You said your *grossdaadi* taught you?"

"*Jah*. And Edna's Ivan taught me his own approach that summer I stayed with them as well. But I've always had my own way of looking at the game. Ivan called it my strategic scattershot approach."

She said that as if she considered it high praise.

He leaned back. "I want a rematch tomorrow."

She stood. "I'd like that. But now I have some mending to do and a supper to prepare."

Had she just dismissed him?

While Seth put away the game, Phoebe went into the living room to find Edna asleep in a recliner, gently snoring.

Leaving her friend to her nap, Phoebe quietly pulled out the sewing basket where the Beilers had placed anything that needed mending. While she sewed on buttons and restitched ripped seams she thought about the time spent with Seth. She was over her irritation at his stubborn attitude about her attempts to make their lunch more enjoyable rather than just something to gulp down and move on from. He would come around in time. And she'd really enjoyed their chess match. It didn't bother her that he'd beaten her because she knew she'd played her best and he'd done her the honor of playing to win. It had been wonderful fun to pit her wits against his and see his measured approach put into practice on more than just lists and schedules.

"You must really enjoy mending."

The dry comment pulled Phoebe's thoughts back to the present. She looked across the room and saw Edna smiling at her. "What makes you say that?"

"I just thought, from that big smile on your face, you must be getting a great deal of pleasure from what you're doing."

"*Mamm* always says a job well done is a pleasure unto itself." Which was certainly true even if it wasn't the reason for her smile.

"That for sure and for certain sounds like Verena Kropf."

What did she mean by that?

Edna let the foot of the recliner down and stood. "Have you given any thought to what you want to prepare for supper? Or do you need me to read from Seth's list of suggestions?"

"I think I'd rather try something new." She knotted the thread and snipped it as she finished with the last button. "There's an idea I had for the pork chops I saw in the freezer." She gave Edna a hopeful look. "I may need a little help."

"Of course."

She closed the sewing basket and stood. "But first, there's something else I want to do before the boys get home."

* * *

Phoebe opened the oven to check on the peanut butter cookies just as the outside door opened.

"Hello." Mark's voice rang out from the mudroom. The salutation was quickly followed by "Mmmm, something smells *gut*."

She placed the sheet pan on the stovetop. "You're just in time. I was looking for a taste tester for these cookies."

"Well, you found one." Mark headed for the stove, his eyes focused on the cookies.

She quickly stepped in his path. "They just came out of the oven—give them a few minutes to cool." She waved to the refrigerator. "Pour yourself a glass of milk while you're waiting."

Mark gave her a mock-pout then moved to the cabinet where the mugs were stored. Once he'd filled the mug he was back at the stove helping himself to two of the warm treats. "These are really *gut*."

Phoebe used a spatula to transfer the rest of the cookies to a platter. "Glad you like them, but leave some for your *brieder*, please."

Mark nodded, then gestured toward her hand. "How's your burn feeling?"

"It stings a little, especially if I forget and grab something heavy with it. But it's not too bad."

"*Gut*. If you need help with anything, don't be afraid to ask for it."

"*Danke*, I'll keep that in mind."

Mark reached for another cookie and she put one hand on her hip. "That's the last one. You need to save some for your *brieder*."

He grinned at that. "I almost feel sorry for them since they won't get this soft, fresh-from-the-oven tastiness." He bit into the treat. "Almost."

She shook her head at him and made shooing motions. "I think it's time you move away from that platter."

He finished off the cookie and drained his mug of milk then set it in the sink. "It's time for me to get to work anyway." He moved to the corkboard. "Let's see what task Seth put at the top of the list today."

A moment later he'd put his jacket back on and headed outside.

When the two scholars made it home from school they were equally appreciative of her baking efforts, wolfing down their share of the cookies as if they hadn't eaten in days rather than mere hours.

After they'd finished and headed out to take care of mucking the stalls, Phoebe looked at the remaining cookies. After waffling for a moment, she finally made up her mind.

She placed four cookies on a saucer, filled a glass about halfway with milk and headed out the door.

Stepping carefully to avoid another klutzy incident, she breathed a sigh of relief when she finally made it to the workshop. She stepped inside and nearly spilled the milk when Checkers jumped up from his spot at Seth's feet to bark a greeting.

Seth looked up and when he saw her, he gave the dog a sharp "Sit" command. "What brings you out here?"

"I baked some peanut butter cookies this afternoon. Your *brieder* have already had some so I thought I'd bring you a few before they're all gone."

"*Danke.* That sounds *gut.*"

She moved to place the saucer and glass on his worktable. "I don't want to interrupt your work, at least not any more than I already have. I'll just set these here and head back to the house."

He reached for a cookie. "There's no need to rush off. I could use a short break."

She relaxed, pleased by the invitation. "What are you working on?"

He pointed to the piece he'd just set down. "The dark queen."

Phoebe studied the piece. The crown and tapered top it sat on were starting to emerge from the block of walnut wood. It was rough still but she could see some of the classic features starting to appear.

She set it back down. "I notice these pieces have a different look than the set we played with. You've added some refinements." She gave him a smile. "Despite how much I like your original, these new sets have a more polished look and feel."

He spread his hands. "I try to improve my skill with each set I make."

That was an admirable goal.

* * *

Seth munched on his cookies, watching her admire his work. He knew it was wrong to be prideful but her obvious admiration of his efforts was quite gratifying. Even Dinah had only seen it as an extra source of badly needed income rather than an artistic outlet for him.

Which, to give Dinah credit, was how he'd started his business in the first place. After he'd made a few sets as gifts he'd gotten some inquiries from folks who'd wanted to buy one, either for themselves or to give as gifts. It had amazed him how much some of them were willing to pay for a set. Dinah had suggested he use his off time in the winter months to make his sets and sell them. But she hadn't been interested in learning to play chess. And when he'd asked her questions about possible design options her only comment had been to ask which design the customers liked best.

He had a feeling that Phoebe would give him a very different answer.

Chapter 14

Seth took his place at the supper table that evening and discovered the meal was once again something she'd come up with on her own. It was a pork chop dish of some sort, accompanied by mashed potatoes that had more than butter added to them, and English peas.

He also noticed that Levi again took the seat to Phoebe's right.

This time, when the bowls were passed around the table he was able to take a generous portion of each dish without hesitation.

When he actually tasted the meal, he was surprised. The sauce on the pork chops had an orangey flavor, the peas had apparently been seasoned with mint, and cheese and bacon pieces had been stirred into the mashed potatoes with perhaps just a hint of mustard. He was still trying to decide what he thought about it when Levi spoke up.

"This is wonderful *gut* food. It's nice to have some variety in our meals, that's for sure and for certain."

Several of his *brieder* added their compliments and agreement. Had having a regimented menu been such a terrible thing? He'd made sure each of their favorite dishes had appeared at least once every week so that it wasn't all weighted one way or the other.

Levi spoke up again, pulling Seth out of his thoughts.

"Tell me," Levi asked Phoebe, "are you settling in okay?"

"*Jah*, this is a wonderful nice home and I feel useful and welcome here."

"*Gut*. Because I think I speak for all my *brieder* when I say we're glad you came."

Seth saw the way Levi's words made her smile, the way her eyes brightened and she sat up a little straighter. Was she falling for his *bruder's* charm?

But the next minute Levi offered her a bit of outrageous flattery and she actually grinned and rolled her eyes at him. Perhaps she had enough sense to see his *bruder's* harmless flirtations for what they were after all. Just in case, though, it would be best if he still had that talk with Levi.

When the meal was over, Seth stood and carried his dishes to the sink. But rather than filing into the living room with his *brieder*, he turned to fill the sink.

Levi, naturally, was the first to notice. "What are you doing?"

"Phoebe needs to keep her bandage dry and since Edna can't help, I'm going to wash the dishes while Phoebe dries."

Levi's lips quirked suspiciously. But all he said was "That's quite noble of you."

Their conversation had garnered the attention of some of his other *brieder*, who were now staring at him in surprise. You'd think they'd never seen him wash dishes before.

Before he could come up with a response, Edna stood and made shooing motions. "Everyone who's not cleaning the kitchen or dishes get out of here and give those who are room to work."

For once Seth appreciated her no-nonsense tone.

Once he and Phoebe had the kitchen to themselves, they got to work on the dishes, chatting about inconsequential things.

"So how did you come to need Edna as a housekeeper? Were you all on your own before she returned to Sweetbrier Creek?"

He nodded. "For a month or so. Our former housekeeper was part-time—she came in for about four hours a day, five days a week. She was with us for ten months before she became engaged." He gave the bowl he was washing a vigorous scrub. "The *gut* Lord was certainly watching out for us when *Aenti* Edna came along. She offered to take the housekeeper's place if we would give her use of the *dawdi haus.*"

"Edna isn't afraid of hard work, that's for sure and for certain."

He cut her a sideways glance. "That seems to be a trait you share with her."

Her cheeks pinkened at that—it was a look he was coming to appreciate. "How did your *eldre* feel about you coming all this way to take the job of housekeeper for a *familye* they'd never met?"

She put away the bowl she'd just dried. "They were hesitant at first—I think they still see me as a *youngie.* But *Daed* came around to the idea and *Mamm* followed his lead, though not happily I'm afraid. It did help that Edna was here, though."

"If you need to speak to them while you're here, you

are welcome to use the phone shanty." He wasn't sure why he'd said that, of course she'd know she was welcome to use it.

"*Danke.*"

By this time they'd finished with the dishes. While Phoebe finished straightening up a few things, Seth headed for the living room.

He found his *brieder* had taken out a couple of sets of dominoes but instead of playing the game, they had lined up two domino runs on the floor and were competing in some fashion. Jesse and Kish were working on one of the runs and Mark and Daniel on the other. Levi was stooped on the floor alternately cheering and critiquing from the sidelines. As Seth watched, the run Jesse and Kish were working on toppled prematurely and there were groans and heckles from the other three.

This looked like an ideal time to have that talk. "Levi."

His *bruder* looked up and met his gaze, his brows raised in question.

"Would you join me in my office please? There's something I'd like to speak to you about."

He saw his *brieder* all exchange glances before Levi nodded and stood from his stooped position. "Lead the way."

When they reached the small bedroom Seth had turned into his office, Seth took a seat behind his desk while Levi dropped into a guest chair and lounged back. "I haven't been singled out for one of your talks in a long time. So am I in some kind of trouble?"

Seth frowned at his *bruder's* amused tone. "I just wanted to talk to you about Phoebe."

His words seemed to have no effect on Levi's mood. "Do you now?" his *bruder* asked. "What about her?"

No point in mincing words. "I notice you've been paying her some particular attention."

Levi shrugged. "Phoebe is an interesting woman. Why shouldn't I pay attention to her?"

"I don't think you realize the effect you have on some of the more impressionable ladies you interact with."

If anything Levi appeared even more amused. "And what effect is that?"

Seth usually ignored Levi's attempts to goad him but this time it irritated him for some reason. "Don't pretend you haven't noticed and even taken advantage of it on occasion. You know very well most of the girls find you charming and attractive. In fact it's beyond me why you haven't found one to court yet."

That remark seemed to finally get under Levi's skin. But he recovered quickly enough. "Don't worry, I'm just being nice to Phoebe, trying to get her to smile a little more. It can't be easy for her to just pick up and leave her *familye* this way."

"Regardless of all that, Phoebe is not just our housekeeper, she's a guest of Edna's and her *eldre* have entrusted her to our care. While she's here she's a member of our household and should be treated as such. Besides, she's going to be returning to Bergamot in a few weeks and we probably won't see her again. I don't want her to leave with a broken heart and unhappy memories."

"I don't want that either." Levi's gaze held a note of challenge. "Maybe you should take charge of seeing that her stay here is a pleasant one since you know how to take care of that without endangering her heart." He stood. "Is there anything else we need to discuss?"

"*Nee*, that was all."

With a nod, Levi left the room.

Seth followed more slowly. He was concerned that he hadn't gotten through to his *bruder*. Was Levi right that he himself should take a more active role in ensuring Phoebe's stay was pleasant? After all he was the oldest, the head of the household.

And that was his only motive, of course.

When Seth reached the living room it was to find that the group had moved to the kitchen and were playing an actual game of dominoes. Phoebe was laughing at something that Kish had said and her whole face was aglow with her mirth. For a moment he imagined her like this, in this kitchen in the midst of his *brieder*, for the long term.

Then he shook his head—it wasn't like him to allow such fanciful thoughts to distract him.

Phoebe glanced up and saw Seth in the doorway watching them. Why did he insist on keeping himself separate from his *brieder*?

She stood. "*Ach*, Seth, you're just in time. *Kum* take my place for a few rounds while I make hot cocoa for everyone."

He straightened and she saw a refusal forming on his lips.

"Unless you think you can make a pot of cocoa that's better than my special recipe."

"I vote for Phoebe's recipe," Levi said.

There was a chorus of agreement from those around the table.

Seth held his hands up palms-out in a sign of surrender and took her place at the table.

With a smile, Phoebe went to work on the cocoa. She'd promised them a special recipe so she looked at the spices in the cabinet and available ingredients in the refrigerator and found a jar of strawberry jelly. Smiling she added a large dollop of the jelly to the pot of milk heating on the stove. Then she added a touch of salt and finally the cocoa.

As she stirred the mixture, she heard Seth let out a mock-protest at a move made by one of his *brieder*. Hearing him really interact with his *brieder* this way brought a smile to her face.

She waited until the current game was over to tell them the cocoa was ready and they immediately abandoned the dominoes to fill their cups.

"There *is* something special about this cocoa." Seth raised a brow. "Is that a hint of strawberry I taste?"

"*Ach*, it's not that easy to get my secrets from me."

Seth merely grinned in response.

What would he think if she told him her actual secret, that she could barely read or write and tried everything to avoid it? She felt a pang of guilt for keeping it from him while knowing he assumed she could. But she needed time to prove herself first.

Besides, if it didn't affect her work, it shouldn't matter. Should it?

* * *

The next morning Phoebe was more comfortable in the kitchen and she had breakfast well under way by the time Seth came in with the milk. This time she was careful to turn the burners off before she went to help him strain the milk. Her hand still gave her sharp reminders that she'd burned it yesterday.

When they were done Seth gulped down a second cup of coffee then went back out to finish up whatever morning chore he'd set himself.

As Seth was going out, Daniel came in from the mudroom

and Edna entered from the back porch. Both headed for the coffee. After they'd each poured up their cups Phoebe noted that the second oldest Beiler quietly went about fixing a fresh pot.

Phoebe decided to take the opportunity to get to know him better. "You work in an orchard, is that right?"

"*Jah*. The Fretz apple orchard. It's located right next door."

"Do you enjoy the work?"

He nodded while he took a sip from his cup. "Someday I'd actually like to have an orchard of my own."

"I'm not familiar with what it takes to maintain an orchard but I would have thought there wouldn't be much to do this time of year."

"Actually, this is the time of year where we do maintenance—trimming away dead growth, lopping off the tops, checking for damage, mulching."

"You said you want to have an orchard of your own someday. Would you plant it here, on this farm?"

"*Nee*. This land is for the farming that supports our *familye*. But I have half an acre here that I've planted with apple and pear trees—if you go out behind the *dawdi haus* and look to your right you'll see them. I use it for experimenting."

"Experimenting?"

"I'm trying to use new growing techniques and grafting of one stock onto another. I'd like to improve the fruit production and quality."

"So you do more than just cultivate and grow the trees."

He gave her a smile that was almost prideful. "*Jah*."

She supposed he had a right to take pride in his work. "Have you harvested any fruit yet?"

He shrugged. "*Nee*, the trees are too young."

The two younger boys arrived in the kitchen just then, ending the discussion on orchards and reminding Phoebe she had to focus on getting breakfast on the table and lunches packed.

For breakfast this morning she'd decided on pancakes, though getting enough batter prepared for this household was a bit daunting.

To go with the pancakes she'd gathered up a jar each of strawberry, blackberry and raspberry preserves, added a little bit of cream cheese, honey and lemon juice and simmered the mixture on the stove for a while. The result was a chunky mixed-berry syrup to spoon over the pancakes. She'd also cooked some bacon to have on the side. By the time she had everything on the table everyone had gathered in the kitchen.

As the Beilers dug into their meal, they made it obvious her efforts at the stove had not gone unappreciated.

"This syrup is wonderful *gut*," Mark said as he grabbed the bowl and ladled another portion on his pancakes.

"Save some for the rest of us," Kish warned.

"I must say," Levi added as he speared another forkful, "I've begun looking forward to your meals. And not just because they're so tasty, but also because of the surprising touches you add to them."

"*Danke*. But, just like Daniel and his orchard, I enjoy experimenting with new ways of doing things when I'm cooking and you all end up with the results of those experiments."

Levi grinned. "Well, let's just hope Daniel's experiments turn out as well as yours."

She cast a quick glance Daniel's way. "*Ach*, I didn't mean to say my cooking efforts compare to Daniel's work in importance, just that they are both experiments."

But Levi shook his head. "I'd say feeding us is every bit as important as Daniel's attempts to improve his fruit trees."

Phoebe decided it was time to change the subject. "Everyone's lunch is packed and on the counter whenever you're ready for it. And I've written your names on them so there should be no confusion."

Levi's grin said he knew he'd gotten to her. But he accepted her change of subject and didn't attempt to tease her further.

Later, as Phoebe finished clearing the table, Seth gestured toward her hand. "I see you're no longer wearing your bandage."

She shrugged. "It was getting in the way when I tried to do my mixing and prepping this morning."

"Let me see it," he said, holding his hand out.

It was really more of a command than a request so Phoebe somewhat reluctantly put her hand in his. His hold was surprisingly gentle despite the rough calluses and large size of his hand. He cradled her hand in a way that made it seem her hand was meant to fit in his. The warm feeling his touch created caught her off guard, made her feel unsettled.

But he was frowning as he studied her injury. A patch about the size of a quarter on her palm between her thumb and index finger was still an angry shade of red and there was a match-head-sized blister near the center.

"It still looks like it could use some extra care," he said without looking up. "I can apply a fresh bandage for you if you like."

She reluctantly slid her hand from his. "*Danke*, but I think I'm okay without it. I'll be extra careful."

He met her gaze then and she saw concern and

something else reflected there. "You know best, but please do take care."

And with that he turned and headed for the mudroom.

Phoebe moved to the sink, her hand still warm and tingly from his touch.

She decided it was best not to attach too much meaning to that. He was just being kind to his housekeeper, nothing more.

And that was as it should be.

Chapter 15

Seth pulled on his jacket feeling oddly deflated. What was wrong with him? It wasn't like he enjoyed doing the dishes. But for just a moment as he held her small, feminine hand in his he'd had the urge to help her, to make her life easier. He could still feel the soft warmth of her hand and the way the pulse jumped in her wrist. Pushing off those thoughts he stepped outside, welcoming the cool blustery wind that whirled around him.

A few moments later he sat in his workshop, trying to focus on carving the light queen. It was delicate work, one cut too deep could ruin the whole piece. But today he was having trouble concentrating.

Perhaps Edna's idea to bring Phoebe here hadn't been such a *gut* one after all. Not only was she younger than what he'd expected, but she was too apt to act on impulse rather than follow a plan or think logically, to the extent that she was a distraction.

Unlike Dinah, whose entire approach had been based on

organization and orderliness. His former wife had brought a structure to their lives, a calming discipline, that had saved him at a time when he was sinking under the weight of smothering responsibilities.

He couldn't imagine Phoebe wrestling order from chaos in the same way.

He gave his head a mental shake. Why was he even thinking of her in those terms? She was just here to help Edna and his *familye* out for a few weeks. Once Edna had recovered the use of her hand, Phoebe would head home and he'd likely never see her again.

His knife slipped, gouging the queen's crown. Grimacing, he studied the damage. He could use wood filler to fix it but if he did that it wouldn't live up to the quality standards he set for himself.

Tossing the piece in the box of seconds he kept on the floor beside his bench, he turned to reach for a fresh block of wood, then changed his mind. Instead he slid a box of the disks he'd cut earlier in front of him.

It would be better to work on the less detailed checkers pieces until he regained his focus.

* * *

When Phoebe went out to collect the eggs, she kept her eyes out for the dog. She didn't want a repeat of what had happened yesterday. But for now Checkers was nowhere in sight. When she entered the chicken yard she repeated the steps she'd gone through yesterday. This time she found nineteen eggs, which was *gut* based on the menu she had prepared for today.

As she closed the gate behind her, she heard the barking that announced Checkers was approaching at a run.

This time she stood right where she was and let the dog approach her. He stopped when he was right at her feet, his barks not at all threatening and his tail wagging.

Phoebe set the basket down and greeted the dog properly, ruffling the fur on his neck and cooing what a *gut* dog he was.

Seth showed up a moment later. Since it was obvious from the tone of Checkers's barking that he was greeting rather than attacking, she wondered why he thought it necessary.

"Is Checkers bothering you?"

She straightened and picked up her basket. "Don't worry, he and I are friends now."

"That's *gut*. But don't be afraid to speak sternly if he gets in your way."

"I don't think that'll be necessary." Then she changed the subject. "What are you working on today?"

"Right now I'm working on the checkers." He waved a hand toward his workshop. "Do you want to see?"

"*Jah*." She was pleased by his invitation.

"Then come along." As they started walking, Checkers danced at her feet. Seth said a stern "Checkers, *kum*!" and the dog immediately abandoned her to trot obediently at Seth's side.

When they reached his workshop she went straight to his worktable and set her basket of eggs down.

With her now-free hands, she picked up one of the pieces he'd completed and studied both sides of it. She looked at the other checkers he'd carved that were lined up on the worktable waiting to be stained and polished. "The star design on the flip side is wonderful nice. And all of these are identical down to the last detail. I can't see any differences other than the wood grain."

He shrugged. "That's what's required by my customers."

"And I imagine they are very well satisfied with the craftsmanship you deliver." Then she met his gaze. "You said your *brieder* don't care much for chess. Do any of them play checkers?"

"*Jah*, they all do."

"It must be quite satisfying to be able to play the game with them with a set you constructed."

There was a look on his face she couldn't quite interpret and then he turned away to fetch a polishing rag. Had she said something wrong?

She roamed the workshop for a little while, impressed by the variety of tools and machines he had. Then she came across several bolts of velvet fabric. Most of them were red but there was a little royal blue and grass green thrown in as well. "Is this what you use to line the drawer and cushion the pieces with?"

"It is." Then he grimaced. "It's my least favorite part of the whole process."

"I could do it for you, at least while I'm here."

He looked surprised at that. "I wasn't trying to make you feel as if you needed to help out."

"Of course not, but I really don't mind. You'd have to show me how, of course, but then I could do it. Truthfully, I'd enjoy feeling that I contributed to the creation of such a lovely set, even if it's just in a small way."

"*Danke*, I'll think about your offer when it's time for me to line another drawer. I have several orders to fill before Christmas and have to admit that I feel as if I'm falling behind."

She straightened and moved to retrieve her basket. "Then I'll get out of your way and let you get back to your work while I go put away these eggs."

She headed back to the house with a bounce in her step.

* * *

When Seth stepped into the mudroom at lunchtime and shrugged out of his coat, he found himself wondering what kind of side dish she'd prepared to go with his sandwich.

Sure enough, Phoebe was at the stove frying something when he entered.

She turned and gave him a welcoming smile. "You're just in time. These are almost ready to come out of the skillet."

He moved to the end of the counter and thumbed through the mail. "And what might 'these' be?"

"Fried pickle slices."

He wrinkled his nose, but she ignored his expression and smiled. "If you don't mind, please step in the living room and let Edna know we're ready to eat. These are best eaten when they're still warm."

"Of course." He was getting used to her assigning tasks to him and his *brieder*.

By the time he and Edna had taken their seats, she was carrying the paper-towel-lined shallow bowl of fried pickles to the table.

And when he tasted the side dish with his sandwich he had to admit the pickles were a satisfyingly tasty accompaniment.

Later, as he carried his dishes to the counter, he met her gaze. "Are you up for another chess match today?"

"*Jah*, I've been looking forward to it all morning."

As had he, truth to tell. "Then I'll wipe down the table and set up the board while you take care of the dishes."

Five minutes later they were sitting across the table from each other with the board between them. She insisted he take the light-colored pieces and the first move since she had that position yesterday. Knowing it was useless to argue with her, he opened by moving his queen's pawn forward two spaces.

She countered by moving the queen's rook's pawn.

And the match was on.

One of the things Seth had learned when playing against her yesterday was that Phoebe didn't believe in keeping chatter to a minimum when playing. Today was no different.

"I've noticed that Jesse is quieter than the rest of you and that he's not as quick to join in when the games come out," she commented as he thought through his third move.

"He's always been that way," Seth responded absently. "Comes with being the youngest I suppose."

She raised a brow at that. "I'm the youngest of my siblings and I'm not sure *quiet* and *thoughtful* are words you'd use to describe me."

He completed his move and looked up with a wry grin. "I suppose that's true. But you're the only girl so that's probably where the difference comes in."

"Maybe." She studied the board and quickly made her move. "Have you ever tried to draw him out?"

Seth frowned as he tried to figure out why she'd moved her bishop. "I told you, that's just the way he is. Some people are more quiet than others by nature. Not everyone can be as outgoing as Levi." Now, why had he said that?

She grinned. "The world would be livelier, for sure and for certain."

Livelier? Did that mean she found Levi's approach to life attractive?

She grimaced good-naturedly. "Of course lively could become very tiresome after a while."

Feeling unaccountably lighter after that, Seth made his next move on the board.

She quickly countered, seeming to give her move very little thought.

He won their match again, but again she didn't make it easy on him. And at the end of the match, he still hadn't been able to follow her strategy.

If she had one.

Chapter 16

Seth looked up from his work to see Phoebe entering the workshop with a saucer of cookies just as she had yesterday. But instead of a glass of milk, she was carrying a mug of something warm from the looks of the pot holder she was carrying it with.

His stomach immediately rumbled in anticipation. "*Gutentag.* That looks and smells delicious."

Her smile also seemed to add to the warmth of the shop.

"I won't keep you from your work, I just wanted to bring this out to you. I thought you might like some hot cocoa to go with your cookies today since it's so cold out." Phoebe set the saucer on the table and turned to hand him the mug. But somehow the handoff didn't work out and the mug ended up on the floor. The cocoa splashed on his pant leg and shoe and the mug broke in four jagged pieces.

A gasp escaped her lips as her eyes widened and her expression was one of someone about to be ill. "I'm so sorry."

Her reaction seemed a bit extreme, even given that she would naturally be embarrassed by the mishap. "Don't worry, the mug is easily replaced. And it was just as much my fault for not getting a *gut* hold on it."

Her tension seemed to ease slightly but she still looked pale. Did she really think he would have been angry?

She finally seemed to snap out of whatever had held her rooted to the floor. "I'll get a broom and clean this up."

"I have one over there in the corner that I sweep up the wood shavings with." He stood. "I'll get a bucket of water from the trough."

By the time he returned she'd picked up the pieces of the mug and had swept the cocoa out the door. He poured the water over the cement floor where it was still stained by the cocoa and she used the bristles of the brush to scrub it further, attacking it with an energy that seemed born of equal parts embarrassment and frustration. She eventually swept the dirty liquid out the door and when she looked up from her work she appeared less shaken than she had earlier.

"I'm sorry for the mess and the interruption of your work. And also that you'll have to eat your cookies without anything to wash them down with." Then she lifted her head. "Although I could make you another cup of cocoa if you—"

His upheld palm interrupted her. "That won't be necessary. And there's no need to apologize. I appreciate you taking the time to come out here and bring me a snack in the first place. And if these cookies are as *gut* as the ones you brought me yesterday, they should be great all on their own."

"If you're sure." She sounded doubtful. "I guess I'll leave you to your cookies and your work before I make a mess of anything else."

He frowned as he watched her leave. He could understand being embarrassed by having such an accident, but this seemed to be something more. He'd noticed it before when she'd had other incidents of this sort. Had something happened in her past to make her this way?

He had a sudden urge to discover what that hurt might be and fix it for her. Which was ridiculous, of course.

He took a bite of one of the cookies and savored the nutty vanilla flavor. She might be a bit accident-prone, but Phoebe could for sure and for certain bake.

* * *

By Friday, Phoebe had developed a routine of sorts. She got up, prepared breakfast, fixed lunches, cleaned the kitchen, swept all the floors, collected the eggs, and tackled any other household chores that needed her attention.

Her favorite moments of the day, though, were the times she spent playing chess with Seth after lunch and bringing him his snacks in the afternoon. It was the challenge provided by the chess games and the chance to indulge her fascination with his chess-making craftsmanship, of course.

She was also forming an attachment to each of the other Beilers. The *brieder* were all individuals in their own right, even the two youngest. She'd remarked on this being Kish's last year of school and asked if he planned to work on the farm with Seth after he graduated or if he planned to apprentice somewhere as Mark had. Kish had immediately said he wanted to one day work as a farrier, something completely different from any of his *brieder*.

But all of the *brieder* shared one defining quality—they were loyal to one another. She was wonderful glad she'd gotten to know them and that Edna had invited her to work here.

* * *

Even though no one had to rush out to their job or school on Saturday morning, the Beiler household rose as early as usual. There were still chores to be done of course—livestock to be fed, cows to be milked, stalls to be mucked out.

Mark all but raced through his chores. His *rumspringa* youth group was spending most of the day together. They were meeting at the dairy farm owned by the *familye* of one of the group's members. According to the teenager, there would be volleyball beginning around ten o'clock, then they would have lunch together. Afterward they'd play more games and, in the evening, have supper and a singing.

It reminded Phoebe of her own *rumspringa* days. She'd been an indifferent player when it came to sports like volleyball and baseball, but she'd always enjoyed the singings. While the hymnals had always been indecipherable to her, she'd memorized the more frequently sung ones and could follow along with the more obscure ones well enough to get by.

Seth had decided after the regular chores were done that he, Levi and Daniel would work on expanding the paddock. The two younger boys were assigned to cleaning out and freshening up the chickens' nesting boxes.

After a morning of such work out in the cold Phoebe was certain they'd be ready for something warm and more filling than sandwiches. So she went to work cooking a hearty chicken vegetable soup. Looking for something to deepen the flavor, she settled on stirring in a generous tablespoon of peanut butter hoping it would add a special nutty flavor. It could simmer on the stove all morning while she went about her own chores.

Just before it was time to serve lunch she decided to fix grilled cheese sandwiches to go with it, because who didn't like fresh-from-the-oven, ooey-gooey cheese, especially on a cold winter day?

They trooped in just as she pulled the toasted sandwiches from the oven. After they'd filled their bowls and settled down to eat, Phoebe asked a question she'd meant to ask sooner. "Is tomorrow a between Sunday or will there be a service?"

"It's a church Sunday. We're having it at the Gerbers' place, which is about a fifteen-minute ride from here so we'll need to plan our departure time accordingly."

She nodded. "That shouldn't be a problem."

Edna spoke up from the other side of Levi. "I'll have a chance to introduce you to my *shveshtra* and some of my other *familye*."

"I look forward to it." Though to be honest, she was nervous. As a newcomer to their community she knew she'd face some scrutiny. Being the center of attention always made her nervous. And when she was nervous, her klutzy tendencies came out in full force.

Levi gave her a reassuring smile. "Don't worry, this is a welcoming community."

Apparently she wasn't as *gut* at hiding her thoughts as she thought she was.

"By the way," Edna said, "it's tradition in this community for several of the women to bring pies or cookies for dessert."

Seth quickly interjected. "But since you're new here you shouldn't feel obligated. I'm sure no one will think anything of it since not every household does it anyway."

"It won't be a problem," Phoebe assured him. "I'm sure I can find time this afternoon to bake something."

After lunch, once the kitchen was cleaned, Phoebe was surprised when Seth brought out the chessboard. "I thought perhaps you'd want to do something with your *brieder* since they're home today."

He shrugged. "They'll still be here after our match. I'm determined to figure out your gameplay strategy."

As they began their match, a few of the other Beiler *brieder* drifted back into the kitchen.

"*Was ist das?*" Levi asked as he took a seat at the head of the table. "Did Seth talk you into playing chess with him?"

"He didn't have to talk me into it," Phoebe asserted as she made her move. "I enjoy the game."

Levi groaned. "*Ach*, don't tell me you're a strategist too."

"I wouldn't call the way I play strategic. I'm more of a spontaneous, instinctual player."

"That explains a lot," Seth said.

Levi lifted a brow but didn't comment further.

When she and Seth finished their match, Levi halted Seth's attempts to pick up the game and turned to Phoebe. "Let's see if you're as good at checkers as you are at chess."

Phoebe spread her hands. "But I lost."

"*Jah*, but you gave him a run for his money. It's more than I've ever been able to do."

That surprised her. "You play?"

"I do. But not nearly as well as Seth. Which is why I don't play him anymore."

"You quit playing because you can't win?"

He shrugged. "It's no fun to play when you know you'll never win."

"I disagree. The fun is in the game itself. I love the

give-and-take, the way I can watch my opponent study the board for the best moves and countermoves, the way conversation seems to go deeper when you're sitting across the board from each other." She leaned forward, trying to make him understand what she was saying. "In all the times I played my *grossdaadi* I only ever beat him once, not counting the times he just let me win while he was teaching me. It was the same with my *daed*. But I cherish my memories of each and every game we played because it was time I spent with just them and me."

Levi raised a brow. "Is that how you feel when you play against Seth?"

She cut a quick glance Seth's way to see he was busy storing the chess pieces in the drawer. "It's how I feel when I play anyone."

"Well, I still intend to see what kind of checkers player you are."

She laughed. "All right. But I warn you, I've won many more checkers matches than I have chess."

"Challenge accepted."

Seth decided not to stay and watch the checkers match. He moved to the mudroom and grabbed his jacket.

"You aren't going back to work, are you?"

He turned to see Phoebe studying him in some concern.

"I'm behind on my orders—everyone wants their sets before Christmas. I need to work on them every hour I can."

He saw that she started to respond but before she could, Daniel jumped in.

"I want the next game," his *bruder* demanded.

With a grin and a shrug, Seth walked out the door. Before he could close it behind him he heard Kish demand the game after that one.

As he trudged to his workshop he thought over what she'd told Levi about liking the game whether she won or not, that the enjoyment for her came from the time she spent with her opponent.

Did that include him—did she enjoy the time they spent together? He certainly did. Mainly because it was nice to have someone willing to play against him, of course.

Some time later, Seth leaned back and rotated his shoulders, trying to ease his cramped muscles. He'd completed the carving on three more pieces and he was quite pleased with the look of them. He reached for another small block of wood then paused when he heard the sound of laughter coming from outside.

Curious, he stood and opened his workshop door. The sight that met his eyes brought a smile to his face. Phoebe and all of his *brieder* except Mark were engaged in an energetic game of some sort—it looked like a version of blind man's buff.

Phoebe was standing at the end of a pair of makeshift obstacle courses. His four *brieder* had paired off into teams with one of each duo wearing a blindfold. And each team was trying to navigate the obstacle courses, with the seeing member giving instructions to the blindfolded one. As he watched he grinned at the missteps and blunders they were making. And those who were falling behind seemed to be having just as much fun as those who were in the lead.

Phoebe spotted him first. "*Kum*, join us," she said, waving him over.

But Seth shook his head. "I have work to do and you all seem to be paired up just fine." He was the odd man out, as usual when it came to his *brieder*. Which was how it should be when one was acting as *daed*.

Levi, who'd just stubbed his toe on a post, pulled a portion of his blindfold up revealing one eye. "You can take my place," he said in mock-disgust. "Kish doesn't seem to know his right from his left."

"Hey," Kish said indignantly, "it's you who can't seem to follow directions."

"Now you have to join us," Phoebe said. "You must settle this dispute one way or the other."

"*Jah*," Kish said. "*Kum* help me show what I can do with a partner who knows what he's doing."

Daniel and Jesse had halted their progress as well and added their own invitations to join in.

Putting aside his deadline worries with only a small twinge of guilt, Seth gave in. "All right, just one round of whatever this is," he said as he sauntered over.

Phoebe clapped her hands. "Back to the start, everyone." She turned back to Seth. "It's an obstacle course game. If you look out across the yard you can see we set up various obstacles with buckets, fence posts, hay bales, and other things we were able to find pairs of. There are also four coffee mugs placed at intervals along each course. The way you play is you try to guide your blindfolded partner through the course without touching him or allowing him to touch any of the items in his path. And you need to talk him through collecting those mugs as he goes. Those can be handed off to his partner, by the way."

Seth stroked his beard. "Sounds a bit complicated."

She raised a brow as her lips twitched in a smile. "Are you saying you don't think you can do it?"

He smothered a grin at her obvious attempt to goad him into playing. But she needn't have bothered—he was ready to go. "Hand me that blindfold."

Before he could put the blindfold on, Levi held up his

hand. "Wait, I think we should change things up. This whole game was Phoebe's idea but so far she's sat it out."

"I was refereeing," she said indignantly.

Levi was having none of it. "Which I view as nothing but an excuse to keep your dignity intact. I say it's time you get your hands dirty, so to speak."

Phoebe pursed her lips in a mock-pout then grinned. "I'm game."

"*Gut.* Now, Kish thinks he can do better with a different teammate. I think he should pair up with Daniel, who is the most logical of all of us." Then he pointed to Phoebe and Seth. "Neither of you has played yet so I think the two of you should form a team and go against Daniel and Kish. Then Jesse and I will play whoever wins."

What was his *bruder* up to? Was he really just trying to even things up? Or did he have some other motive? But his *brieder* were already shifting around to pair up as Levi had suggested.

Phoebe approached him, her expression uncertain. "Do you trust me to guide you?"

He'd actually prefer to be the one doing the guiding, but her expression was so tentative, so uncertain, that he nodded. "I do."

With a smile, she held her hand out for the blindfold. As she tied it behind his head, she suggested an approach. "I find it more effective to use a clockface to give directions, rather than just say right or left. Assuming the direction you're facing is twelve o'clock, if I need you to move in a different direction I may say two o'clock or nine o'clock or some such." She knotted the blindfold behind his head. "How's that?"

"It's fine." Wearing the blindfold made him feel vulnerable in a way he hadn't in quite some time. But as soon as Levi gave the signal to start, Phoebe began to direct him in an unhurried, confident voice that gave him the assurance to step forward. Her directions were clear, her approval when he made the right moves bracing and before long he was moving through the course with unexpected confidence.

Thanks to her direction he only made one mistake— stepping outside his lane—forcing a go-back-four-paces penalty that Levi gleefully enforced. But in the end they finished first anyway. Seth removed his blindfold to see Daniel and Kish still a few steps behind them.

Seth joined the rest of the group in some good-natured heckling as the pair finally made it across the finish line.

Levi quickly claimed his and Jesse's right to challenge the winners. This time Seth insisted Phoebe wear the blindfold. They didn't do as well this time, probably because he wasn't as adept at the direction system she'd used. The few times he used right or left it seemed to confuse her, no doubt because she was expecting clock-based instructions.

In the end they finished just a few steps behind Levi and Jesse. Phoebe good-naturedly congratulated the pair and then began organizing everyone into cleanup details to disassemble the obstacle courses and put the various posts, hay bales and other objects they'd used back where they belonged. And doing it in such a way that it all seemed part of the game.

She truly was amazing. And wonderful *gut* for his *brieder*.

And perhaps for him as well.

Chapter 17

Sunday morning Phoebe felt more jittery than she had since her first day here. Today she would meet the Sweetbrier Creek community. And even more intimidating, they would meet her.

Please, Gotte, *don't let me have one of my clumsy spills or falls today, not in front of all of Seth's friends and neighbors.*

Forcing herself to get out of bed, she dressed quickly, then hurried to the main house to get breakfast ready.

As she reached the kitchen she thought that Seth would be happy to see she'd finally be serving oatmeal for breakfast. She'd prepared it for baking last night and just had to slide it into the oven this morning. While it was baking, she cooked a large batch of scrambled eggs, adding a bit of cheese to it just before it was ready to come out of the skillet.

By the time the Beilers were ready to take their seats she had everything on the table.

"What's in this oatmeal?" Kish asked as he served himself. "It doesn't look like walnuts and raisins."

"It's not. I used applesauce and blueberries. It's my favorite way to have it. But I can use walnuts and raisins next time if you prefer it that way."

Jesse scooped up a bite. "I've never had it with fruit instead of nuts before."

She paused as Seth passed her the platter of scrambled eggs. "Surely you've had it more than that one way?"

"*Nee*," Mark said. "Just with raisins and walnuts. That's how I thought it was supposed to be." Then he brightened. "Sometimes we put preserves on it when we eat it, though."

Phoebe nodded. "*Gut*, then you do have some variety, even if it's after the fact." She spread her hands. "But if you prefer me to make your oatmeal the way you've always had it, I can certainly do that."

"We didn't say that," Levi protested. "At least I didn't. Every meal has become an adventure around here and I find myself looking forward to seeing what you'll come up with next."

Phoebe wasn't really sure if that was a compliment or not.

"Actually it's not exactly true that we've only ever had it one way." Seth pointed his fork Mark's way. "You're too young to remember, but when *Mamm* was alive she used to make it many different ways." He moved the food around on his plate. "When she passed it was just easier to do whatever was quickest."

If Mark had been too young to remember, how old had Seth been when his *mamm* died? It must have been very difficult to lose his *mamm* so young. Was that why he had trouble letting himself just relax and enjoy spending time with his *brieder*?

That appeared to be one more puzzle piece she needed to fit in place to help her figure out what had made Seth into the man he had become.

After breakfast it was a scramble to get everything cleaned up and everyone ready. Finally, they were all prepared. Just to be safe, Phoebe asked Seth to load the buttermilk raisin pie she'd baked into the buggy. She, Edna and Jesse rode in the buggy with Seth. The other four *brieder* rode together in a second buggy.

Because it was easier for Edna to climb into the front with her arm in a sling, Edna sat beside Seth while Phoebe sat in the back with Jesse. She tried to draw the boy out in conversation but while he was polite and answered all of her questions, he didn't elaborate or introduce any topics of his own. She was concerned that there was more to his reticence than shyness and made herself a promise that she was going to do her best to get this youngest of the Beilers to open up to her before she left.

When they reached the Gerbers, Phoebe took a deep breath before she moved from her seat. Telling herself these were all friends of the Beilers and Edna and they had no reason to wish her ill, she pasted a smile on her face and stepped down.

Jesse had already helped Edna climb out of the buggy so the older woman stepped beside Phoebe and placed a hand on her arm. "*Kum*, we're a little early. I'll introduce you to some of the ladies."

Phoebe nodded and allowed Edna to escort her into the home's parlor. First her friend introduced her to Bernice Gerber, the hostess for today's gathering. The woman was somewhere between Phoebe's *mamm's* age and Edna's. She was plump with lots of laugh lines and a broad smile. She took the pie from Phoebe and led her into the kitchen where other desserts were already set out. It quickly became obvious that the woman loved to talk. Not that Phoebe pried or asked a lot of questions. But within minutes Phoebe knew how many *kinner* and *kins-kinnah* she had, how many years she'd known Edna and how long it had taken her to get her home ready for this service.

Edna finally pulled her away and took her to meet two other women, introducing them as her baby *shveshtra* Hilda and Trudy. They looked quite a bit younger than Edna and although they were twins and remarkably similar in appearance, the women had very different personalities. Hilda seemed somewhat flighty and was a bit of a babbler. Trudy, on the other hand, seemed more grounded and practical.

At one point Trudy turned to Phoebe. "You need to meet some of the women your own age. *Kum*, I'll introduce you."

She walked up to two young ladies who were chatting together. "Margaret, Constance, this is Phoebe Kropf. She's helping out at the Beiler place while Edna recuperates. Phoebe, this is Margaret Chupp who makes the most beautiful baskets, and Constance Fischer, our schoolteacher." Then Trudy walked off, leaving Phoebe with Margaret and Constance.

"Welcome," Margaret said warmly. "I hope you're enjoying your time here in Sweetbrier Creek."

Phoebe nodded. "The Beilers have been wonderful *gut* to me and I've enjoyed getting to spend more time with Edna."

The teacher smiled. "That's right, you're from the same town as their *aenti*."

"*Jah*. I've known her for most of my life."

Margaret nodded. "I'm sure the Beilers are grateful that you were willing and able to come on such short notice."

Before Phoebe could respond the signal came that it was time to line up to enter the room set aside for the service. She made a mental note to broach the subject with Constance of how Jesse and Kish were doing in her class if the opportunity presented itself.

Phoebe took her place with her new friends and the other single females behind the married ladies of the community.

After the service was over and they'd filed out, she followed the others to the kitchen. When it became known that she was currently serving as housekeeper in the Beiler household, she found herself getting some unexpected attention. As they worked together in the kitchen, Phoebe picked up from bits and pieces of conversation that Levi was a favorite among the single ladies. There was no surprise there. She was more surprised that she didn't hear similar talk about Seth. Was it because he was a widower? Or that he was quieter, less outwardly charming? Whatever the case, she thought perhaps the local women were overlooking someone who would make a *wunderbaar mann*.

Once they'd finished serving the men, Phoebe had a chance to speak to Constance. "You must know Kish and Jesse very well."

"*Jah*. They are both *gut* boys. Kish is a bit rambunctious, but not at all mean-spirited. And Jesse is more quiet but wonderful smart."

Just what she would have expected to hear. "I assume you'll be doing a Christmas play that all the students participate in, just like we do in Bergamot."

"*Jah*. Kish will sing with the group. And Jesse will read the Christmas story from the Bible. I think you'll enjoy the program."

Phoebe grimaced. "Unfortunately I won't get to see it. I'm returning home to be with my own *familye* for a few days at Christmas."

"Being with *familye* is important but I know the Beilers will miss having you with them." Then Constance turned to the counter. "Would you mind grabbing that other pitcher and helping me replenish the empties?"

Phoebe froze, worried that she would spill something if she agreed. But how could she refuse? Then she squared her shoulders and picked up a pitcher. She could do this— she just had to focus.

While she was down among the diners she spotted Seth deep in discussion with two other men, all of them looking solemn. Levi was farther down the table, wearing his usual charming smile. He looked up and caught her eye, giving her a grin before turning back to his friends.

She saw another young lady standing near the table where Levi was seated. The girl, whom Phoebe had not yet met, gave her a look that was distinctly unfriendly. But she turned away quickly and offered to refill the glasses of Levi and his friends.

Phoebe resisted the urge to roll her eyes. Apparently the young lady was one of Levi's admirers. Little did she know that Phoebe was no threat to her whatsoever.

She made it back to the kitchen without one trip or spill and breathed a sigh of happy relief.

Later, when it was time for the women to sit down and eat their lunch, Phoebe found herself at a table with Margaret, a friend of Margaret's named Clara, Edna and Edna's *shveshtra*.

"So you arrived Tuesday I believe," Clara said. "What do you think of Sweetbrier Creek so far?"

Phoebe picked up her fork. "Other than coming here

today, I haven't left the Beiler farm since I arrived. But I like what I've seen so far."

Hilda looked dismayed. "Oh, but our town has so much to offer. Seth mustn't take up all of your time this way. Tell him you need time to get out and about more."

She hadn't meant for her admission to reflect poorly on Seth. "Actually, he's going to town to run errands on Tuesday and I plan to accompany him so I can get groceries."

This time it was Trudy who spoke up. "That's right, the Beilers are hosting the next Sunday service so I imagine you do have some shopping to do."

Hosting? Phoebe's stomach suddenly was a mass of butterflies. Why hadn't Seth or Edna told her about that?

"Have you ever hosted a service before?" This question came from Margaret. Phoebe was beginning to feel like a ping-pong ball as she turned from one speaker to the other.

"My *familye* has and naturally I helped *Mamm* get the house and food ready." But of course she'd never had the responsibility for the whole thing. Thank goodness she had Edna to lean on for direction.

Trudy nodded. "Then you'll be fine."

Would she? She'd certainly have something to say to Seth when they got home this afternoon about keeping her informed.

* * *

Seth stood near one of the horse paddocks speaking to Homer Gerber and Calvin Detweiler, the cabinetmaker Mark was currently apprenticing with. Lunch was long over and the ladies had left the kitchen and were mingling about, keeping an eye on the *kinner* at play or holding *bopplin* on their hips or shoulders. While Homer discussed

whether to repair or replace an older buggy that had seen
better days, Seth let his gaze wander across the grounds.
He spotted Levi and Daniel with a group of other young
men checking out a friend's new buggy horse. Mark and
some of the other young people in his *rumspringa* group,
in spite of the cold weather, had set up a volleyball net and
were playing an energetic game.

Kish was playing cornhole toss with another group.

It took him a little longer to spot Jesse. His youngest *bruder* was with a group of kids who were standing
together and just talking. Not unusual for the boy. As he'd
told Phoebe, Jesse was naturally quiet. Which didn't mean
he wasn't social, as was evident from his interaction with
this quieter group of *kinner*.

But Phoebe's concerns nagged at him. He looked closer
and even though Jesse was *with* the group, his body lan-
guage made it obvious he didn't feel *part* of the group. He
wasn't engaging in conversation and the others didn't seem
to be making any effort to include him. And while Seth
was sure none of the others were deliberately excluding
him, none of them so much as looked Jesse's way.

Was Phoebe right? Was there more to this than Jesse's
nature?

Then he spotted Phoebe, who seemed to be walking
about aimlessly, and a moment later just happened upon
Jesse. She paused to speak to him and the two of them
moved to the porch, where they sat side by side on one of
the benches.

Curious, Seth moved closer where he could see what
she was up to without interfering.

Phoebe pulled a couple of sheets of paper from her tote
bag and handed one to Jesse. "Now," she said, "fold your
paper just the way I do."

Seth watched as she carefully made a number of complicated folds, pausing after each one to give Jesse time to copy her. If the boy made a mistake, she patiently showed him what he did wrong and let him make the correction himself. When at last she was done, the two each had a very sleek-looking paper airplane.

"Let's see how far these things will fly, what do you say?" And with that she counted down to three and the two of them tossed their paper projectiles.

Seth's eyebrows shot up as the airplanes traveled an astounding distance—hers went at least sixty feet, maybe more.

"Did you see that!" Jesse's voice had an enthusiastic edge that Seth had never heard from him before.

"I did," Phoebe answered calmly. "Why don't you fetch them and we'll try again and see if we can make them go farther."

With a nod Jesse took off to retrieve them.

Seth saw the satisfied smile on Phoebe's face. It was wonderful kind of her to look out for Jesse. Too bad this did nothing to help him engage with the other kids.

The two of them tossed the planes again, but this time Phoebe spent a bit of time coaching Jesse on how to aim and why it mattered. Seth was actually impressed with her understanding of aerodynamics. This time when they flung the planes, each gained several more feet.

By now they'd attracted the attention of several of the other children of various ages. Daniel Glick, a boy about Kish's age, approached Phoebe. "Can you show me how to do that too?"

Several other children echoed the request.

Phoebe stood. "Actually, there's something I need to take care of inside."

At their disappointed reactions, she turned to Jesse. "If I leave these sheets of paper with you, do you think you could teach them how to fold it to make a plane like ours?"

Jesse seemed to shrink inside himself for a moment.

Then Phoebe smiled. "I have faith in you."

Jesse straightened and met her gaze. "*Jah*, I can do that."

"*Gut*. I'll leave you to it then." And with that she turned to go inside the house.

Seth stood where he was a little longer, watching Jesse teach the other *kinner* and *youngie* who crowded around him. He saw how even the older ones took direction from him.

Did this mean Phoebe had been right about Jesse? Or was this merely proof that he'd been right, that Jesse was okay, just quiet by nature?

Whatever the case, she'd done something to help build his little *bruder's* confidence and for that he was grateful.

Chapter 18

Seth set the buggy in motion. Phoebe's first outing seemed to have gone very well. It appeared she'd made some friends, and he'd even had a few of his own friends congratulate him on having found such a pleasant housekeeper.

"I heard something interesting today." Phoebe's words brought him back to the present.

"Oh?" He sent a quick smile her way. If she was bringing up community news then it appeared she truly was settling into her role here.

"It seems your *familye* is hosting the next church service."

"*Jah.*" Then something in her tone caught his attention. He straightened and cut her a sideways glance. "Didn't I mention that to you already?"

"*Nee.*" This time he heard the steel underlying her mild tone.

He turned his gaze forward again. How upset was she? "There's still two weeks, plenty of time to prepare."

"Of course. Now that I know about it."

It sounded like he *was* in trouble. "We'll all help with the preparations of course." Though he and his older *brieder* would need to focus on the grounds and outbuildings.

"I'm familiar with what's required. I helped my *mamm* get our home ready for a church service several times before. I just need to make sure I have enough notice."

"Is two weeks not enough?"

"It's more than enough, now that I have that notice."

"*Gut.* And I'll help you make a list and a schedule to keep things on track."

"That's not really necessary."

"Oh, it's no trouble. I'll be doing the same thing for all the work we need to do on the grounds and outbuildings."

* * *

Phoebe didn't protest further. Seth and his lists. What would he think if he knew she couldn't read well enough for them to be of help to her? Would it change the way he viewed her, the way he gave her free rein to run the household?

Well, once she demonstrated that she could manage the task of getting the house ready for the upcoming service he wouldn't have any reason to doubt her abilities.

Surely that would be enough to prove herself.

Wouldn't it?

That evening, Phoebe lay in bed staring up at the ceiling. Overall, it had been a *gut* day. She'd survived the community gathering without making a fool of herself. And she thought she might have made friends in Margaret and Constance.

Seth had been looking at her more kindly too.

So long as no one knew about her reading and writing challenges she could stand on her own with them.

One of the nicest things about today was that she'd managed to shine a spotlight on Jesse without causing him any undue discomfort. She'd come up with the paper airplane idea last night when she'd glanced at the bag that held her origami and paper-cutting supplies on the dresser across the room.

She'd suspected Jesse would be *gut* if placed in the role of teacher. Not that she believed this would cure him of his shyness overnight, but perhaps it was a step in the right direction.

Phoebe adjusted her pillow and rolled over on her side. Time to get some sleep. There would be a lot to do tomorrow.

Including talking to Seth about an idea she had to make his life easier. Assuming he'd be open to change.

* * *

The next morning Seth leaned against the kitchen counter, drinking down the last swallow of his third cup of coffee. His *brieder* had all headed out to their various destinations and Edna was in the living room. Phoebe was across the room, her back to him as she wiped down the stove.

He found himself strangely reluctant to leave the warm coziness of the kitchen for the *kalt* winter morning that awaited him outside. But he had deadlines to meet so there was no time for those sorts of indulgences. Just as he set his cup in the sink, though, Phoebe turned to him. "If you have a few minutes I'd like to speak to you about something."

"Of course." He crossed his arms and leaned back against the counter. What was on her mind now?

She stood there chewing her lip for a moment, as if trying to make up her mind. Whatever she wanted to discuss with him must be serious.

Then she straightened and met his gaze. "You said on Saturday that you were behind on your orders."

"*Jah*." That was certainly an unexpected topic.

"I've been thinking about your situation and I have an idea about how you might be able to work a little faster to get caught up."

Her statement got his back up a little. What made her think she could help with the way he worked? "I won't compromise on quality," he warned. "Word of mouth is the only advertising I do."

"My idea wouldn't require you to compromise on quality."

She sounded mighty sure of herself. But he figured she meant well. "I appreciate you wanting to help, but there's no need for you to worry yourself about it. I'll catch up on the orders I've already accepted. I just need to put in a few more hours each day." He shrugged. "After all, it's only eleven days until the last day I can ship them out for Christmas."

She gave him a direct, unblinking look. "You're putting in too many hours already. You almost fell asleep over supper yesterday." She put a fist on her hip. "What you need to do is change the way you're working."

Her stern demeanor almost made him smile. "What do you mean?"

"There are certain parts of the process you use in creating these chess sets that take more skill and craftsmanship than others, ain't so?"

"Of course."

"In fact, some can be easily taught to someone who has no carving skill whatsoever."

He rubbed his jaw. "I don't know—"

She waved a hand. "I've already offered to help with the lining, which is one of those tasks that requires a different kind of skill than creating the board and pieces."

She'd get no argument from him on that score. "True, but—"

"So what other steps in the process can you think of that fall into the same category?"

He wasn't used to having someone interrupt him the way she did. But he thought about her question a moment then shook his head. "There aren't any."

Her frown deepened. "Are you telling me that there's not one thing that can be done by someone else without affecting the quality of your product? What about the staining? Or the packaging? Or cutting the wood you build the board and drawer with?"

Seth rubbed the back of his neck. "I suppose those do require different skills." Was she actually thinking about volunteering to do those tasks as well? The packaging, maybe, but he couldn't see her working any of the cutting and pressing equipment. "Those tasks really don't take a lot of my time, it would probably take longer to train someone else than to go ahead and do it all myself. And I'd just as soon make sure it's all done properly." Realizing how that sounded, he quickly added, "Not that I think you wouldn't do your best."

"As would any of your *brieder* you recruited to help you."

"My *brieder*?" She kept surprising him with her jumps from idea to idea.

"Of course, who else? The whole *familye* benefits from the sales of these chess sets, ain't so? Why shouldn't they help produce them if you need them to?"

"Levi, Daniel and Mark already have other jobs that contribute to our *familye* income."

"As do you with the operation of the farm. You wouldn't be asking any more of them than you ask of yourself. Besides, your two youngest *brieder* can certainly take on some of these tasks."

She seemed to have an answer for everything. What she didn't understand, though, was that he *did* ask more of himself—it was what you did if you were the head of the household.

Phoebe waved a hand. "But back to what you said about it taking longer to teach than to do. I think you aren't giving your *brieder* enough credit. And how difficult would it be to learn how to package a chess set for shipping, or to line the tray or cut the lengths of wood?"

He started to respond but she held up a hand. "Yes, I know there are consistency and quality issues that whoever helped would need to be aware of, but that's something that can be emphasized. In fact, you can check behind us the first few times we perform the task."

He shifted slightly, unable to find a strong argument to counter her proposal. But apparently she wasn't done yet.

"There's something else I'd like you to think about."

What now? "I'm listening."

"When I'm doing the mending, I like to work on all the pieces that need to have buttons sewn on first, then all the ones that need to have seams restitched, then all the ones that need to be patched, and so forth. Do you know why I approach it that way?"

She was comparing mending to carving chess sets? Didn't she know how to stay on topic? "I suppose it's because it's easier to do one type of task at a time than to switch back and forth."

She beamed at him as if he were wonderfully clever. "*Jah*. And what if you approached your work the same way. Rather than doing one set from start to finish you did it by part?"

"I'm not sure—"

Before he could finish, she again jumped in. "Suppose, for instance, you made all the boards and storage drawers first? Then, while you move on to making the chess pieces, I could line all the drawers. And someone, say Jesse, could hand-polish the finished boards and pieces. And Kish could cut the blocks you need. Levi, Daniel and Mark could help as available and as needed."

He stroked his beard. It wasn't the way he liked to work, but how to let her down gently? "It sounds like you've given this a lot of thought."

She nodded. "Most of last night. To be honest, I wasn't sure you'd really want to listen to my advice on matters of business."

That hit him wrong. "I like to think I'm always willing to listen."

Her chin came up. "That's *gut*. Because I decided if *Gotte* had placed it on my heart, I had no business keeping it to myself. What you decide to do with my suggestions, however, is up to you."

He could tell she was earnest and obviously meant well but she had no idea what implementing this would take. "I appreciate you trying to help. Changing my entire process might be a *gut* idea if I had time to play with this awhile and could take the time to get everyone trained and make tweaks to the process where needed. But since I'm already backlogged, I don't see that I could take the risk right now of getting even further behind."

He saw the disappointment clearly displayed on her

face and posture but she nodded. "It's your business so of course you must do it as you see fit." She moved to the sink. "Now I need to get the breakfast dishes clean and then tackle the laundry. And I'm sure you have things to do as well."

Seth headed out into the windy day, turning his jacket collar up against the cold. It wasn't raining or snowing but there was a touch of moisture in the air.

He knew his response had disappointed her but there was no help for it. What she'd proposed sounded *gut* on the surface but she really didn't understand the way he worked.

Besides, he liked to have his hands on the whole process, it was important to him to know that his standards of quality were upheld in every part of it.

That would be impossible if he parceled out the work.

Did that make him prideful?

Chapter 19

Phoebe attacked the dishes with a little more vigor than was absolutely necessary. That conversation hadn't gone as well as expected. He hadn't brushed her suggestions off entirely but she suspected that was just him being kind. From his demeanor she didn't think he would ask for much help even after Christmas when his backlog was under control.

But she would respect his decision and just do her best not to add anything extra to his workload. And maybe she could help him in other areas so he had more productive time for his work on the chess sets.

For now she would make sure she got her own work done. Which meant tackling the laundry, and with a household of six active men and boys, that was quite a chore. But Phoebe tackled it with gusto.

Because it was too cold to hang the laundry outdoors and have any chance it would dry, she planned to use the lines that were hung in the basement for just that purpose.

She tackled the clothing first and then went on to wash and hang the towels and bedding.

By the time she finished, it was nearly lunchtime. She barely had time to throw together a fruit salad, complete with some chopped pecans tossed in, to go with their sandwiches.

She hoped when Seth came in for lunch there wouldn't be any awkwardness based on their earlier conversation.

* * *

When Seth entered the house for lunch, he nodded Phoebe's way as he headed for the stack of mail on the counter.

There were three envelopes addressed to him. The first two contained final payments for chess sets he'd shipped last week. The third was an order from someone who wanted to know if he could produce four sets for him before Christmas. The man even said that since it was a last-minute order, he would pay a 50 percent premium.

"Is something wrong?"

Seth looked up to see Phoebe watching him with a worried frown as she set the small platter of ham on the table. He grimaced as he moved to fetch the bread. "I just received a generous offer for four of my chess sets."

"Isn't that a *gut* thing?"

"*Jah*, normally it would be." He set the loaf on the table. "But since I'm already so backed up, I can't possibly accept another order."

"*Ach*, that's too bad."

To her credit she didn't bring up their earlier conversation, but the memory of it hung in the air between them. Especially since this order could have made a big difference for him and his entire household.

Once they'd served their plates, Phoebe brought up a different subject entirely. "I realized this morning that I never asked you what space you hold the service in when it's hosted here."

"The basement. It's a bit crowded but we manage."

"Then I need to study the space and figure out what can be moved somewhere else temporarily."

"*Jah*. But my *brieder* can help with that. And there's a spare room upstairs that can be used for temporary storage."

"*Gut*. Now, I know different communities have different traditions around the luncheon after the church service. Will I be expected to provide the entire meal?"

Edna spread mayonnaise on her bread. "Other ladies in the community will provide the desserts. We'll be expected to provide the main meal as well as tea, lemonade and coffee."

"The meal yesterday consisted of church spread sandwiches, bologna and cheese sandwiches and coleslaw. Is that also traditional here?"

This time Edna nodded. "*Jah*, that's what most will do. But there are those who prefer to cook a potato casserole or have another type of sandwich and that's all right too."

Seth decided to join the conversation, complimenting her on her fruit salad. "This would be *gut* to have instead of the coleslaw if you'd like to do that." Not wanting to sound as if he was pushing her in one direction or the other, he quickly added, "But I'll leave the menu up to you."

She nodded. "Edna and I will be walking through the house this afternoon," she said. "We plan to make note of everything that needs to be done before everyone arrives the day of the next service."

Perhaps she was starting to see the benefits of making

lists and approaching work in an organized manner. "Making plans is a *gut* thing. And when we go to town tomorrow you can pick up any extra supplies you might need." He reached for his glass. "While you're doing the walkthrough, if you see anything that needs repair, let me know and I'll see that it gets taken care of."

"We'll keep our eyes out."

After lunch Seth set up the chessboard. They hadn't played a match yesterday since they'd been away from home. He was surprised now by how much he was looking forward to playing again. It was a sign of how much he enjoyed playing the game, he supposed.

And from the smile on her face as she sat down across from him, he could see she enjoyed it as well.

"Your turn to go first," he said as he turned the board so the light pieces were in front of her.

Later, as Phoebe made another of her out-of-left-field chess moves, Seth shook his head. But he was beginning to see something of her strategy, or rather her lack of one. She seemed to play purely on instinct, reacting to the current situation on the board. Her ability to read the board and its implications, however, was amazing.

"You say your *grossdaadi* taught you the basic moves—did he also teach you strategy?"

"*Actually* it was Edna's Ivan who tried to teach me strategy and taught me how to play fearlessly."

Fearlessly, is that what she called it? "They both taught you well." Regardless of the end result of their matches she never made the wins easy for him.

"*Danke*. They've both been wonderful *gut* influences on my life as well as my game."

He moved his rook, capturing her queen's bishop. "Check."

She studied the board and made the only move open to her. Then quizzed him about what time they would be heading for town in the morning and how long the outing normally took.

He answered absently. It would be checkmate in two moves but if she realized that she didn't seem at all concerned. Apparently she'd meant what she said about enjoying the game for the company, not whether or not she won.

And though he kept waiting for her to bring up the conversation they'd had this morning she never did.

* * *

When Phoebe stepped inside his workshop that afternoon with her offering of cookies and milk, Seth almost stood to take the saucer and glass from her. He had an urge to protect her from a repeat of the painful embarrassment she'd experienced with the cup of cocoa. But instead he kept his seat and let her proceed unaided.

And her pleasure when she succeeded was worth it.

"Did you finish making your list yet?" he asked as he took one of her cookies.

"We just have the basement left to go through. And we've identified a few things in the house that could use repair or a touch-up."

"Just put the list on the corkboard and I'll take a look when I get in this evening."

Rather than responding directly, she pointed to the flat, square wood tiles stacked on his worktable. "Those are what you use to make the squares on your chessboards, aren't they?"

"They are. I'll glue them in place later today and then tomorrow I'll stain and seal them."

"That certainly seems like something me or one of your *brieder* could do." There was a very pointed tone in her voice.

He should have known they weren't done with this topic, especially after the new order he'd received today. "They need to be cut, stained and placed in a certain way."

"So, you're saying none of the rest of us could quickly learn to do a task that is mostly repetitive."

She just didn't understand what this job took. "I'm very particular in how I want the boards to look."

"You like to control the process from start to finish because you take pride in your work." It was a statement, not a question.

"Exactly." Maybe she did understand.

"One should be careful that such pride doesn't blind one to how *Gotte* would wish him to conduct himself." Before he could respond she added, "Did you consider that you might be robbing your *brieder* of the chance to feel a part of what you do? And robbing yourself of the opportunity to be more a part of their lives?"

And with a raised brow, she turned and made her exit.

Seth ate the last cookie, mulling over her words. Was that really what he was doing—letting his pride get in the way of asking for much-needed help? And in the process robbing himself and his *brieder* of the chance to spend time together?

He picked up the rook he'd been working on when she entered and rubbed the surface with his thumb. He reached for a piece of sandpaper and went to work.

But he couldn't get her words out of his head.

Phoebe walked back to the house, pleased with how the conversation had gone. She'd had a difficult time speaking up that way but she really did think if he tried out her suggestions, it would not only help him meet the deadlines he was worried about but also bring him and his *brieder* closer together, which in her mind was every bit as important if not more so. Because while she could tell that they all really loved one another there was some kind of wall that had been erected between Seth and the rest of them.

And before her time was up here in Sweetbrier Creek, she would really like to do what she could to tear that wall down.

Once she was inside, Phoebe went in search of Edna. Earlier in the day the two of them had come up with a list of the basic things that would need to be done to get the house ready for the upcoming service. Then they'd walked through every room on the first and second floors to see if there was anything that required special attention that wasn't already on the list. Edna, of course, had been in charge of actually writing the list, even though she had to do it left-handed.

Now it was time to look over the basement so they could make note of anything that might need sprucing up or moving out, or requiring extra attention down there.

At the end of the day the list was extensive. There were the normal tasks involved when you were going to give a home a thorough cleaning—scrub the baseboards, floors, counters and fixtures, take the rugs outside to be vigorously beaten, wash the windows and curtains, polish the woodwork and so forth. Added to that were repairing the hems on one pair of curtains, polishing the silverware, getting out the extra pitchers and platters that were used for large gatherings and making sure they were clean.

The list they'd made for Seth included tightening a loose tread on the porch steps, replacing one of the porch rails, repairing two spindles on the banister between the first and second floors, fixing a sticky window sash and taking care of a squeaky tread on the basement stairs, along with a few other odds and ends.

And they had two weeks to complete it all. *Gut* thing there were six Beiler *brieder* and her and Edna—it would take all of them to get it done.

* * *

That evening at supper, Seth waited until everyone had filled their plates and they were settling down to eat before he cleared his throat to get their attention.

All eyes immediately turned his way. He almost changed his mind. But then he caught Phoebe's gaze on him—questioning, hopeful, supportive.

"I have a request to make," he started. "As you've probably heard me say, I've gotten quite a few more orders for the chess sets this Christmas season than I'd expected. That's a *gut* thing since we can use the extra money. But it's also put me behind schedule."

"Surely you're not asking us to make some of the sets for you," Levi said. "There's no way we can do half as *gut* a job as you do."

"*Nee*. But I can't carve any faster than I already do, not without compromising on the quality. Since most of my business is word of mouth, that would be self-defeating."

"So what are you asking us to do?" Daniel asked quietly.

"Phoebe suggested a way to speed things up that I'd like to try, at least until I'm caught up on the Christmas orders. It's an assembly-line-type approach to getting the work done. I'd continue to carve the pieces and lay out the boards. But Phoebe has volunteered to line the storage

drawers for me. And there are other things, like the staining, polishing, sealing, packaging and such that someone
else could do."

There was silence for a moment—no one spoke, no one
ate or drank, they just stared at him. Then all of a sudden,
they were all speaking at once, volunteering to handle various aspects of the process, even arguing over who would
do what.

Seth sat back and let the talk swirl around him. He
hadn't admitted, even to himself, that he'd expected his
brieder to be less than enthusiastic about helping him out.
They all had their own chores to tend to and to be honest
none of them had ever seemed to take much interest in his
craft.

Was that because he hadn't given them reason to, had
shut them out of that part of his life?

He finally allowed himself to meet Phoebe's gaze. She
was looking at him with understanding and perhaps a bit
of an I-told-you-so edge. Which he supposed he deserved.

* * *

Phoebe found herself humming as she did the dishes.
She'd suspected, given time, Seth would come around, but
it felt *gut* to be proven correct so quickly. This would work
out for the *gut* of everyone involved, she was sure of it.

"You seem to be in a pleasant mood."

Phoebe looked over her shoulder to see Edna standing
in the doorway.

"I am," she said as she turned back to the basin of
dishes. "It's been a *gut* day."

"Did you perhaps have something to do with that surprising request Seth made at supper tonight?"

"I don't see how Seth requesting help from his *brieder* would be so surprising."

"It's not something he's done before. And you didn't answer my question."

She should have known Edna was not one to be put off. "I may have said something to him about there being a way he could work better to make those deadlines he was so worried about."

"And he actually listened to you. That's *gut*."

Something about Edna's tone struck Phoebe as odd. But when she turned around to look at her friend, she couldn't read anything in her expression. Had it just been her imagination?

"What do you mean?"

"Just what I said—it's *gut* that Seth took your advice on this. Change is difficult for him."

Phoebe nodded and turned back to her work. But there'd been just the hint of a satisfied smile on Edna's face that made her think there was something else on her friend's mind.

Chapter 20

Tuesday midmorning Phoebe entered the kitchen to see Seth leaning against the counter, a cup of coffee in hand. "Sorry if I kept you waiting. I wanted to retrieve something from my room."

He shrugged, seeming unconcerned by her tardiness. "I needed this coffee anyway."

She noted the stack of mail near his elbow. Edna must have gotten it early today.

He set the coffee cup in the sink and straightened. "Ready?"

She nodded and moved to the door.

"Aren't you forgetting something?"

She turned to see him holding up the notebook that held the shopping list. He tore out the top sheet of paper and handed it to her. "Here. You'll need this if you don't want to miss anything."

"Of course." With Edna's help she'd committed it all to memory when everyone went their separate ways after breakfast. But she couldn't tell him that, not yet anyway. She wanted to make sure Seth, all the Beilers really, got to know her without any cloud of her embarrassing challenges coloring their perception of her—not to mention proving to herself once and for all that she was indeed capable of standing on her own—before she confessed. If she ever said anything at all.

So she meekly accepted the list from him, folded it in half and slipped it into her tote.

"Do you need a pen or pencil so you can cross items off as you purchase them?"

"I have a pen."

"Then I think we're ready to go."

When Phoebe stepped outside, she saw he already had the horse hitched to the buggy. Checkers ran up and danced around their feet. She and the dog had become fast friends. He'd actually kept her company as she'd gathered the eggs earlier.

They traveled down the lane in companionable silence for a while. It was an open buggy, but she had her coat on and they shared a buggy blanket so she was really quite comfortable.

Finally, she spoke up. "I met Margaret Chupp and teacher Constance on Sunday."

"I'm glad you're making friends here."

"Constance seems to have a *gut* opinion of Kish and Jesse."

"Glad to hear it."

"She told me about the parts they'll have in the Christmas program. I'm for sure and for certain sorry I'll have to miss it."

He frowned. "That's right. You'll be going home for a few days to be with your *familye* at Christmas." His expression cleared quickly. "But you'll get to see your own school's Christmas program."

"*Jah.* And I have three nieces who'll be in it so it will be wonderful *gut* to see them perform." Though if she had to choose between the two, for some reason she'd be tempted to choose the one here.

Phoebe glanced around. "I'm looking forward to seeing more of Sweetbrier Creek."

He smiled at that. "I apologize for keeping you so close to home since you've been here. If you want to take a day off to see more of the area or visit with your new friends, just let me know."

"*Danke.* But I've been quite happy to spend my time at your home. It's why I came after all." Her answer seemed to please him.

Then she changed the subject. "Have you figured out how you're going to involve your *brieder* in your work?"

"Since Mark is apprenticing for Calvin Detweiler, I think he would be the one who could be the most help the fastest."

"But surely you're going to involve more than just him?"

"I'm planning to start with Mark and make sure getting him to do some of the work doesn't affect the quality of the sets or prove too distracting. If that works out, then I may get one or more of my *brieder* to help out."

"May get? I seem to remember all of them volunteering to help in any way they could."

"And I appreciate it, but I have to make sure I can still get the chess sets out on time."

She could understand that. She just wished he would have more faith in their ability to make this work.

The discussion turned to small talk as he pointed out areas of interest along their route—the orchard where

Daniel worked, the schoolhouse, Edna's *shveshtah* Trudy's *familye* home and the like.

When the countryside changed and the first signs of the town itself began to appear, Phoebe studied the buildings they passed with interest. She noted one with a large sign proclaiming it to be Detweiler's Cabinet and Furniture Store. "Isn't that where Mark works?" she asked as she pointed.

He nodded. "*Jah*. Calvin Detweiler is who Mark apprentices with, and across the street is Rosie's Diner where Margaret Chupp works."

Seth finally turned the buggy into the parking lot of a business whose sign proclaimed it to be Spellman's Grocery Mart. Then he handed her an envelope. "This contains what should be enough cash to cover the cost of the items on your list."

She slid the envelope carefully into her tote and stepped down from the buggy.

He gathered the reins, then hesitated. "I know this place is unfamiliar to you. I could go inside with you if you like."

"*Danke*, but I'm sure it's very similar to the grocery store we use at home. And I'm perfectly capable of doing the shopping myself." At least she hoped she was.

He nodded but still didn't set the buggy in motion. "Make sure you follow the list and double-check it before you finish your purchases. We don't want to forget anything and have to make a return trip."

She rolled her eyes. "I won't forget anything."

"I just have a few errands to run so you shouldn't have to wait on me."

"Don't rush through anything on my account. It'll probably take me a little while to figure out the layout of this store. And I don't mind waiting."

He waved to an area that had obviously been set aside for buggies rather than cars. "When I return, I'll park the buggy on that side of the store. That way I can get out and transfer your purchases to the back of the buggy."

This time she just nodded, and he finally headed the buggy back toward the road.

Phoebe took a deep breath and entered the store. Truth to tell, she'd asked Edna to accompany her this morning. It would have been *gut* to have someone read labels, especially if there was a favorite brand they wanted. But Edna had claimed that getting in and out of buggies was too difficult for her with her arm in a sling. Not that it had seemed to give her much trouble Sunday.

So Phoebe did her best. The layout was somewhat different from the market at home, and it was a bigger store with a wider selection. Since the order she'd memorized the list in was not the same order as the items were stocked on the shelves it took a bit of mental reorganizing, but by the time she'd finished she was confident she'd gotten everything from the list. However, she wasn't sure she'd gotten the requested size or brand in each case.

There were also a few things she'd deliberately added to her cart that weren't on the list. She'd found she liked to be a little adventurous with her cooking so she'd sought out produce and herbs that looked like they would be interesting to try. But those she paid for out of her own pocket.

When she walked out of the store with her loaded grocery cart, she pushed it to the side where Seth had said he'd park the buggy, and sure enough he was already there. He leaned against the back of the buggy in a relaxed pose with his arms crossed.

But as soon as he saw her he straightened and marched forward, meeting her halfway and taking the cart from her.

"I hope I didn't keep you waiting long."

"*Nee*, I've only been here a few minutes." They arrived at the buggy and he started transferring the bags. "Did you have any problems finding anything?"

Phoebe shook her head. "This store is laid out a little differently from the one at home, but I'm confident I got it all." She just hoped it was in the right form.

"*Gut*." He unloaded the last bag. "I'll put the cart away if you want to go ahead and climb inside the buggy."

Once they were headed out of the parking lot, Seth spoke up. "It's almost lunchtime. Why don't we eat in town before we head back. We can pick up something to bring Edna as well."

A warmth spread through her chest at the invitation. "That sounds *gut*."

"There's a place on our way home that's quick and has tasty hamburgers if that's okay with you?"

She nodded. "I like hamburgers but I haven't had one in a while."

He negotiated a turn. "Then you'll enjoy this one," he said without taking his eye from the road but with a smile in his voice.

When they arrived, Phoebe discovered the name of the place was King's.

Once they were inside Seth waved to a menu board above the counter. "Those are your choices. Just let me know what kind of burger you want and then pick one for Edna."

Phoebe didn't bother to look at the menu. "I'm in the mood to try something new. Is there one that's considered their specialty?"

"I like the western burger—it has bacon, cheese, crispy battered onions and barbecue sauce."

"Oh, that sounds wonderful *gut*. I'll have one of those and I think Edna would like a plain bacon cheeseburger."

Seth nodded and placed their order, adding sodas for the two of them and a large order of wedge fries to share.

When the burgers arrived, he led her to a small rectangular table. As they took their seats across from each other Phoebe thought that this felt almost like a celebration. Appropriate since she felt like celebrating—after all she'd survived her first solo shopping trip.

Seth found himself smiling for no particular reason except that Phoebe's *gut* mood was contagious. And she did seem to be in wonderful *gut* spirits. Her demeanor was open and warm—her eyes sparkled, her smile made frequent appearances, and her hand gestures were light and expressive.

Was it just the change of scenery that had brought out this cheeriness in her? Or was it something else?

Whatever the case, her mood was infectious.

All through the meal and on the ride home she chatted away about anything and everything. And in the process, he learned a lot of little things about her.

Like how folding paper airplanes wasn't her only paper-related talent—she had a fondness for origami as well as paper-cutting crafts.

Like the fact that her favorite color was yellow—the color of sunflowers and buttercups.

Like the fact that she liked to ride a bicycle when the weather allowed.

Of course, she hadn't only wanted to talk about herself—she'd asked him questions about himself as well. And he found himself telling her things he'd never told anyone before—small, silly things.

Like how much he missed fishing in the springtime, a favorite pastime from his childhood.

Like the way he sometimes wondered if it mattered to his *brieder* that he was only their half *bruder*.

And how his favorite memory was of the day his future *shteef-daed*, a man he'd grown to love with all of his six-year-old heart, had asked his permission to marry his *mamm*.

He wasn't sure why he'd told her so many deeply personal things. She was just so easy to talk to, so sympathetic and nonjudgmental.

* * *

Later, when they'd arrived back at the Beilers' home and unloaded all the bags, Seth headed back to his workshop.

As soon as he was gone, Phoebe pulled the shopping list out of her tote and handed it to Edna. "I'm pretty sure I got everything on the list, but would you mind checking items off as I unpack the groceries?"

"Of course."

Humming her favorite hymn, Phoebe held up each item as she unpacked it. Sure enough, she'd gotten the wrong brand of soap and she'd bought the wrong-sized box of rice, but that still didn't darken her mood. She was sure she could explain that away if anyone remarked on it.

"Ach du lieva."

Something in Edna's tone made her stomach drop and her humming died away. "Is something wrong?"

Her friend met her gaze with a mix of apology and sympathy. "This wasn't on the list earlier. Seth must have added it after we went over it this morning."

That bad feeling in the pit of her stomach intensified. "What wasn't on the list?"

"Rhubarb."

For him to add it this morning must mean he had a plan for her to cook it in some form or another sometime soon. There was no way she would just be able to casually explain this away. Which left her with only one thing to do—she'd have to let Seth know she'd failed to purchase it.

And worse still, she'd have to let him know why.

Chapter 21

Phoebe squared her shoulders. Best to get it over with now.

Giving Edna a smile that no doubt looked more like a grimace, she turned and grabbed her coat from one of the mudroom hooks. Buttoning it with clumsy fingers, she slowly trudged across the distance between the house and Seth's workshop.

The wind that had felt bracing and playful a few minutes ago now seemed to pound against her.

These next few minutes would change everything. She dreaded the thought of seeing pity and condescension in his eyes when he looked at her.

Or maybe something even worse.

* * *

"I have something to tell you."

Seth could hear the seriousness in her tone. What had happened since he'd left her a few moments ago?

He turned and gave her his full attention, noting how distressed she appeared. "Is something wrong?"

"I didn't get everything on the list like I thought I did. I missed one item—the rhubarb."

He felt a flash of irritation—it would mean another trip to town this week. Next week would be too late, they needed to have it for Sunday. But getting angry wouldn't serve any *gut* purpose. And she seemed to be berating herself more than anything he could say would. "That's unfortunate. I'll go into town tomorrow and pick it up."

She was still wringing her hands, so he tried to soften his tone. "It's an annoyance but not anything to get distressed over. You just need to be more careful in checking the list in the future."

She didn't seem to have heard him. "Apparently you added that item sometime after breakfast and before we left for town." Her voice still had that flat, defeated tone.

"*Jah.* I added it while I waited in the kitchen for you to join me." Was she trying to shift the blame to him? "But I don't understand why that would matter."

She let out a long breath. "It matters because, with Edna's help, I spent thirty minutes this morning memorizing what was already on the list."

He sat up straighter, studying her in surprise. "Why would you do that?"

She looked down and brushed at her skirt, and he noticed her hands trembled slightly. "Because I can't read or write very well. Actually, barely at all."

It took a moment for her words to register. "Of course you can."

As soon as the words left his mouth, he realized how ridiculous it was of him to argue with her. Memories of her going her own way rather than referring to his lists, of her having Edna jot down notes when there were lists to be made, of her ignoring the menu at King's all flashed through his mind. How had he missed the signs?

"I'm sorry, I know I should have told you as soon as I arrived." She lifted a hand and then let it drop. "I know it's vain of me and I should accept the way *Gotte* made me. But I just wanted to pretend to be normal for a little while—to be someone without these shortcomings. Besides, I've developed ways to compensate. Like memorizing the things I need to know."

But how could this be, she seemed so bright, so independent? "And you say Edna knows about this?"

"She does." Then her eyes widened and she rushed to add, "But she didn't think it was her place to speak of my problems. She told me that the choices of if and when I told you were up to me. So please don't blame her."

Still trying to wrap his mind around what she'd confessed, he nodded. "Don't worry, I understand her discretion. I just wish you'd come to me sooner and not waited until you were backed into a corner."

She nodded, her expression even more miserable than before if that was possible.

Seeing her distress, he tried to clamp down on his annoyance over the fact that she hadn't trusted him enough to tell him earlier. He supposed he could understand her reluctance to admit such a thing. "What's done is done. There's no need for us to dwell on it. It's *gut* that you've learned ways to work around this issue. And now that I know, I can make allowances and help make things easier for you." He was surprised to see that his words, rather than ease her distress, only made her stiffen.

"That is wonderful kind of you," she said, her tone anything but relieved. "But I'm not looking for any special treatment. I'm the same person I was before I walked in here and I'd for sure and for certain appreciate you continuing to treat me the same. If I need help, I'll ask for it."

He was taken aback, as much by the firmness of her tone as by her actual words. How could he not see her differently given what he knew now? It was brave and admirable of her to want to do this on her own, but since she was in his care while she was in Sweetbrier Creek he had a responsibility to keep her safe. Perhaps he could strike a balance. "I will try."

She gave a dignified nod. "*Danke*. And again, I apologize for not getting the rhubarb. Are you sure it's not something that can wait until next week's shopping trip?"

"*Nee*. Jesse's birthday is Sunday and strawberry rhubarb cake is his favorite."

Her jaw dropped slightly. "Jesse's birthday is Sunday?"

"*Jah*. He got a card in today's mail, that's what reminded me."

She placed a hand on her hip. "And this is another thing you were going to wait to tell me."

"As I said, I only remembered myself when I saw that card this morning."

"This morning, before we went to town. Didn't you think I might want to get him a little gift?" Then she threw up her hands. "Of course you didn't." With an audible huff, she turned and walked away.

How had she so quickly managed to turn this around so that he was the one on the defensive?

As Phoebe slowly walked back to the house her irritation with Seth faded to the background. Instead, an uneasy feeling settled in her chest. Seth had said he would try to treat her as he always had but there was something about the way he'd said it that made her wonder if it was even possible. Things would change, she didn't doubt that for a minute. But to what extent?

Which brought up another question. Since Seth now knew the truth, should she tell his *brieder* as well? Did she even have a choice or would Seth feel it was his place to tell the rest of the household?

And how about others in the community? How much longer would it be before this was just an echo of the community she'd left behind in Bergamot?

When she stepped inside the kitchen, Edna was sitting at the table waiting for her. "How did it go?"

Phoebe went to the counter to finish putting away the groceries. "The rhubarb was on the list because it's an ingredient in Jesse's favorite cake. Did you know his birthday is this Sunday?"

"*Nee*, I did not."

"It is. So I need to figure out something to give him for a present."

"Phoebe, sit." There was both command and irritation in Edna's voice. "Stop talking around the issue and tell me how your talk with Seth went. How did he take the news?"

Phoebe slowly crossed the room and then dropped heavily into a chair at the table. "He was very kind. He said there was no need to dwell on what had happened and that he would do what he could to help me." She had to swallow past a thickness in her throat.

Edna's gaze softened. "You don't sound as if you think that was a *gut* outcome."

She drew invisible circles on the table with a finger. "I'm afraid everything is going to change now."

"Well then, I say it's up to you to make sure it doesn't change for the worse."

Phoebe looked up at that. "What do you mean?"

"If you want to be treated as someone who can take care of herself just as well as anyone else, then you have to prove that it's so. Your *familye* and friends in Bergamot treated you like a small child because you allowed them to. There's a difference between obedience to your *eldre* and making sure they see you as a young woman who can take care of herself." With that Edna stood and turned toward the living room.

As Phoebe went to work preparing the cookie dough for the boys' afternoon treat, she thought over Edna's words. She made it sound so simple. How did she actually go about shaping the way people saw her?

* * *

That evening at supper, Phoebe waited until everyone had served their plates and then cleared her throat and sat up straighter. "If I could have everyone's attention, there's something I'd like to tell you all."

As had happened at supper the night before when Seth had asked for their attention, there was an immediate pause in the conversation and eating as everyone looked at her expectantly. Trying to be as matter of fact and direct as Seth had been, she placed her hands in her lap and sat up straighter. "There's something about me you don't know. It's something Edna already knows and it's something I told Seth about this afternoon. But I think the rest of you should know as well."

She paused a moment and realized she now had everyone's undivided attention.

Kish leaned forward. "Please don't say you're leaving us already."

She allowed herself a smile at that. "*Nee*, it's nothing like that. It's just something that's part of who I am." She took a deep breath then blurted out, "The thing is, I can't really read or write well—hardly at all in fact."

She didn't have long to wait for their reactions.

Jesse, of course, didn't say anything, just looked at her as if trying to puzzle something out.

Kish had a wide-eyed, slack-jawed expression.

Seth gave her a small nod of approval.

Mark was the first to actually speak. "But how's that possible? You aren't slow-witted—you can do all kinds of clever things."

Before Phoebe could respond, Seth spoke up. "There's no need for that, Mark. Of course Phoebe can do lots of things—not everything requires the ability to read."

She noticed he didn't say she wasn't slow. But she kept her focus on Mark. "I learn a lot of things from watching others and then imitating what they do. And when it becomes important to know what a list or document says, I will have someone read it to me and I'll memorize it."

"Well, I for one think learning that way is a remarkable skill." Levi gave her an admiring smile. "I myself was never *gut* at memorizing."

Levi's words seemed to ease some of the tension around the table.

Jesse asked her how many words she could memorize. Kish asked if her unusual menus were because she couldn't read recipes and Mark asked how she could do her lessons when she was in school. Before long the conversation moved on to other topics and Phoebe breathed a small sigh of relief to have it behind her. And realized it hadn't been as bad as she'd imagined it would be.

She'd thought about asking them to not share the news

with anyone outside the *familye*, but then decided against it. She wanted to provide a *gut* example for these boys and young men, and that included honesty.

When there was a lull in the conversation, she turned to the youngest Beiler. "Jesse, I understand you have a big day coming up."

His gaze, when it met hers, was startled, wary. And the mood around the table seemed to have subtly shifted. Why?

"Seth tells me your birthday is Sunday," she continued. "You'll be thirteen, is that right?"

"*Jah.*"

Apparently the youngest Beiler wasn't excited about his upcoming birthday. She definitely needed to ask Seth for an explanation.

"John thinks we'll have at least a dusting of snow by morning," Daniel said.

Levi forked up another serving of vegetables. "Then it's a *gut* thing our crew has inside work tomorrow."

Seth nodded. "Perhaps we should put some extra hay out for the livestock after supper, just in case."

And just like that the subject had been changed.

Why had talk of Jesse's birthday garnered such a strange reaction?

She was determined to do some digging to find the answer to that question.

Chapter 22

Sure enough, when they rose on Wednesday morning there was a dusting of snow on the ground and occasional flurries still falling.

Phoebe made sure to pack a little extra in everyone's lunches—*Mamm* always said a full stomach would help provide the energy to stay warm.

Once the younger Beilers had scattered for the day, she turned to Seth. "Before you head out, do you mind if I ask you a question?"

"Not at all. What would you like to know?"

She noticed he had a wary look on his face—what was he expecting? "I was wondering why things got a little uncomfortable when the subject of Jesse's birthday came up last evening?"

He frowned, clearly puzzled. "What do you mean?"

"I mean, Jesse didn't seem at all excited or even interested in the subject, and none of the rest of you wanted to talk about it either."

"That's just Jesse being Jesse. As for the rest of us, I didn't notice anything out of the ordinary, we just don't dwell on such things. I think it must have been your imagination."

She frowned at his tone. Had he already started to dismiss her opinions?

After he left Edna spoke up. "It wasn't your imagination."

Thank goodness she wasn't the only one who'd seen it. "Then what was it?"

Edna waved her to a chair. "To understand you need to know a little bit about this *familye's* history."

Phoebe shifted in her chair. "I don't want to pry into their private business."

"You aren't prying. And this is something most everyone around here already knows."

She supposed that was different. "All right."

"Back before Jesse was born, this was a different household. I remember visiting here and how warm and welcoming it was. Reba, their *mamm*, was a wonderful *gut* cook and always had extra food available for anyone who dropped in. Boaz, their *daed*, was an outgoing man, full of *gut* humor and a generous spirit. He loved to tell stories to anyone who would listen and to sing as he worked."

This was the man Seth had spoken so fondly of yesterday.

Edna's expression grew serious. "Then Reba died giving birth to Jesse and everything changed. Boaz lost his joy and began to focus all his energy on the farm. He left the raising of his sons to his elderly *mamm*, who lived in the *dawdi haus* at the time, and Seth, who was only sixteen back then. To Boaz, Jesse was a reminder of the love he'd lost, and while I'm sure he tried not to be cruel, he could barely stand to be in the same room with Jesse."

Phoebe felt her heart break for both *daed* and *suh*. "That's a terrible burden for a *kinner* to bear."

"*Jah*. And while his *daed* was alive, Jesse's birthday was seen more as the anniversary of Reba's death than as a celebration of his birth. I don't think Seth and the others are even aware of it, but I believe there's still some shadow of that sadness and discomfort whenever Jesse's birthday comes around."

That explained a lot, including why the boy always seemed to stand on the fringes of things rather than joining in.

She sat up straighter. "We must make this year different for Jesse, for all of them."

Edna eyed her speculatively. "Did you have something specific in mind?"

Phoebe slowly nodded. "Perhaps. Let me think about it a little longer."

Edna reached across the table and patted her hand. "I have faith that you will come up with exactly the right thing."

Phoebe certainly hoped she was right.

* * *

Phoebe sat back as Seth studied the chessboard. "Are you ready to start involving the rest of us in creating the chess sets?"

Lunch was over and they'd just started their chess match. It had become one of her favorite parts of the day.

He nodded absently, his focus obviously still on the chessboard. "Almost. I have a little more to do on the current set I've been working on." He made his move and leaned back. "After that I'm going to sit down and come up with a plan for how to make this new process work. That includes writing out instructions for each of the pieces that I think can be handled by someone else."

She shook her head. "You for sure and for certain like to make plans."

He shrugged. "It's the only way I know how to make sure things stay on track and get done."

She let that go. "Have you lined the drawer yet?"

"*Nee*. That's one of the last steps."

"Then perhaps this would be a *gut* time to teach me how to do that task for you."

"Are you sure you still want to do that?" She heard a note of hesitation in his voice.

Was he still fighting against letting go of total control of his pieces? Then perhaps getting her to help him let go of this one piece would make it easier for him to let go of others.

"For sure and for certain. And there's no need to wait until you can write out instructions since I won't be able to read them anyway."

He shifted, rubbing the back of his neck.

She'd tried to lighten the mood but apparently he wasn't comfortable talking about her shortcomings yet. Then she stiffened. Had that been at the heart of his hesitation—her ability to perform the task given she wouldn't be able to read his directions?

Trying to push down the knot in her stomach that that thought had generated, she smiled. "If you'll talk me through it this first time, I should be able to handle it with very few questions when working on the ones after that."

She saw a flash of skepticism in his expression, there and gone in a heartbeat. Then he nodded. "If you have the time, when we finish our game, I'll show you how to do the job."

Actually, she'd prefer she did the work while he directed, rather than him doing it while she watched. But now was not the time to argue the point.

His hesitation was understandable. She'd just have to prove her abilities to him by following through. If he gave her the chance.

Now that she'd won that point—sort of—it was time to change the subject. She moved her bishop, capturing one of his pawns. "By the way, how do you and your *brieder* celebrate birthdays?" She kept her tone as casual as she could.

Seth shrugged. "The way most *familyes* do, I imagine. We have a cake, give gifts, invite some friends and relatives over to help celebrate. Why?"

"I wanted to know what to expect when we celebrate Jesse's birthday on Sunday."

"That's not something you need to worry too much about."

That was a strange thing to say. "What do you mean?"

"Because Jesse's birthday falls so close to Christmas we don't usually have a big party, just a quiet celebration within our household—a nice meal with a strawberry rhubarb cake and some gifts."

"Well that hardly seems right."

He waved a hand. "Jesse's never liked to make a big production out of his birthday so there's no need to worry—it will be all right with him."

Did he really understand what he was saying? "Whether he shows it or not everyone, especially *kinner*, like to have their special day recognized and celebrated."

Seth shifted in his seat. "With me being so busy trying to get my orders finished and having to get the place ready for hosting the church service, I don't—"

Phoebe didn't let him finish. "His birthday is on a between Sunday, ain't so?"

"*Jah*, but—"

"So there won't be any work being conducted that a celebration would interfere with," she said patiently. "And I can make sure there's enough food prepared for a nice party on my own."

She saw another protest form on his lips and held up a hand.

"Before you say anything more, there's something I'd like to say."

Seth sat back in his seat, surprised by the set determination of her features. Why was she so focused on Jesse's birthday? Why couldn't she just drop the subject? But she obviously wasn't to be deterred so he waved a hand, indicating he was listening.

"Edna told me the circumstances of Jesse's birth."

He stiffened, not sure how he felt about them discussing that particular subject behind his back. "If you'd asked me I would've told you. There was no need to go to Edna."

"I did try to speak to you about why everyone shied away from talk of Jesse's birthday. And I didn't ask Edna, she volunteered."

That was quibbling the point but he let it go. "I guess what happened is common knowledge anyway."

"I know that must have been a difficult time for you and your *familye*, especially your *daed*." There was a soft earnestness to her expression. "Edna also told me how it changed your *daed*, which I'm sure made it even more difficult for the rest of you. Under those circumstances it would be natural for a *kinner*, at least on some level, to blame it on the new addition to the *familye*."

Seth took immediate exception to that. "*Nee*. I don't blame Jesse. He was innocent in what happened." He tugged on his sleeve. "And I wasn't a *kinner* when Jesse was born, I was sixteen."

"Of course you were. But how did it color the way your *daed* viewed that day? The way some of that feeling splashed over on you? And how could Jesse not help but feel something was off as he got older?" She leaned forward. "Think about how you celebrate every other birthday in this *familye* and compare it with how you all are treating Jesse's birthday, have apparently always treated Jesse's birthday—are they the same? If so, then I won't say anything more on the subject." She sat back and folded her hands in her lap.

Seth tried to search his heart. Was she right? Had he been guilty of making his little *bruder* feel he had no right to celebrate his birthday? The thought almost brought him to his knees. How could he not have realized this before?

He looked up and met Phoebe's gaze. "Please ask Edna to invite her *shveshtra* and their *familyes* to join us for Jesse's birthday lunch on Sunday."

She rewarded him with a broad smile. "*Wunderbaar!* We'll do that today. And I saw an ice-cream freezer in the basement so we'll get that out as well."

He smiled at her childlike anticipation.

"Do you normally give homemade or store-bought gifts?"

"It depends on what each of us feels like doing."

"And do you think the gifts for Jesse have been bought or made already?"

"I'm not sure what my *brieder* have done."

"Well, what have you done?"

He was ashamed to say he hadn't given it a whole lot of thought. "I plan to carve a whistle for him."

She smiled. "I think homemade is always a *gut* way to go, it shows you care enough to put in the effort. I'll have to come up with something myself."

"I'm sure whatever you come up with he'll appreciate."

Then she fiddled with one of the captured pieces. "If you don't mind, I'd like to add a couple of little birthday traditions we have in my *familye*. But only if you think it would be okay."

He sat back and folded his arms. "And what would those be?"

"In my *familye* we each make a homemade card for whoever's birthday we're celebrating. And also, before we cut the cake, each person hands over their card and says one thing they admire about the person whose birthday it is."

That sounded like a step too far. "I don't know…"

She didn't let him finish. "Why not? Making a card isn't difficult. It doesn't have to be fancy or well drawn, just a festive drawing with the words *happy birthday* is enough. And surely you don't have a problem coming up with something you admire about your little *bruder* to share?"

He straightened defensively at that. "Of course not. I'm just not sure about the time involved. As I said, this is a very busy time for me."

Phoebe raised a brow at that. "This is something you should be able to do one evening after supper. Is that too much to ask?"

She was right. "Of course not. And it sounds like a *gut* idea." It was more than a *gut* idea—he owed Jesse this and so much more. And there were so many things about his youngest *bruder* to appreciate, finding something to say shouldn't be any trouble at all.

"*Gut.* I'll pass it on to the others. This will be a wonderful nice celebration for Jesse." She clasped her hands together in her excitement and unfortunately overset the board. "*Ach.* I'm so sorry."

He stood and began putting away the pieces. "That's okay, we spent more time talking than playing today. And it's time for me to get back to the workshop."

"Should I go with you now to work on that drawer?"

Seth had hoped Phoebe, with all she had to do to get the house ready for Jesse's birthday and hosting the church service, would decide she didn't have the time right now to work with him. He knew she meant well but if he had to stop and give her verbal directions constantly, how much help could she be?

Then again, this whole parceling out of the tasks had been her idea—it wouldn't be fair for him to not give her an opportunity to participate. And he just couldn't see doing something that would hurt her feelings.

When they entered the workshop a few minutes later he moved to the shelves where the fabric was stored and grabbed a bolt of the green velvet. "When someone orders a chess set, one of the few options they have is whether they want the drawer lined in red, blue, or green. Most customers want red but I occasionally get an order for blue or green." He'd originally intended to just tape a note on the board as to what color she should use. He'd need to come up with a new plan now.

But she was a step ahead of him. "I saw some crayons in the house. I'll pull those three colors from the box and you can color a slip of paper and place it in the drawer to indicate which fabric to use."

"That'll work." He carried the fabric to a smaller work-table situated in the back of the shop. "This mark on the edge of the table is what I use to measure how much fabric I need to cut. And the fabric is twice as wide as what I need so I can get two squares from every length I cut." He grabbed a pair of scissors to demonstrate but she held her hand out.

"Let me. I learn better by doing rather than just watching."

He hesitated. The fabric was thick and expensive—he couldn't really afford to have her mess up the measurement.

She seemed to read his mind. "Don't worry. I've cut lots of fabric for quilts and my *mamm* wouldn't have let me do it if I couldn't be precise."

Feeling a twinge of guilt for having made her feel she needed to reassure him, he placed the scissors in her hand and stepped back. As he watched, she cut the fabric with surprising speed and precision. Then she cut the piece she'd cut from the bolt in half.

"There." She held the two squares out for him to see. Then she put a finger to her chin. "I'm thinking, when I have time between lining the storage drawers and doing my housework, I could pre-cut a stack of these so they'd be ready to go whenever needed."

That made a lot of sense—he should have thought of it himself. Then again, he didn't have any spare time between his tasks.

Shaking off that thought, he moved back to the main worktable and picked up the storage drawer. "If you look closer there's an insert here in the bottom."

She obliged by looking inside the drawer, her head dipping below his chin. He inhaled the scent of cinnamon and apples, saw the single wispy tendril escaping the crisp white folds of her *kapp*, heard her soft breaths as she studied the insert.

Then she looked up and placed her hands on the side of the box.

Her face was so close to his he could clearly see the individual flecks of gold in her brown eyes, and now their fingertips were touching.

"May I?" she asked.

Chapter 23

It took Seth a moment to realize she was asking to take the box from him. He quickly released it and took half a step back.

She tilted the box forward and slid out the bottom insert. Then she set the box aside and turned the insert this way and that, studying it.

She finally looked up. "So how do you attach the velvet to this tray?"

He gave his head a mental shake, uncomfortable with the direction his thoughts had taken. Trying to bring himself back to the present, he reached to take it from her but then remembered she wanted to do it all herself.

He cleared his throat and gestured to the velvet. "You fold over the fabric and glue it to the bottom." He grabbed the bottle of glue and set it on the table in front of her. "The trick is not to pull it too tight—it has to be loose enough to allow the pieces to nestle inside their individual compartments."

She nodded, her brow furrowed as she considered what he'd said. "All right. You talk me through each step of the process as I do it."

As they worked together Seth noted how well she took directions and picked up on not only what they were doing but why it was being done a certain way.

When the tray was finally covered to his satisfaction he leaned back. "We'll leave the tape in place so the fabric stays put while the glue dries. The last step is to draw an X on the bottom with the glue and then place it in the drawer with the section for the checkers at the front."

She did as he directed then sat back with a smile. "That wasn't so bad. Do we put the game pieces in now?"

"*Jah*, that's the next step, but I can take care of it myself."

She gave him one of those stern-schoolteacher looks. "Of course you can, but the point is, if you want to speed up your process, you should delegate such things."

He rolled his eyes, but he nodded. "The pieces are over here."

"I assume you place them in the drawer in a certain way?"

"Of course. The chess pieces are stored in the same order as they are positioned on the chessboard. And then the checkers are placed in the appropriate slot with all the dark pieces together and then the light ones."

"That sounds easy enough."

He watched as her nimble fingers carefully placed the pieces in the proper slots. Then she met his gaze again. "What's next?"

He pointed her to the shelf below the fabric. "I put a double layer of that Bubble Wrap in the drawer to keep the pieces in place during shipping."

As she complied, he anticipated her next question.

"Once that's taken care of, you slide the drawer in place below the board. And that's it—we're done and it's ready for shipping."

Phoebe slid the drawer in place with a triumphant push and grinned. "That was quite satisfying." She gave him a raised-brow look. "Handing over that piece of your work wasn't so bad, was it?"

"*Nee*, not bad at all." Actually, he'd quite enjoyed watching her work, seeing those little spurts of satisfaction light up her face when she successfully managed a task.

"Have you decided what other parts of your work you can hand off?"

"I'm still trying to work it all out, but since Mark is a furniture maker's apprentice that means he already knows how to use most of this equipment. He can cut the wood I need to build the board and storage drawer. Maybe Kish can learn how to polish the finished pieces. And Jesse can work on the packaging."

"What about Daniel and Levi? They offered to help as well."

He shrugged. "Neither of them gets home until suppertime."

But she wasn't ready to give up. "They're usually home on Saturdays. I know there are only two Saturdays left before Christmas but I'm sure they'd be willing to put in some time to help for those two days. In fact, I imagine they would be quite *gut* at creating those inserts that go into the drawer." She cocked her head to one side. "I'd guess you already have a template drawn up for that."

He rubbed the back of his neck. "*Jah*, I do. It goes quicker if I don't have to measure each time."

She nodded and then straightened. "Since you don't have any other drawers for me to work with right now I'll head back to the house." She grinned. "I don't want your *brieder* to get home and not have any warm cookies."

Then, as she moved to the door: "Besides, I know you must be eager to create those lists and instructions you were talking about earlier." And with that she was gone.

Seth just stood there for a few minutes after she'd made her exit, a smile lingering on his face. Phoebe was such a ball of contradictions. Just when he thought he had her figured out, she did something to surprise him.

She'd definitely surprised him yesterday when she'd confessed her inability to read. He hadn't really known how to react at the time. Still didn't, if push came to shove.

But he wanted to support her. And he knew he could do that by being her safety net, making sure her lack of reading ability didn't hamper her in any of her tasks here. The tricky part would be to do it without being too obvious about it.

But he felt he was up to the challenge.

* * *

As Phoebe worked on mixing her cookie dough she thought about how natural it had felt to work with Seth. Sure, he'd been hesitant to let her cut the fabric and she was aware enough to realize it had a lot to do with him having found out about her shortcomings yesterday, but as they'd worked he'd relaxed. By the end of their session he seemed to have forgotten he felt the need to hover.

Perhaps he was coming to see that she was the same person she'd been two days ago with the same capabilities.

Before supper, Phoebe managed to corner the four middle *brieder* and let them know the plan for Jesse's birthday. Her ideas were met with varying levels of enthusiasm but in the end they all agreed to do their part.

Then at supper she attempted to bring up the subject again, trying to put a more positive tone on it than the one she'd encountered the day before. "Jesse, since Sunday is your birthday, I thought I'd let you decide the menu. Do you have a favorite meal or dish you'd like to have served? Besides the strawberry rhubarb cake, I mean." Seth had made a quick trip to town this morning so the rhubarb was already in the refrigerator.

The boy shrugged. "I'm not particular."

But she wasn't going to let him get away with that. "Come now, you can't tell me there isn't some dish you really like above the others."

He looked up and met her gaze. "Well, I do like fried chicken."

"*Wunderbaar.* And what do you like with your fried chicken?"

This time he didn't hesitate. "Cheesy mashed potatoes and stuffed eggs."

"*Gut* choices. Anything else?"

He hesitated a moment. "Well, I really like the way *Aenti* Hilda cooks collard greens but none of my *brieder* like it cooked that way so maybe some baked beans instead."

Phoebe ignored the groans coming from several voices around the table. "But it's not their birthday, it's yours. Edna, perhaps you can get the recipe from your *shveshtah.*"

Edna raised a brow. "It's actually a recipe of my *mamm's* so I already know it."

Phoebe nodded. "Then that's settled." She changed the subject. "I notice you've received some birthday cards recently. Would you like me to set up a string so we can hang them in the kitchen or living room?"

He frowned. "We don't usually do that."

"Oh, but you should. It's what my *mamm* does with all the cards we receive. It looks quite festive—it makes me smile when I see it, especially since some of them are mine." She stabbed some green beans with her fork. "And it would also make me smile to see some of that same kind of decoration here."

That did the trick. He nodded. "All right, I'll get them for you right after supper."

She watched him sit up a bit straighter and attack his food with more energy.

The fact that he'd held on to the cards he'd received showed that he wasn't as unconcerned with his birthday as Seth had assumed. Had Seth picked up on that at all?

She glanced toward the head of the table and saw the eldest Beiler watching his youngest *bruder* with a speculative look on his face.

* * *

As Seth helped her string the blue yarn across the kitchen wall that evening, he wondered if Phoebe might be homesick for Bergamot and felt the need to re-create some of her *familye* traditions here.

He supposed he couldn't blame her if that was the case. She was young, after all, and home probably represented something safe and comfortable for her. It was likely that her *familye* and friends had grown accustomed to her inability to read a long time ago and made accommodations for her, sheltering her from any unpleasant consequences. If she wanted to re-create some of that homey feeling here he could give her a little leeway.

After they'd finished attaching the yarn to the wall, Jesse brought out the cards he'd received to date. Phoebe made a big production of positioning them just right and he saw how pleased Jesse looked as he caught sight of the finished banner. Perhaps Phoebe had been correct in her assessment of Jesse actually wanting to celebrate his birthday.

Phoebe stepped back and admired her work with a glowing smile. "Doesn't that look just *wunderbaar*! And when you start getting Christmas cards we can hang them up as well."

Seeing her smile, he thought it looked *wunderbaar* indeed.

* * *

When Seth stepped inside the kitchen at noon the next day he smiled at the sight of the garland of birthday cards. Phoebe had been right—they definitely brightened the room.

She was at the counter working on a dish of some sort—what interesting side would they have to go with their sandwiches today?

He moved to the other end of the counter where the day's mail was stacked. He spotted a new issue of a wood-carving magazine he subscribed to. Normally he would have dived into it right away while he ate his sandwich. But today he set it aside to read after supper.

There was another card for Jesse and the rest of the mail appeared to be mostly sales flyers. Then he spotted an envelope mixed in with the flyers. Another card for Jesse? He turned it over and paused. It was addressed to him, and the return address indicated it was from his cousin Zilla.

For a moment he froze. It had been just a little over a week since he'd sent those letters out to his cousins, but so much had happened in the time since that he'd completely forgotten about his request. Until now.

Had his cousin identified someone who met the criteria for a *fraa* that he'd stated in his letter? Or was she writing to tell him she hadn't been able to find anyone? There was only one way to find out.

He slowly opened the letter, not sure what he hoped Zilla would have to say.

Seth, I received your letter requesting help in finding a possible fraa. *I'm so happy you've decided that you're ready to take this step—you deserve to be happy. Having known Dinah and based on the requirements you listed, I think I have the perfect match for you. Fannie Yoder is a fine* Gotte-fearing *woman. She's a widow with a sweet five-year-old* dochder. *Fannie was a schoolteacher before she married Philip, which means she's used to working with groups of* kinner *so she won't be deterred by the number in your household. She keeps a very orderly home and she has a pleasant personality. I know Dinah made baskets to sell in order to supplement your* familye *income. Fannie can't do that but she does make very* gut *goat cheeses that she sells at a local market if goats are something you want to include in your livestock.*

Fannie is about three years older than you, closer to my own age, but I assume that won't be a problem since I know Dinah was a little older than you as well.

She will be accompanying me and my familye *when I go back to Sweetbrier Creek to visit* Mamm *and* Daed *for Christmas so you will have a chance to meet her and her you. She understands there are no commitments at this point and is viewing this as a pleasant getaway since she has very little* familye *of her own.*

I appreciate you entrusting me with helping you in this way and I know that whatever the outcome, things will work out as Gotte *wills.*

I look forward to seeing you soon.

Zilla

Chapter 24

Seth refolded the letter and placed it back in the envelope. It was the news he'd hoped to receive when he'd sent his letters out and he should be excited at the prospect of meeting this friend of Zilla's.

So why wasn't he?

He glanced up and caught Edna watching him with an assessing, speculative look on her face.

Then the sound of Phoebe's off-key humming caught his attention. She was flitting between the counter and the table and the stove. There wasn't any kind of economy of motion in her actions, yet there seemed a sort of flighty grace. It was like watching a damselfly darting from here to there.

Zilla's friend would no doubt have a more calming presence then Phoebe had had. And if Fannie was like Dinah as Zilla had said then she would have no trouble organizing and setting up dependable routines. But would she like to play chess or want to help him work on his chess sets or surprise him with unusual side dishes?

Perhaps he should have added those things as requirements.

All through lunch he found himself turning things over and over in his mind. Finding a new *fraa* had seemed like a *gut* idea when Edna had brought it up a week and a half ago but now that things were moving forward it suddenly felt like it was all happening too quickly.

"You're being very quiet today." The concerned note in Phoebe's voice brought him back to the present. "Are you still worried about completing your orders on time?"

He nodded. After all, he had been concerned about that too. "Even with my *brieder's* help I'm going to be cutting it close." He gave her an apologetic smile. "Speaking of which, between that and preparing the house and grounds for the upcoming church service I'm afraid there won't be any free time for our after-lunch chess matches, at least not until after I complete my orders."

She leaned back. "I'll miss our matches but I understand." Then she smiled. "But once you get your assembly line going I can use that time to do my part on the chess sets."

She made that sound like something she was going to enjoy doing.

And perhaps she was.

As he'd told Phoebe earlier, Seth had recruited Mark as the first of his *brieder* to help him in his workshop. When the boy got home from his apprenticeship job, after grabbing a handful of Phoebe's fresh-baked cookies, he went straight to Seth's workshop.

Seth showed Mark the planks of wood he used to build the basic box of his chessboards, what he looked for in the grain and what dimensions and angles to use for cutting it. Though he'd written it all down in great detail, Seth demonstrated by cutting the pieces to put together a board.

Afterward Mark took over and cut enough wood to use in constructing four more boards.

His *bruder* also watched him work on assembling the first one, asking questions at various stages of the process that encouraged Seth to consider letting him build the next one while he looked on. Perhaps Phoebe had been right about how much of the work he could delegate.

* * *

Over the next few days Seth included his two younger *brieder* in the process. He also adjusted his own work sequence. Mark was now making the basic box of the chess boards, including the drawer and inserts. And the boy was doing a wonderful *gut* job—Calvin was training him well.

Seth had taught Kish to glue the checkerboard squares to his exacting specifications and to add the felt feet to the bottom of the board box. Jesse was helping with the staining. All that was really left for him to do was to carve the chess pieces, his favorite part of the process.

Now that everyone was trained and doing their part, the process had definitely speeded up and there didn't seem to be any drop in quality.

Which was a *gut* thing, because he'd taken a leap of faith and accepted that late order for four additional boards.

He truly missed the lunchtime chess games with Phoebe. But to help him fill his orders she now accompanied him back out to the workshop as soon as they finished their meal, and she spent an hour or so working on lining the drawers and adding felt to the bottoms of the individual chess pieces. And in the afternoon when she brought him his cookie snack, she spent a little time cutting sections of velvet and stacking them neatly on an empty shelf she'd cleared for just that purpose.

* * *

On Saturday afternoon, Homer Gerber delivered the church wagon containing the benches and songbooks. Seth showed him where to park the wagon and they, along with Levi and Daniel, unhitched the draft team and gave the animals feed and a good grooming.

While the men were occupied with that Bernice Gerber, who'd followed behind in her buggy to give Homer a ride home, arrived.

Phoebe bustled out to greet her. "*Kum* in out of the cold," she invited. "I have some hot cocoa on the stove for us to enjoy."

"That sounds wonderful *gut*," Bernice said as she climbed down. Then she reached back inside and fetched something from the floor of her buggy. "And I brought you just the thing to go with that cocoa—a big batch of chocolate chip peanut butter cookies."

As the woman took off her coat and entered the kitchen, she looked around with a broad smile. "*Ach*, Phoebe, what a wonderful *gut* job you are doing here. This is beginning to look the way it did when Reba was still alive."

"*Danke*. But I haven't done much."

"Let's have none of that false modesty." Edna's voice held a note of exasperation. "You've added warmth to this home, and I don't mean the kind you get from the stove."

Phoebe didn't know how to respond to that so she avoided saying anything at all, instead pouring up the cups of cocoa while Edna and Bernice chatted about some community news.

Later, when the menfolk trooped in, Phoebe brewed some coffee and gave everyone their choice of that or the rewarmed hot cocoa.

Once he'd finished his coffee, Homer stood. "*Danke* for the coffee but we'll be going now. I know you're busy getting everything ready."

Once they'd seen the Gerbers off, Phoebe turned to Jesse. "I thought I'd make some paper snowflakes to hang around the wall like we did your birthday cards. Would you like to help me?"

Jesse nodded enthusiastically.

"*Gut.* I'll go get my supplies. You can get the scissors from the sewing basket."

When Phoebe returned to the kitchen, Jesse was seated at the table, waiting for her. "Have you made paper snowflakes before?" she asked the boy.

"*Jah.* Teacher Constance showed us how to make them last year." Then he frowned. "I'm not sure I remember exactly how to fold the paper, though."

"I'll show you." She handed him a piece of paper while she took another. Then she walked him step by step through how to square it off and then how to make the folds. Once they had the folded triangle she picked up her scissors. "Now comes the fun. We create our own patterns by making cuts on the edges."

"I remember this part." And Jesse began snipping at the snowflake-to-be, cutting out triangles, slashes, half circles and shapes that had no definition.

Taking her cue from him, Phoebe decided to just have fun with it. When they unfolded their creations, Phoebe gave a pleased exclamation. "These are *wunderbaar!*" she said as she smoothed them out. Then she picked up another sheet of paper. "What do you say we make the next ones a little smaller so we can have some variety?"

Between the two of them they made a dozen snowflakes

of various patterns and sizes. They'd just finished taping them to the string when Seth stepped back inside the house.

"You're just in time," Phoebe said by way of greeting.

He gave her a wary look. "In time for what?"

She held up part of their handmade decoration. "We need to hang this snowflake garland."

His expression cleared. "Of course. Where do you want to hang it?"

"I think in the living room over the open doorway would be best." She turned to Jesse. "What do you think?"

"I agree." His expression was thoughtful, as if he'd given the question careful consideration.

Seth was already moving toward the basement stairs. "Let me grab my hammer and some small finishing nails and I'll be right back."

When he returned he quickly hammered in a nail on either side of the doorway, then handed the hammer to Jesse as he turned to Phoebe. "Give me one end of the string and I'll tie it off."

Phoebe stepped forward with the hand holding the string outstretched. But in the process of Seth reaching for the garland he grabbed her hand as well.

Phoebe froze as her gaze flew to his. The warm tingly sensation where his hand touched hers made her pulse jump, sent the heat to her face.

Confused, she pulled her hand back and tried to gather her thoughts.

Then she realized Seth was watching her, a puzzled look on his face. Whatever it was she'd felt, he obviously hadn't experienced it himself.

She gave him as serene a smile as she could muster and handed the other end of the string to Jesse. "Here. I think the two of you can finish this up without me. I need to get started on supper."

And with that she made her exit.

As Seth watched Phoebe leave the room the word *escape* came to mind. Was it because she'd also felt that little spark when he'd accidentally grabbed her hand? It had certainly been disconcerting, but only because it was so unexpected. Surely it hadn't meant anything more than a reaction to surprise or static electricity.

Had she read more into it than that? And for a moment, had he?

Chapter 25

Sunday morning, as soon as the youngest Beiler stepped into the kitchen Phoebe was ready to help him celebrate. "Happy birthday, Jesse. In honor of your special day I made some cinnamon rolls for everyone."

Jesse's eyes lit up. "*Danke*. They smell wonderful *gut*."

That sentiment was echoed by several of the others who'd already made it to the kitchen.

Phoebe smiled as she set the platter in the middle of the table. "If you all help set the table we'll be able to eat that much sooner."

The boys took the hint while Phoebe pulled the cheesy hash-brown-and-bacon casserole from the oven.

Within a few minutes everyone was seated at the table with bent heads.

Then, before they served their plates, Seth stood. "A few days ago Phoebe mentioned some traditions she and her *familye* share when they have a birthday to celebrate. They create homemade cards for the birthday person and as they hand them to him or her they mention something they appreciate about that person. It sounded like a *wunderbaar* tradition and we thought today would be a *gut* day to try it out." He picked up a handmade card that rested by his plate and carried it over to Jesse. "What I admire and appreciate about you, little *bruder*, is the way you are always willing to jump in to help whenever you see a need, without waiting to be asked."

Jesse's eyes widened and his jaw loosened. He used a finger to shove his glasses up higher on his nose and he looked down and focused on the card. "*Danke.*"

"My turn." Levi stood and carried his card to Jesse. "And I appreciate the way you can add up the points in a domino play in your head faster than anyone I know," he said with a cheeky grin.

That earned him a return grin from Jesse.

The rest of the *brieder*, each in turn, presented Jesse with a card and a word of appreciation.

Then Edna took her turn, stating that she admired Jesse because he was such a *gut* listener.

Finally it was Phoebe's turn to rise and hand him a card. "I appreciate lots of things about you, but if I had to pick just one thing, then it would have to be your curiosity. You're always so eager to learn new things and to look at things from different perspectives. It makes me look at things in new ways too."

Jesse's stance had a new air of confidence and now his shoulders drew back just the tiniest bit more. He opened her card and his eyes got even rounder. "Look at this," he said, holding it up for everyone to see. She'd fashioned the card using an intricate cutout design of a bird on a branch using two colors of paper.

Uncomfortable with the praise, Phoebe returned to her

seat and picked up her fork. "I suggest we get to our breakfast," she said. "I need time to get the kitchen cleaned up and ready for our luncheon guests." She turned back to Jesse. "We can hang up all of the birthday cards you got after breakfast so they can be on display for your party. But for now we should eat before our breakfast gets cold."

They all settled in to eat their meal and there was a jovial mood around the table. Jesse received some good-natured ribbing about not getting a big head. And Phoebe was pressed to tell them more about how birthdays were celebrated in her household.

Afterward, while Phoebe cleaned the kitchen and prepared for the upcoming party and meal with all the extra guests, the Beilers were dispatched to take care of the remaining Sunday chores and to set up the basement as a game area for the younger guests. Seth and Daniel brought up an extension for the table as well as a number of extra chairs.

It seemed no time at all before the guests started to arrive.

Edna's two *shveshtra*, along with several of their *kinner* and *kins-kinnah*, arrived to help Jesse celebrate his special day. Phoebe had added the handmade birthday cards Jesse had received that morning to the banner and it now looked quite festive.

The meal, which included everything Jesse had requested, was well received. And Jesse pronounced the strawberry rhubarb cake that Phoebe had baked to be the best he'd ever had.

Even though it was cold and wet outside, the space they'd prepared in the basement with the cornhole boards, a ping-pong table and horseshoes was more than enough to keep the young people entertained.

The adults stayed upstairs and sipped on hot cups of

coffee and tea. The conversation bounced around from topic to topic as normally happens at family gatherings. Phoebe was unfamiliar with most of it but let it all swirl around her, enjoying the insights into both Seth's and Edna's lives. Then Hilda said something to Seth that made her sit up straighter.

"My Zilla tells me you're finally ready to look for a new *fraa*. I'm glad to hear it."

It was all Phoebe could do not to turn and stare at Seth.

But Hilda had more to say. "And she tells me she's bringing someone along when she and her family come to visit for Christmas." The woman settled more comfortably, a self-satisfied smile on her face. "Who knows, my Zilla may turn out to be as *gut* a matchmaker as her *mamm*."

Edna gave her *shveshtah* an exasperated look. "As far as I know, the only successful match you've ever made was between Zilla and Jude."

Phoebe missed the next few minutes of conversation as she tried to process the idea of Seth looking for a *fraa*. It had caught her completely by surprise, but it shouldn't have. It made sense that a man such as Seth would want a helpmeet by his side. The only surprise was that he hadn't started looking before now.

He must be serious about moving forward if his cousin was bringing a woman to Sweetbrier Creek to meet him. Was she the only person who hadn't known? Of course Seth had already demonstrated he wasn't always *gut* about giving her a heads-up on things.

What sort of person was this potential match for him? Would she be a woman who'd challenge him or would she be someone who would be more biddable? One thing for certain, she'd be able to read and write, which meant she'd have no trouble with reading Seth's lists.

Whoever he selected to marry would have a *gut mann* to spend her life with. And since she would have moved back to Bergamot by the time any of this happened it was really none of her concern other than to wish the couple well.

Then she noticed Levi and Daniel exchanging glances. From their expressions it seemed this was a surprise to them also.

Based on Edna's demeanor, though, not only had she known about it but she wasn't happy that Hilda had brought the subject up.

Hilda seemed blind to her *shveshtah's* disapproval and continued her chattering on the subject. "If Zilla's friend doesn't work out for you, you just let me know and I'll see if I can find someone for you myself."

Seth shifted in his seat and Phoebe felt a twinge of sympathy. This couldn't be a comfortable conversation for him to sit through.

Trying to switch the focus of the conversation away from Seth's search for a *fraa*, Phoebe stood. "I think it's time to see if Jesse and his friends would like to have more cake and hot cocoa. Seth, would you mind helping me?"

Seth popped up at once. "Of course." And with that he headed to the kitchen, barely waiting for her to precede him.

When they reached the kitchen Seth realized he'd traded one uncomfortable situation for another. Having his *aenti* discuss his personal matters in the room full of people had been awkward. But being alone with Phoebe after the abrupt announcement of his search for a *fraa* felt awkward in a completely different way.

He wasn't sure why—after all he didn't owe her any kind of explanation. Not only wasn't she *familye*, but she was only here temporarily.

But as they worked together to gather up saucers, forks and mugs, the silence drew out between them. He could feel the tension growing, stretching, tightening until he was sure it would snap with a physical recoil.

As he helped her get everything ready for Jesse's guests, he searched for something to say, anything, just to dissipate the tension. "*Danke* for calling me in here. *Aenti* Hilda doesn't always think before she speaks."

"You're welcome. And I'm sure your *aenti* means well." She hadn't met his gaze even once since they'd entered the kitchen. "Besides, looking for a *fraa* is nothing to be embarrassed by. It's *gut* for a person to have a helpmeet to go through life with." She grabbed the milk from the refrigerator and moved to the stove.

Something seemed a little off with her voice, though he couldn't quite say what. But before he could respond, she continued. "I think that's everything. Would you mind calling the *kinner* up here while I make the hot cocoa?"

He hesitated a moment, feeling as if he needed to say something to her, but he wasn't sure what. So instead he left the room to do as she'd asked.

Once Jesse and his guests had trooped up to the kitchen Seth slipped out of the house. Ignoring the cold, he leaned a hip against the porch rail and stared unseeing across the front yard. The brief conversation he'd had with Phoebe had left him feeling oddly dissatisfied.

The door opened behind him and a moment later Levi joined him at the porch rail. "It seems *Aenti* Hilda let the cat out of the bag."

Hearing the note of amusement in his *bruder's* voice did nothing to improve Seth's mood. "I wasn't trying to keep it a secret."

Levi turned and leaned back, his elbows resting on the

rail. "Yet you failed to mention your sudden interest in finding a *fraa* to any of us." His eyes narrowed. "Then again, perhaps it's not quite so sudden. Apparently you've been planning something like this for a while if Zilla's had time to find you a candidate."

Seth heard the undertone of accusation in his *bruder's* tone. Or maybe it was just his guilty conscience acting up. "I wrote both Zilla and Caleb letters asking them to help find someone just before Phoebe arrived." He clasped his hands together and leaned forward against the porch rail. "I thought it was time I married again."

"*Gut*, I've been thinking the same thing about you lately. But are you sure you want someone else doing the looking for you?"

"It's not so unusual a thing." He heard the defensiveness in his tone and tried to moderate his voice. "And I know enough about what I want in a *fraa* to describe it to someone else." A little voice in the back of his head questioned that statement.

Levi crossed his arms. "Did Phoebe have anything to say when you two went in the kitchen after *Aenti* Hilda made her announcement?"

Seth shrugged. "Not that it's really any of your business but the only thing she had to say was that she thought it was *gut* for a man to have a *fraa*."

"I see."

Seth glanced over at his *bruder*. "What is it that you think you see?"

"A lot more than you do, obviously."

There was that annoying note of amusement again. But before he could say anything Levi straightened and rubbed his upper arms.

"It's *kalt* out here. I think I'll go back inside and get some of Phoebe's hot cocoa."

Once Seth was alone again he stared out over the front yard without really seeing it. Why did he have this edgy, dissatisfied feeling? The fact that he was looking for a *fraa* was not only a very personal matter but also something that was entirely normal for someone his age and in his situation. He didn't need either Phoebe's or Levi's approval.

Perhaps he should have said something, should have forewarned them, but the fact that he hadn't didn't require any sort of apology.

So why did he feel so guilty?

Later, as the guests donned their coats and bonnets to leave, Trudy took Phoebe's hand. "Edna tells us you and Seth's *brieder* are helping him with his chess sets and have gotten a little behind on preparing your home for the service next Sunday. So if you don't think we are overstepping, Hilda and I, along with some of our *dechder*, would like to come on Wednesday for a workday to help you out."

"*Ach*, that is wonderful kind of you. And I would definitely appreciate it."

"Then plan on it. We'll be here right after breakfast and we'll bring our own cleaning supplies."

Edna stepped in to add her thanks to Phoebe's. "And we'll provide the food."

Despite her intention to focus on other things, as Phoebe cleaned the kitchen that afternoon, her stubborn mind turned to thoughts of what this woman Seth's cousin was bringing would be like.

"Nothing is settled yet."

Phoebe's gaze shot up to see Edna watching her sympathetically.

"I have no idea what you're talking about." Phoebe carried a stack of dirty saucers and forks to the counter.

"This woman Zilla is bringing with her, she and Seth may decide they don't suit."

It would be wrong to hope Edna was right. "I'm sure his cousin wouldn't get his hopes up if she didn't think they'd be a *gut* match."

"But still, there's no certainty when it comes to matters of the heart."

"I think Seth is looking for a match that is more a matter of the mind rather than the heart. Besides, it's none of my business. I'll be gone in a few weeks and will probably never visit here again."

Just saying those words made her chest ache. But enough of these heavyhearted thoughts. She just had to focus on other more productive things, things that were within her own control.

Which definitely excluded Seth.

Chapter 26

They had a simple supper that evening composed mostly of leftovers. On the surface everything seemed pleasant and normal, but Seth sensed a formality in Phoebe that hadn't been there before. And most of her conversation was directed toward the other end of the table.

Surely she wasn't upset that he was looking for a *fraa*? No doubt it had more to do with how she had learned the news. She seemed to take it very personally when she heard news secondhand or late—perhaps that's all this was.

Afterward, as the table was being cleared, Phoebe met his gaze and finally spoke directly to him. "After the kitchen is cleaned I plan to work on making the Christmas cards that I want to mail out. I'm not sure how you handle that for your household but since you're so busy with your chess sets, I would be glad to help work on yours as well."

Pleased to hear some of her positive spirit back in her voice, he smiled. "*Danke*. I'm afraid we haven't sent out cards the last year or two but I think it would be *gut* to start the practice again."

She gave him a challenging look. "Then I propose a trade. If you'll let me know how many cards you need, I'll make them. In return you agree to write the greetings and address them for me." She turned to Edna. "And I'll be happy to make some for you as well."

Then she looked around the table at Seth's *brieder.* "And any of you who want to participate can help with either making the cards or writing in them."

Phoebe's lips twitched up in a smile as most of Seth's *brieder* avoided eye contact and left the kitchen as soon as possible.

After she'd set the kitchen to rights, Phoebe slipped away to the *dawdi haus* to fetch her origami and cutting supplies then returned and spread them out on the kitchen table. She needed to make seven for her own use, and Edna had asked for four. Depending on how many Seth needed she might have her hands full.

A few moments later Seth set a box on the table beside her supplies. "This is the Christmas box left from when Dinah was in charge of this." He opened the box and pulled out some red bows in various sizes, a spool of green wire, some pinecones that had been lacquered, and several sheets of paper with notes written on them.

He picked up the papers. "These are the people she sent cards to." He placed that one aside. "And this one is a menu for our Christmas meals along with a shopping list for the ingredients. And this one is a recipe for a special fruitcake—Dinah always made several to give away as gifts for our neighbors and friends."

"That sounds like a wonderful *gut* tradition, it's a shame to let it die out. Perhaps I should bake some Christmas cookies for you to give away this year."

"You have so many other things to do—"

"Nonsense. I enjoy baking."

He lifted his hands palms-out. "I'll leave it up to you to decide."

She smiled, pleased he was willing to leave at least a few matters in her hands. She pointed to the last sheet of paper. "What's that one for?"

"It lists the sizes and placements for the wreaths she always made."

"Goodness, she sounds as if she was even more organized than I imagined."

"*Jah.* It was one of her best qualities."

She knew he liked structure and being able to feel that there was an order to things. Still, knowing that he was well aware that she was more spontaneous than organized, the comment stung. Telling herself he hadn't deliberately intended to make her feel bad made it hurt marginally less.

She grabbed a sheet of paper and her scissors. It would be best if she just focused on making the cards.

While Phoebe worked on the cards she wanted to send, Seth reviewed Dinah's list. He scratched off a few names and added a few more. "Is eleven too many?"

She smiled at that. "No number can be too many when you're sharing your appreciation or your joy." Then she gave him a warning look. "I just may not get them all created tonight."

"I can help you make them," Levi offered. "You just need to show me how you make those fancy cutouts."

Phoebe grinned at that. "They don't all have to have the cutouts—a simple drawing will work just as well. But *jah*, I can show you how to make the cutouts if you like."

Seth watched as Phoebe and Levi put their heads together

over the paper, heard their give-and-take discussion and easy laughter. And when Levi finished his first one, a simple cutout of a candle, Phoebe applauded his efforts.

Then, without warning, Phoebe looked up and caught him watching her.

He cleared his throat. "I see you have some cards finished. Would you like me to write a greeting inside?"

She nodded and pushed the three completed cards to him. "I'd like the greeting inside of each of these to read *Wishing you a very joyful and blessed Christmas*, and then add my name to the bottom."

He looked at the designs on the cards. One was a wreath, one was a mantel with a lantern and one was the candle Levi had made. "These are *wunderbaar.*"

"*Danke.*"

"Do you care which card goes to which person?"

"*Nee*, I don't have time to really personalize them this year."

Did that mean he was working her too hard? After all, she'd agreed to be his housekeeper, not to help with his chessboard-making efforts or to try to fix some of the things that were broken around here.

He grabbed a pen and carefully wrote the inscription she'd requested.

"Do you have the addresses of where you need to send these?"

"I've memorized the addresses for my *brieder.*" She sat back a moment, biting her lip. "I don't have the others." There was a defeated air about her as she admitted that. And he had a sudden urge to do something to perk her up.

"Perhaps you could call your *mamm* tomorrow and get the addresses from her."

She immediately brightened. "*Jah*, she would have

them." Her expression softened. "And it would be *gut* to speak to *Daed* and *Mamm* again."

He felt a little stab of guilt. "You know you can use the phone whenever you need to, don't you?"

"That's very kind of you. *Danke*."

Did that mean she hadn't believed he'd allow her to use it? Thinking she could believe he'd be so hard-hearted gave him pause. Was that what others saw in him? Was that what *Phoebe* saw in him?

Perhaps it was time he paid more attention to those around him.

* * *

"I have a favor to ask you."

Seth was in the mudroom getting ready to head outside. He paused buttoning his jacket and looked up to see Phoebe facing him, her hand kneading her apron. His *brieder* had already scattered for the morning and Edna had headed back to the *dawdi haus* so it was just him and her in this part of the house.

"Of course. What is it?" Why did she look so nervous?

"In a few minutes I'm going to go call my *daed* and tell him I need the addresses, just as we discussed last *nacht*. Then I'll call back in an hour so he or *Mamm* can find the addresses and give them to me."

He thought he knew what this was about. "If you're asking permission to use the phone, I already said last night—"

"*Nee*." She took a breath and lifted her chin. "When I call back, would you mind going with me? I need someone to write down the information. I'd try to memorize the addresses but I'm afraid I might mess up."

Seth mentally kicked himself. He should have realized that would be an issue for her. Being forced to ask for help this way couldn't have been easy. So he answered as matter-of-factly as he could. "I can do that. Just come by the workshop when you're ready." He grinned. "I may lose track of time."

He saw some of the tension ease from her demeanor.

"*Danke*. I know you're very busy—hopefully this won't take too much of your time."

He gave her a self-deprecating smile. "No doubt I'll be ready for a little break by the time you need me."

As Seth made his exit he wondered about the protective urge she kept bringing out in him. He'd like to say it was because she was in his care while she was here but he knew it was more than that.

He thought of the way she'd looked as she'd asked for a favor. Unhappy about having to ask but willing to put her fears aside and push through to do what needed to be done.

He finally decided it was that odd mix of vulnerability and courage that tugged at him, made him want to slay her dragons. Or in her case, stand beside her to slay those dragons together. Because she always seemed ready to face her problems head-on.

* * *

About five minutes before the scheduled call time, Phoebe stepped into Seth's workshop.

"Be with you in a moment," he called out without looking up.

She took advantage of his attention on his work to watch him at his craft. He was totally focused on what he was doing—the vertical lines between his eyebrows were pronounced, his gaze was locked on his carving and his head was bent over his work. But it was his hands that captured her attention. The sight of his large, callused hands that could somehow make such sure, delicate movements as he brought the dark king to life from the cylinder of wood was fascinating, mesmerizing. As he paused to run his thumb across the surface of the wood, she saw a faded scar that she hadn't noticed before—what was the story behind it?

When he finally sat back she moved farther into the room. "Is this a *gut* time?"

"*Jah*." Seth set the piece and his gouge down, stood and worked the kinks out of his neck and back. Then he grabbed a small notepad and pencil from his worktable.

"Let's go, we don't want to keep your *eldre* waiting."

The wind had picked up and Phoebe pulled her coat closer as they tromped down the drive. Seth thoughtfully adjusted his long stride to match her shorter one.

"I appreciate you taking time away from your work to do this for me."

"Glad to do it. I needed a bit of fresh air to clear my head anyway."

When they arrived at the phone shanty Phoebe ignored the bench and stood in the middle of the small shelter to place her call. It only rang twice before her *mamm* answered.

"Phoebe, is that you?"

"Hello, *Mamm*."

"*Ach*, it's so *gut* to hear your voice. Have you been getting on okay? Are you ready to come home yet?"

Phoebe winced but tried to keep her irritation out of her voice. "I'm doing well. And I'll be home for a visit on Christmas Eve, just like we planned."

"A visit." There was a definite note of disappointment in her *mamm's* voice. "So Edna isn't healed yet?"

Stay positive. "Not entirely. She has a doctor visit sometime this week I believe. That'll tell us how long I'll be needed here." She made a mental note to remember to ask Edna just when her appointment was.

"Well, at least a hurt arm doesn't affect her ability to give you direction. I'm sure that's been a blessing to you."

Phoebe decided not to respond to that and instead got down to business. "Did you get the addresses I needed?"

"*Jah.* These are for Christmas cards, ain't so?"

"They are."

She heard a deep sigh come over the line. "Rhoda and I are working on ours. I certainly miss those pretty little touches you contributed in the past." Then she added, "But Rhoda is a *gut* artist, her drawings are *wunderbaar.*"

"That's nice." And she meant it. Now that she'd put some time and distance between her and her *familye* she could see that *Mamm* needed a *dochder* she felt comfortable sharing the running of the household with. And it would never be her. "Are you ready with the addresses?"

"*Jah,* I have them right here. I can read them to you if you're ready. And I can go over them as many times as you need me to so you can memorize them."

Her irritation faded. *Mamm* might think of her as a *kinner,* but she was patient and loving still. "*Danke,* but that won't be necessary. I have someone here who will write it down for me. His name is Seth Beiler and I'm going to give him the phone now so you can speak directly to him." And with that she passed the receiver to Seth.

As soon as Seth began speaking to her *mamm* Phoebe realized she should have swapped places with him and stepped outside the shanty, no matter how cold and windy it was. With him drawing closer to be able to hear her *mamm* and write the information down, the shanty quickly felt crowded. They weren't touching exactly, but his presence seemed to fill the small space and she had nowhere to go.

She was surrounded by the scent of wood and stain and him, by the sound of his rich voice, by the sight of his strong hands flowing fluidly across the paper as he wrote down the addresses. Where the shanty had felt cold a moment ago, Phoebe now found it almost uncomfortably warm. She had to fight to control her breathing, to not let it turn into gasps.

These feelings were new, unexpected, unsettling. What was wrong with her?

Seth finally turned back to her and held the receiver out. "I have all the information written down. Your *mamm* would like to speak to you again."

It took Phoebe a moment to react, then she quickly nodded and accepted the handset, fumbling it a moment before recovering. To her relief Seth stepped back and gave her some space. But she found she now missed his presence.

The cold air cleared her head, and she focused on the telephone. "Hello."

From the corner of her eye she saw Seth walk off. No doubt he was in a hurry to get back to work. Hopefully he hadn't noticed too much out of the ordinary in her reaction.

Seth left her to say her goodbyes and headed back to his workshop. He'd wait to address her cards for her when he went back to the house for lunch.

Right now he needed to put some distance between them.

There'd been a moment back there in the shanty when

he'd felt…something. He wasn't ready to put a name to it yet. The hitch in Phoebe's breathing hadn't helped things either.

But now that he'd stepped away, had had the blast of cold wind to clear his senses, he realized it had been no more than the unexpected intimacy of that small shanty. It had been inappropriate of him to step in so close and he wouldn't make such a mistake again.

Phoebe was under his care while she was here. As he'd told Levi, she was a guest of Edna's and her *eldre* had entrusted her to his care. While she was here, she was a member of his household and should be treated as such.

With that bracing thought, he had himself back under control and continued on to his workshop.

But a niggling voice in his head said he wasn't as in control as he was telling himself he was.

Chapter 27

Phoebe had washed and hung up one load of laundry between phone calls. Now she went down to the basement and began a second. While she worked on the task that she could basically do by rote, her mind kept returning to that moment in the phone shanty. In her mind she knew it had only lasted a few minutes but at the time it had seemed to stretch out for much longer. She wanted to believe it had affected her because she'd never found herself in such a situation before or that perhaps what she'd felt was a sense of being trapped. But if she was being honest with herself, there was only one answer for why it had affected her so strongly.

She had developed feelings for Seth Beiler.

Which was totally inappropriate, especially given that the man was due to meet a potential match in just a week or so. And she was obviously not the kind of woman he was looking for.

So the best thing she could do was try to forget the

whole thing and under no circumstances let on to Seth how she was feeling.

She was afraid the second part of that was going to be a whole lot easier to accomplish than the first.

At supper that evening, Phoebe finally remembered she had a question for Edna. "Don't you have a doctor visit coming up soon?"

Edna nodded. "*Jah*. Tomorrow morning as a matter of fact."

Seth immediately reacted. "*Ach*. You should have said something sooner, *Aenti*." He turned to Mark. "Can you take her—"

But Edna cut in. "That's not necessary. I know you're all very busy so I've already arranged for a car to take me."

Phoebe felt a little stab of guilt. Had she been ignoring her friend? "I'll go with you."

Edna smiled as she shook her head. "*Danke*, but that's not necessary." Then she lifted her chin. "I may be old enough to be your *grossmammi* but I'm still able to get around on my own when I need to."

"Of course you are," Phoebe said quickly. "I just thought you might want company."

"That's a wonderful nice thought but you're needed here." The older woman raised her hand, palm-out. "My mind is made up. Let's hear no more about it."

Phoebe, who knew what it felt like to have everyone around her doubt her abilities, smiled. "You know best."

She cut a quick glance Seth's way and could tell he wasn't happy with the corner Edna had backed him into, but at least he let the subject drop.

Poor Seth, he didn't like it when someone in his household didn't let him take care of them as he thought he should.

He had a *gut* heart and strong protective instincts, but

he certainly needed to recognize when his actions crossed the line from protective to smothering.

* * *

Phoebe looked up from the stove as Edna stepped inside. "Welcome back. What did the doctor say?"

Edna hung her coat on a hook in the mudroom then lifted the arm with the sling. "That I need to wear this thing for two or three more weeks and then, if all goes well, I should be able to get back to normal."

"That is wonderful *gut* news." For Edna at least. Because it also meant she herself had only two or three more weeks here and then she'd be going home permanently. She'd known the day would come, of course. And given the feelings she was having for Seth perhaps it was better that it came sooner rather than later.

But oh, it was going to be so difficult to say goodbye to this *familye*—every single member.

And perhaps one in particular.

Later that day Daniel placed an armload of pine branch cuttings on the counter in the mudroom. "I hope these are what you were looking for."

Phoebe wiped her hands on her apron as she bustled over. She lifted a few of the sprigs and nodded. "These are perfect—they'll make wonderful *gut* wreaths."

Daniel rubbed the side of his jaw. "I'd offer to help you make them but Seth needs me in the workshop."

"Of course." She waved him away. "I can do this on my own. Go, help your *bruder.*"

Jesse, who'd been in the mudroom shedding his coat and hat, spoke up. "I can help. Seth says he won't need me again until tomorrow."

"*Wunderbaar. Kum*, help me sort through these. We'll make three piles—the bigger pieces, the medium-sized pieces and the scraps." They worked in companionable silence for several minutes, the only sounds were the muted scratches the pine switches made as she and Jesse shuffled them around.

Finally she dusted her hands. "I think that should do it. While I move this pile of larger pieces to the kitchen table, would you fetch Dinah's Christmas box from the sideboard?"

Jesse did as she asked and then took a seat beside her at the table. He looked over the small branches and sprigs set out on the table with a what-do-we-do-now look on his face. "How did you learn to make wreaths?"

"My *mamm* taught me." She picked up a couple of the cuttings. "I can teach you if you want to learn."

He sat up straighter. "What do you need me to do?"

"You see where I'm holding these two sprigs together? If you would take it from me and hold it just like that then I'll have my hands free to tie them together with a bit of green wire we'll pull from Dinah's Christmas box—*jah*, just like that." Phoebe fetched the thin green wire from the box, cut a length and twisted it around the woody parts that overlapped. Then she tested it to make sure it was secure. They repeated the process several more times and each time Phoebe gently tugged the connected pieces into a curve. Then she turned back to Jesse. "What do you think? We can add either three or four more cuttings depending on what size we want."

Jesse nudged his glasses farther up on his nose. "I think we should add four."

She grinned. "I believe you're right, let's make it big and full." Then she gave Jesse a challenging look. "Would you care to swap jobs, I'll hold the pieces and you twist on the wire?"

Jesse nodded enthusiastically and held the partially completed wreath out to her. "*Jah*."

He studied the stack of cuttings. "Which should I pick?"

"It's up to you. We can make any of them work." When he still hesitated, she added, "Look for one that's full and that has a sturdy main stem."

Jesse's gaze sharpened and he pulled one from the stack and held it out.

"That's perfect," Phoebe said as she took it from him. Then she put it in place and held it out for him to secure with the wire. Once he'd done that she instructed him how to shape it so that the end result would be a circle.

After that it went quickly. Jesse selected cuttings with growing confidence and then placed, secured and shaped them as she'd taught him. Before long they had a nearly completed circle of green.

"Now let me tell you how to finish it off and secure the ends together." And as Edna had done with her, she talked the boy through doing it himself rather than doing it for him.

Once that was done, she had him set it on the table and they both studied it for a moment. Finally she cut a glance his way. "What do you think?"

He rubbed his neck. "It's okay I guess."

"You're right, it's just okay. But we want it to be *wunderbaar*."

"Do we need to redo it?"

"Not at all. We just need to make it look fuller."

"How do we do that?"

"The trick to making it look fuller is to take some of those smaller sprigs, especially the ones that have pine-cones attached, and weave them in."

Jesse popped up from his seat. "I'll get them."

When he returned with his armload, Phoebe again showed him how to add them in and the two of them worked together until it was pleasingly full. "I think this is enough. It doesn't have to be perfectly even all around, in fact I like it better if it isn't." She adjusted one of the added pinecone sprigs. "It gives it a touch of character and uniqueness."

She hid a smile as Jesse rubbed his chin and nodded. "I can see that."

"We just need to add one of those red bows from Dinah's box and it'll be complete."

Jesse reached into the box and pulled one out.

Phoebe tugged one of the ends and fluffed the folds until it looked almost like new. Again, she felt a little imperfection helped give it character and a sense of *familye* history.

She talked Jesse through how to attach the bow and then stepped back and admired the finished product. "You are a quick learner," she told the boy. "Next year you'll be able to make these on your own for the *familye*."

Jesse's smile faded at that. "I wish you were staying with us forever."

His words touched her in a way that was bittersweet. "I'm afraid that's not possible but I'll think of you all often after I leave. Besides, it seems Seth is looking for a *fraa* so there may be exciting changes to your household after I leave. I'd be honored, though, if you would write to me occasionally to tell me how you and your *brieder* are getting on."

That didn't bring the smile back to Jesse's face as she'd hoped but he nodded.

Phoebe gave him a bracing smile. "Now, it looks like we have enough cuttings to make another, smaller wreath. Shall we?"

While they worked Phoebe found herself imagining this household with someone new in the role of lady of the house, part of the Beiler *familye*—cooking the meals, interacting with the six *brieder*, taking care of things like these wreaths and the greeting card garland—in other words, making this house a home.

And no matter how hard she tried, her stubborn mind—or was it her heart—kept putting her image in that role.

Chapter 28

The next morning, almost before Phoebe had the breakfast dishes done, Edna's *shveshtra* and six nieces descended on the Beiler home with mops, brooms, rags and other cleaning supplies in hand.

Mark and Daniel had both stayed home from their respective jobs to provide assistance with the repair work and any heavy lifting that might be required.

They divided up the house among them. Edna took two of Trudy's *dechder* upstairs. Trudy and Hilda took two of Hilda's *dechder* and began work on the first floor. That left Phoebe to tackle the basement with the other two girls, along with Mark and Daniel.

While Priscilla and Annie, cousins who both looked to be in their late teens, worked on cleaning the shelves of canned goods and bulk supplies, Phoebe sorted through the odds and ends that could be moved out to make more room for the church benches. As she identified items— like the outdoor games, drying racks and miscellaneous hardware—she called for Daniel and Mark to carry them out to the spare room upstairs or to one of the outbuildings.

When the room was finally cleared of the unnecessary items, Mark and Daniel moved on to tackling repairs and touch-ups in and around the house. All three women went to work scrubbing the basement floors, wiping down the walls and cleaning the windowpanes until they sparkled.

As they worked the two girls chattered away without missing a beat. The talk ranged from boys to Priscilla's precious new nephew to upcoming Christmas preparations. At one point it rolled around to the fact that Annie was excited by the fact that all of her siblings, some of whom apparently lived quite a distance away, would be home for Christmas the following week. Apparently it would be the first time they would all be together in several years.

Annie wrung her cleaning rag out in a bucket. "Zilla is wonderful excited to be bringing her friend Fannie to meet Seth. *Mamm* says he's been single too long."

"*Jah.*" Priscilla wiped her brow with the back of her hand. "I just wonder why he couldn't find someone right here in Sweetbrier Creek."

Annie shrugged. "Who knows the ways of a man's heart?"

"What do you know about Zilla's friend?"

Phoebe wasn't comfortable with gossip, but she was guiltily glad Priscilla had asked that question.

Annie paused a moment. "Zilla isn't one to gossip, of course, but I understand Fannie is a widow and has a five-year-old *dochder*. Oh, and she was a schoolteacher before she married." Then she went back to work. "The only other thing I know is that if she's a friend of Zilla's then she's for sure and for certain a *gut* person."

It sounded like this Fannie would be perfect for Seth.

Then Priscilla changed the subject. "Speaking of needing a *fraa*, I know Levi is only twenty, but I wonder if he's ever going to settle down. As far as I know he's never singled any girl out for his attention."

Annie laughed. "Mark my words, when Levi finds the right girl he's going to fall big. And that's going to be one lucky girl."

Phoebe missed the rest of that discussion as she tried to picture this household with the addition of a five-year-old girl. Having a little girl in the house would certainly change the whole set of relationships within the *familye*. But she could see the child bringing out a tender side in Seth. The oldest Beiler *bruder* would bring the girl into the fold as if she were his own, especially since he had had the same thing happen to him at a similar age. And the other Beiler *brieder* would take the *kinner* under their protective wings as well.

The little one would get a new *daed* and five doting *onkels* all at once. And perhaps she would soon be joined by some siblings as well.

Phoebe scrubbed the baseboard a little harder, doing her best to scrub those images from her mind at the same time.

* * *

When Seth stepped inside the kitchen at lunchtime he found Phoebe checking something in the oven. His cousins Annie and Priscilla were there as well, helping her get the table set and glasses filled for lunch.

When he said hello both girls gave him sly, speculative looks. It puzzled him at first and then he realized that they no doubt knew about the friend Zilla was bringing home and why.

Trying to mask his irritation at this intrusion into his personal life, Seth turned to Phoebe. "Something smells wonderful *gut*."

Phoebe smiled over her shoulder. "*Danke*. It's just a chicken and pasta casserole. And I've got stewed tomatoes and peppers on the stove to go with it."

Before either of them could say more the rest of the group began arriving. Seth lent a hand and it only took a few more minutes for them to get the food to the table.

Once everyone filled their plates, Seth led them in a moment of silent prayer.

When everyone looked up it wasn't long before the kitchen was filled with talk of what work had been completed and what remained to be done. Then someone complimented the wreath Phoebe and Jesse had made and the conversation turned from there to a discussion of Christmas preparations. This year Hilda was having a large *familye* gathering at her home.

Seth let the talk flow around him, enjoying the simple pleasure of having his home filled with the warm comfort of an extended *familye* gathering. That hadn't happened in quite some time, not here in this kitchen.

And it didn't escape his notice that Phoebe seemed to fit right in.

About halfway through the meal Phoebe turned to him, pulling Seth back into the discussion. "Daniel and Mark have been wonderful *gut* helpers this morning, but most of their work is done now if you need their help in the workshop."

Seth shook his head. "Everything is done but the carving of a few more chess pieces, which I need to take care of myself. So feel free to take advantage of their help for whatever you might need."

Mark groaned. "Don't we get any say in this?"

"Of course you do," Seth said drily. "You can say *jah*, you'd be glad to help."

Mark rolled his eyes but smiled Phoebe's way.

After lunch Seth found himself reluctant to leave the group and return to his workshop. But there was work to be done if he wanted to complete his orders on time. So as the ladies resumed their work he made his exit.

* * *

Trudy helped Phoebe clean the kitchen while the others resumed their work on the rest of the house. As Trudy wiped down the counter she studied the garland of birthday cards that was strung across the mudroom entrance. "That's a lovely card," she said pointing to the one Phoebe had made. "It's quite unique. Do you know who sent it to him?"

Phoebe felt her cheeks warm. "I did."

Trudy eyed her approvingly. "I've never seen one like it. Where did you get it?"

That question made her even more uncomfortable. "I made it."

"Now I am for sure and for certain impressed. That is quite a talent you have there." She finished wiping the counter and moved to the sink to rinse out the cloth. "Have you ever thought about selling them?"

"*Nee*. It's just something I do for the enjoyment of it." Then Phoebe wiped her hand on a dishcloth. "I think I'll let the dishes soak for now so we can join the others and finish up the housework."

To Phoebe's relief, Trudy accepted her change of subject and no more was said about her papercraft skills.

The rest of the work was accomplished quickly and they were able to wrap things up within a couple of hours. Phoebe sent the ladies home with her thanks and tins full of cookies she'd baked the night before for just that purpose.

Then she turned to Edna. "Your *familye* is very generous with their time."

"They enjoy getting together this way, even if it's to do housework."

"Well, I certainly feel more prepared now than I did before." She gave Edna a tentative smile. "We might actually pull this off without having to apologize for anything."

"Of course you will. I never doubted it for a moment."

Phoebe wished she had that same level of faith in her abilities.

Chapter 29

Thursday afternoon, when Phoebe entered the workshop to bring Seth some of the oatmeal raisin cookies she'd baked, she found him cleaning his tools.

He glanced her way and put the tools down. "You'll have to eat one of those with me to celebrate—I've finished the last of the Christmas orders."

"Oh, Seth, that's *wunderbaar!*"

He nodded. "I counted the sets, went through every drawer and counted the pieces, just to make sure. They're all there." He sat back and rubbed the back of his neck. "I actually made the deadline, even with the addition of that last-minute order for four sets." He met her gaze. "Or I should say *we* made the deadline. Your suggestion of the assembly-line process did the trick."

"Actually it had more to do with all the help you received from your *brieder.*" She grinned. "Even if you did have trouble accepting that help."

He had the grace to look a little sheepish at that. "I'll

admit I was reluctant to give up control of my process. But I didn't have a lot of choice and, in the end, I actually enjoyed having my *brieder* around and seeing the way they took ownership of the finished product."

"Well, I think this calls for not only a *familye* celebration but also a frolic of sorts to get these all packed up and ready for shipping."

True to her word, Phoebe set up a frolic-like atmosphere that evening for the final packaging of the sets. She had prepared a pan of snickerdoodles and popped a big bowl of popcorn for snacking and the whole household was recruited to get the job done. Even Edna declared she wanted to play a part, if only to read through Seth's checklist.

Though grateful for everyone's enthusiastic willingness to help, Seth found himself unable to relax. He hovered over everyone, making sure the right sets went to the right recipients, that the inner packaging was such that the contents were well protected and secured, that the outer packaging was absolutely perfect so that nothing would come open in transit. Despite that, the mood among the others in the room was lighthearted and even playful.

When at last it was finished, everyone just sat back and stared for a moment. Then Levi grinned and let out a loud whoop, tossing some popcorn in the general direction of his *brieder*. "We did it!"

With a laugh, several of the others reached for the bowl and retaliated. Quite a bit of popcorn ended up on the floor as kernels were tossed back and forth.

Seth let them go at it awhile—they deserved a little bit of horseplay after putting in so many hours to help him out. A moment later he got hit with a handful of the salty white snack himself.

Caught by surprise, he glanced around the room and

realized Phoebe was the culprit. "I don't believe you did that."

"Why not?" She didn't look at all repentant. "Someone needed to do it—you were looking much too pompous."

"Was I now?" He plucked some of the popcorn from his lap and bent to put it on the side table. Then at the last minute tossed it in Phoebe's direction.

She laughed as most of it landed in her lap, and the sight of that delighted merriment held him entranced for a moment.

It was only when Edna stood and called a halt that he came back to himself. "I think that's enough for tonight." She managed to include them all in her stern gaze. "I'm going to bed but I expect every one of you to help Phoebe clean up this mess."

As they worked to comply with Edna's demand, Seth announced to his *brieder*, "I plan to take these to town tomorrow to have them shipped and Phoebe is going to go with me to do her shopping. So make sure if there's anything you need from town it makes it to the list." Even if she couldn't read it, a list was a *gut* thing to have. And he'd help her check everything off.

It was the least he could do.

* * *

Phoebe made certain she was on time the next morning—she didn't want to keep Seth waiting like the last time they'd gone to town.

Still, when she stepped outside she found him standing beside the buggy, blowing on his gloved hands, no doubt trying to warm his face.

"I'm sorry if I kept you waiting," she said as she approached.

"*Nee*," he answered with a smile. "I only just finished getting Chester hitched to the buggy."

The lightness of his tone made her smile. Having finished all his work by the deadline had definitely put him in a *gut* mood this morning. When she grabbed the frame to climb into the *familye* buggy she noticed that the ready-for-shipping cartons he'd loaded inside earlier almost filled the entire back.

Once she'd settled inside, Seth set the buggy in motion. Phoebe lifted her face and inhaled deeply. Despite the cold it was a beautiful day—the sun was out and there were only a few clouds dotting the blue sky.

The silence between them was companionable, comfortable, as if they were two old friends. But after a while she decided she wanted to hear his voice. And learn more about him at the same time. So she hit on a subject that would accomplish both. "You said that the chess set we use for our games was one of the first ones you made. How old were you at the time?"

"Fourteen."

"Fourteen? *Ach*, so young. How did you learn such a skill at such an age?"

"When I was a boy, even before he married my *mamm*, *Daed* liked to whittle little trinkets for me and other *kinner.* Watching him make these little animals and whistles out of a bit of wood always fascinated me. Then, when I was about eight years old, he gave me my first whittling knife and patiently taught me how to carve without cutting myself. Then other things, like how to carve actual figures and make whistles, how to choose the right piece of wood, how to smooth the pieces out." He shrugged. "After a while I found myself experimenting on my own and making other things. I liked to challenge myself with each new project. The chess set I made for *Daed* was a result of that."

He liked to challenge himself—she could see that in him. "So is that when you started selling the chess sets?"

"*Nee.* I made another set a couple of months later for an *onkel* who had seen *Daed's* set and admired it. And then I made a few more as I had time and gave them away as gifts. I did it more because I enjoyed carving the pieces and wanted to try to improve my skill." He shifted in his seat. "Eventually I did get the occasional request from people who had seen them and wanted one. So, if I could fit it in with my workload on the farm, I made them for just the cost of the materials."

"That was generous of you. Did you ever try to make other games?"

"*Jah.* Once I started making chess sets I knew that's what I wanted to do, but I also tried a few things like tops and tic-tac-toe games. *Daed* said he would speak to a toymaker he knew about me apprenticing with him, and I knew if I did that I might have to do more than just chess sets."

"And that was something you wanted to do, apprentice with a toymaker, I mean?"

"*Jah.* I only liked farming because it was a chance to work with *Daed*, but I had no real love for the vocation itself. Whittling and carving, however, were things that really spoke to me."

She could see that passion for his craft not only in the quality of the items he produced but also in the way he approached his work. "So you honed your skills through an apprenticeship."

"*Nee.*"

His answer surprised her, as did the note of regret in his voice. "What happened?"

"That first year after I graduated from school *Daed* hurt his foot right at planting time. It was a really bad injury, it had him in a cast for about four months, and he needed me to help him around the farm. The next year I was actually about a month into my apprenticeship when *Mamm* died." His hands tightened on the reins.

She touched his arm briefly. "I'm sorry, I know that must have been hard on all of you."

He nodded, his lips compressed. For a moment he didn't say anything and she figured the subject was closed. But then he started up again. "*Grossmammi* already lived in the *dawdi haus* and was able to help some. But she was seventy-one years old with arthritis and my *brieder* were so young—Jesse was a newborn, Kish was just one and a half and Mark was three. Daniel and Levi were school age but just barely." He flicked the reins. "It meant I was needed at home full-time."

"So you gave up your apprenticeship and took on some responsibility for your *brieder*, all while grieving your *mamm*."

He shrugged. "One does what one must for *familye*. And they were grieving, too, especially my *daed*. I was glad to be there for them—I love my *familye*."

"Of course you do." Phoebe had never doubted that.

Seth kept his gaze focused straight ahead. "I helped out as much as I could. But three years later *grossmammi* passed away as well and at age twenty I felt as if I were drowning." He paused while he stopped at a crossroads and then negotiated a turn.

She pictured a twenty-year-old Seth trying to hold his whole *familye* together with no one to turn to for any sort of relief. Without him having to say so she knew he'd felt that to turn to others, even extended *familye*, would mean admitting his *daed* was not handling things well.

No wonder he'd felt as if he were drowning. How had he gotten through that? But it wasn't her place to ask.

Once they were moving forward again, however, he answered her unspoken question. "One day, not too long after *grossmammi* passed, Dinah approached me. She had somehow recognized that I was struggling, and she said she thought she had a solution to both our problems. It turned out she couldn't have any *kinner* of her own. So if we married, I would gain some much-needed help with taking care of my household. And she would have a house full of *kinner* to raise as her own."

Phoebe tried to absorb what he'd just told her, but mainly she was just grateful *Gotte* had sent someone to share his load. "It sounds like Dinah was a very determined kind of woman."

"*Jah*, which I appreciated. I was grateful for her forthrightness and I agreed to her proposition almost at once. I never had reason to regret it. Dinah brought order and discipline to our home, but with a loving hand. My *brieder* respected her and for the younger ones at least, she was like a *mamm* to them. And she was very respectful and kind to my *daed*."

"I'm so glad you had someone like Dinah to help you."

He nodded. "Me too. I'll always be grateful she found the courage to approach me as she did and for the way she brought order and grace to our household."

Order and grace—two qualities no one had ever accused her of possessing.

Better not to think of that.

Instead she went back to the original topic. "So when did you decide to make a business of your chessboard making?"

He smiled. "That was actually Dinah's idea. After we

married and things settled down a bit I felt I could spare a little time to make a few sets again. When Dinah saw that I was getting requests from others to make a set she thought I should start charging for them so we could earn some extra income. In addition to being very organized, Dinah was a very practical person."

"I take it that's something you admire—organization and practicality."

"It certainly stood us in good stead while we were married."

So how did he feel about the way she was managing the household?

"As it turned out, once *Daed* passed away a few years later and I couldn't produce as much income from the farm on my own, the extra income from the chess sets certainly came in handy."

He turned the buggy into a parking lot just then and Phoebe frowned. "This isn't the grocery store."

"It's the shipping company I use. I decided to stop here first because I want to make sure these go out as soon as possible."

That made sense. "Of course. I'll help you unload."

"There's no need." He secured the horse to one of the stanchions provided on this side of the building. "They have large pallet carts inside that I can use. Just stay here with the buggy. I won't be long."

Phoebe settled back in her seat.

A few minutes later Seth came out with the cart and loaded it up then pushed it back inside.

She didn't mind sitting here alone—it gave her time to think over what he'd told her. And he'd revealed quite a lot about his history. It felt *gut* that he'd trusted her with so much personal information.

It took a while before he returned, at least fifteen minutes. But she could tell from the parking lot that they weren't the only customers, and he did have quite a few packages.

When Seth finally returned, he quickly untied the horse then climbed in the buggy. As he took the reins he gave her a smile. "Next stop, Spellman's."

When he pulled into the grocery store's parking lot, Phoebe prepared to step down. "I'll be as quick as I can. But feel free to take your time running your other errands."

Seth smiled as he climbed down. "I have no other errands today so I'm going inside with you."

"Oh." She was surprised he didn't have other things to tend to in town. Was it because he was done with the chess sets, or at least the Christmas orders for them?

Seth secured the horse and then accompanied her inside the store.

He held up a sheet of paper. "I brought the list so I can help."

She had memorized the list but if he wanted to use it she supposed that was okay. "Then why don't we split the shopping. You take care of everything on the aisles to the left of that one with the rice and pasta and I'll take what's on the right."

He shook his head. "*Nee.* There's no need to be in a hurry. I'd rather we just do it all together."

She felt her mood lighten. It was nice that he wanted to spend time with her.

But as they pushed the cart down the aisles Seth seemed to pay more attention to the list than to her. He would often reach for an item before she had a chance to do so herself. Whenever she did place an item in the basket, he'd scrutinize it and then mark it off the list. A couple of times she reached for the wrong item and before she could correct herself, he gently corrected her himself.

By the time they'd finished shopping she was convinced he'd only maneuvered events to shop with her today because he didn't trust her to get everything they'd need to feed the attendees on Sunday.

He, however, seemed to be in a *gut* mood. Once he'd loaded everything in the buggy, he climbed in and took the reins. "I think we should stop for burgers again today."

"That sounds *gut*."

"And don't worry, today I'll let you know everything that's on the menu so you can make a proper selection."

That was kind of him, but the tone of voice he used tightened a knot in her chest. It was very close to the pat-the-*kinner*-on-the-head tone her *mamm* often used. Surely she was being too sensitive.

Once they arrived at King's, Seth began reading the menu to her, just as he'd said he would. But he spoke with such slow, heavy-handed deliberation that she quickly picked something just to put an end to it. She turned and headed for an empty table, leaving Seth to deal with waiting for the order.

Their conversation during lunch was over inconsequential things such as the food, the weather and the remaining tasks ahead of them to get everything ready for Sunday.

She could tell Seth was still feeling upbeat, but though she tried to hide it, her own mood had sobered.

Be patient, she told herself, *you just need to let him see how capable you are. This shortcoming of mine takes some getting used to.*

But the disappointment that he still didn't trust her to know her own abilities and limits stung more than she wanted to admit.

Chapter 30

As they headed back toward home Seth felt *gut* about how the morning had gone. He'd managed to join her for the grocery shopping in a natural way that didn't require him to go into any explanations or excuses. He'd assisted in the shopping itself so she didn't have to rely entirely on her memory. Which was *gut* because she'd reached for the wrong item a couple of times. And he'd given her options at King's she hadn't had the first time they'd gone there.

He could sense a little tension in her but it was no doubt due to the stress of doing the shopping for a luncheon that included around 130 people. He was determined to make that event as worry-free as possible for her as well. One way he could do that would be to offer to make a list for her of everything that needed to be done to feed such a group. Edna could help her stay on track and give her confidence that nothing would get overlooked.

He thought lately that he'd seen signs that she was

beginning to appreciate having some structure. And she'd picked up on that when they discussed Dinah earlier. This would just be one additional safety net for her.

All in all, things were going quite well.

* * *

Once she arrived back at the Beiler place, Phoebe's emotions ping-ponged back and forth. On the one hand she was exceedingly pleased that Seth had felt comfortable enough to share his personal history with her. So much of it had been heartbreaking, all the more so because of the matter-of-fact way he'd delivered it.

On the other hand, she couldn't shake the hurt and frustration when she thought of how he'd treated her like someone incapable of getting the shopping done on her own and who needed to be given her menu choices in a slow, patronizing manner.

So when Jesse approached her later that afternoon she wasn't only happy to have him initiate a conversation, but also happy to have something else to focus on.

"Can I talk to you for a minute?"

"Of course." She turned and leaned back against the counter, giving him her undivided attention.

"I talked to teacher Constance today."

"And was this conversation about something in particular?"

"*Jah.* You."

Phoebe froze, not sure she was going to like the rest of this conversation. Had Jesse talked to his teacher about her inability to read? Of course he had—why else would the subject have come up? "What about me?"

The boy rubbed one of his upper arms nervously. "Not about you exactly because I didn't use your name, so you don't have to worry about that. I just told her I knew someone who was really smart and clever but who had trouble reading and writing."

Phoebe did her best to keep the smile pasted on her face, but she knew Constance had probably figured out who the boy was talking about. After all, she was the only new person who had entered the boy's life in the last few weeks. This was unwelcome news, but she couldn't find it in herself to be upset with the boy.

But Jesse was still talking. "Teacher Constance is really kind and wonderful smart and I know you are, too, even if you can't read. So I asked her how that could be." He scuffed the floor with the toe of his shoe. "I thought maybe she could help. 'Cause you do so much for others I wanted to do something for you."

Phoebe was touched by the sincerity of his efforts and intention, even if she was uncomfortable with his approach. "That was very thoughtful of you. But as my *mamm* always says, we must be thankful for both the talents and the challenges *Gotte* has given us and not look with envy on what He gave to others."

Jesse met her gaze head-on. "But what if He gave us challenges so that we can overcome them?"

His question surprised her in both its simplicity and its depth. Not knowing how to respond, she went back to the original topic. "And did your teacher have any insights?"

Jesse nodded enthusiastically. "She says you might have something called dyslexia. It means your brain processes words and letters differently than other people's brains do. And it has nothing to do with how smart you are." His eyes were bright with his enthusiasm for the information he was relaying. "She's been doing a lot of reading about it because she has a cousin who is in the same situation."

Phoebe's pulse jumped at that. "And has she been able to help him?"

Some of Jesse's enthusiasm dimmed. "Teacher said that there's no real cure, but there are ways to help the scholar learn in different ways from the other students."

The little flicker of hope that had ignited momentarily fizzled out. What *gut* did it do to put a name to her problem if there was no cure?

But Jesse had meant well so she offered him a smile. "I appreciate you looking into this on my behalf," she told him. "Now I know what it is that makes me this way."

"But there's something else. She said it was important to know that having dyslexia has nothing to do with how smart you are. She said there have been some very intelligent and very clever people through history who had the same issue—inventors, scientists, artists, doctors. It's not any different from being very tall or very short. It might make you different, but it doesn't make you slow-witted."

His earnest effort to make her feel better about herself touched Phoebe deeply. This boy had such a big heart, such a genuine empathy for others. Before she could stop herself she reached out and gave him a hug. "*Danke*," she said softly. Then she released him and went back to her cooking.

And as she stirred the pot she realized that somehow the news he'd brought her *had* made her feel better about herself.

Chapter 31

Saturday was a very busy day. While the Beilers made sure the yard was tidy and the barn was swept clean, that fresh straw was added where appropriate and the hay bales were neatly stacked, Phoebe and Edna worked on giving the basement one last cleaning.

Yesterday Seth had sat down with her and quizzed her on what all remained to be done to get ready for Sunday. Then he'd written it down and organized it in what he felt was the best approach. Afterward he'd handed it off to Edna, saying it was a checklist to help them stay on track. Phoebe had borne it all with what she considered admirable patience.

This morning, after the Beilers had headed outside, Edna had placed her hand on the list and looked at Phoebe. "We can do what needs to be done without worrying about this list, ain't so?"

Phoebe smiled. At least Edna continued to treat her as a fully functioning adult. "Agreed. Working from a list would just slow us down."

Later, while she and Edna worked in the kitchen getting the food ready for Sunday's lunch, the Beiler *brieder* unloaded the church wagon and carried the benches and songbooks to the basement.

As the final touch to getting the room tidied up, she and Edna had come up with a way to curtain off the area where the washer was located. Now Phoebe could picture Seth and his *brieder* setting rows of benches facing each other along the length of the spotless room. The hymnals would be placed on the benches, ready for the people who would file into the room and take their seats.

Later, when all the work had finally been completed, everyone trooped in and took their seats for supper.

As Kish served himself some of the cheesy chicken and dumplings with bacon that Phoebe had prepared, he inhaled deeply. "This smells *wunderbaar.*" Then he glanced at Phoebe. "What are you planning to cook for Christmas dinner—a ham or a goose?"

Before Phoebe could answer Seth spoke up. "We'll be having Christmas lunch with *Aenti* Hilda's *familye* this year."

Mark looked up at that. "I thought we'd have Christmas lunch here since we have Phoebe and *Aenti* Edna with us."

This time Phoebe spoke up. "But I won't be here for Christmas. I'm returning to Bergamot on Tuesday to spend Christmas with my *familye* and won't be back until Friday morning."

"But that means you'll miss the Christmas program." Jesse seemed both disappointed and accusatory.

"I'm for sure and for certain sorry that I'll miss the program but I promised my *eldre* I'd spend Christmas at home with them." She looked toward Kish. "I'm sure your *aenti* will have a very fine dinner for you and I'll be happy to bake a cake or a couple of pies for you to bring."

Kish didn't seem appeased by that. "But I—"

Seth cut off whatever protest his *bruder* was about to make. "Enough, Kish. Phoebe gave her word to her *eldre* that she would be home for Christmas and it's not proper to ask her to break her promise."

Phoebe tried again to appease them. "You'll have Edna here and you'll have lots of *familye* to visit, so you won't be lacking for either food or company."

No one at the table seemed happy with that answer, including Phoebe, but she'd given her word and she wouldn't go back on it.

No matter how much she might want to.

* * *

Phoebe barely slept Saturday night. Though she knew the house was ready for the service tomorrow she wasn't sure that *she* was ready.

During one of her middle-of-the-night bouts of staring up at her darkened ceiling, Phoebe had decided that it actually made sense for Edna to stand in as hostess rather than her. After all, Edna was actually part of the *familye* and she wasn't. And if she hadn't hurt her hand, Edna would be in charge and Phoebe wouldn't even be here. So first thing when she got up she would let Edna know.

When she woke up for the third time and saw it was just under an hour before the time she normally rose, she decided to get up. But before she even sat up she paused to offer up a prayer of thanks and petition.

Gotte, Who is the creator of all things, Whose power is immense but Who concerns Himself with the smallest details of our lives, I am truly grateful to have been able to prepare to receive the gmay *into this home.*

Please, if it be Your will, help me to get through this day in such a manner that it will not embarrass the Beiler familye *and that the* gmay *can focus their thoughts on worship of You rather than any mistakes I may make.*

When she finally got out of bed she dressed quietly and quickly, her mind already swirling with thoughts of what needed to be done before people started arriving for the service.

She stepped into the kitchen to find she wasn't the only one up extra early. Seth stood by the counter, kettle in hand, making a pot of coffee.

He looked up when she stepped in the room. "*Gut matin.*"

"*Gut matin.*" She plucked the apron from its hook on the wall and tied the strings behind her back. "I thought for once that I'd be the first one up this morning."

Seth grinned. "You'll have to try harder."

Phoebe went straight to the stove and turned the oven on. She planned to make a breakfast casserole with potatoes, eggs, cheese, peppers and sausage. Something that she could cook now and keep warm until the *familye* was ready to eat.

As she cracked the eggs into a bowl, she kept having to fish out pieces of eggshell. If her nerves didn't settle down soon she'd for sure and for certain make a mess of things. And to make matters worse Seth was still in the kitchen. Hopefully he hadn't noticed her clumsy handling of the eggs.

She heard him place his cup in the sink and cross the kitchen, headed for the mudroom. To her surprise he paused by her side.

She looked up to meet his gaze and his expression was warm and supportive.

He touched her arm briefly. "Don't worry yourself, all will be well."

And then he was gone.

She stood there a few moments, just staring at his back until he'd stepped outside. That had been so unexpected, so kind.

She went back to work and there were no further problems with pieces of shell in the bowl or other signs of nervous clumsiness.

Edna arrived in the kitchen a few minutes later and Phoebe immediately relayed her idea about Edna serving as hostess.

"Nonsense," was Edna's immediate response. "You said you could handle preparing the house for the service and part of that is ensuring everything in the house goes well, including greeting our guests." She gave Phoebe a stern look. "You can't do that by retreating into the shadows. Do you want to be viewed as a capable adult or not?"

Feeling properly chastised, Phoebe dropped the subject.

"Now," Edna said, "since I'm no help to you here I'll go check on the boys and make sure they straighten their rooms properly before they come down."

The rest of the Beilers appeared soon after and all grabbed coffee before they headed out to do Sunday-morning chores.

They were back for a quick breakfast and then headed out again for last-minute checks to make sure the drive and parking area were ready to handle all the buggies and horses that would soon fill the free spaces around the place.

Thirty minutes before the first of their neighbors would likely arrive Seth and his *brieder* were properly dressed for Sunday service and were in place, ready to help their neighbors park their buggies and tend to their animals as they arrived.

The first arrival was Edna's *shveshtah* Trudy and her

familye. While Trudy and her three *dechder* joined her and Edna in the house, the menfolk headed for the spacious, cleared and freshly cleaned barn.

"We have two apple pies, a gingersnap pie and a shoofly pie," Trudy said before they'd even shed their coats. "Where would you like us to put them?"

Phoebe waved a hand toward the kitchen. "In here." She led the way and had them set their desserts on the expanded kitchen table.

They had just done so when Hilda and her *familye* arrived. They also came bearing pies. As soon as they entered the house, Hilda turned to two of the women with her. "This is my *dochder* Zilla and her friend Fannie and Fannie's *dochder* Beth. They arrived here in Sweetbrier Creek yesterday afternoon."

Exchanging greetings, Phoebe did her best not to stare at the woman who'd come here to meet Seth with the hopes of marrying him. Fannie was a pretty woman, with cornsilk-blond hair and deep-blue eyes. She had a heart-shaped face, a pleasant smile and an air of quiet confidence about her. Her daughter was a mini version of herself with a sweet touch of shyness.

"Where would you like these?" Hilda's question brought Phoebe back to the present.

"*Ach*, I'm sorry. Please, *kum* this way."

It wasn't long before the living room and kitchen were filled with women and girls milling about in shifting clusters, visiting with one another. More pies had shown up as well and now the kitchen table practically groaned under the weight.

Even as she mingled among the other women, Phoebe was aware of Fannie wherever she was. The woman was personable, friendly and well received.

At some point Margaret and Constance arrived and Phoebe was delighted to renew her acquaintance with them. She was pleased to find that Constance didn't treat her any differently, even after Jesse's artless reveal of her shortcomings. These were two girls she could see herself forming long-term friendships with if she didn't live so far away.

All available chairs had been placed in the living room so there would be seating for those who wanted it prior to the start of service and some of the elderly and women carrying *bopplin* had taken advantage of that.

At the appropriate time, Phoebe lined up with the single women and headed into the basement and took her place on one of the benches.

After the service was over the ladies returned to the kitchen to get the food ready while the men worked on converting the benches to tables for the meal.

Baskets of bread, pitchers of tea, water and lemonade, bowls of peanut butter spread, cheese spread and pickles, along with bologna and bowls of coleslaw with apples and raisins mixed in were transported downstairs.

Fannie pitched in along with everyone else. She was helpful and moved with confidence and efficiency. It made Phoebe feel clumsy by comparison. In fact, when Phoebe had a near accident, knocking her elbow against a large pitcher of water, Fannie was right there to set it to rights before it could spill. She couldn't help but like the woman and she could easily picture Seth liking her as well.

And she couldn't find it in herself to take joy in that.

After the meal was over and the dishes and food had been cleared, Phoebe spotted Zilla taking Fannie over to introduce her to Seth. After a few minutes, Zilla walked away, leaving the couple to speak alone.

Phoebe forced herself to look away. She had no business

spying on their activity. But she couldn't shut off her imagination.

She went back inside and grabbed a damp dishrag. It wouldn't hurt to give the counters an additional scrubbing.

She was still at it a few minutes later when Edna walked in.

"I believe those counters are probably clean enough," she said mildly. "Don't you think you should be visiting with our guests and getting to know the people of this community better?"

"Why? I'll be gone in a few weeks anyway." Phoebe mentally winced when she heard the sulky tone in her voice.

Edna put a fist on her hip and her eyes narrowed. "Phoebe Kropf, what kind of talk is that? Are you feeling sorry for yourself?"

So what if she was? Didn't she have a right to feel that way occasionally? But she kept her thoughts to herself.

Edna shook her head. "Were you not taught to be thankful for what you have and not to look to what others have?"

Phoebe stopped going through the motions of cleaning and placed both hands on the counter. "*Jah*. I'm sorry. I don't know why I'm so out of sorts."

"Don't you?"

What did that mean?

Then Edna straightened. "Don't worry about the future. *Gotte* will work things out for the *gut*."

And before Phoebe could form a response, Edna was gone.

Chapter 32

Seth strolled beside Fannie, unsure how to open the conversation. When she remained silent he decided to start slowly. "Is this your first trip to Sweetbrier Creek?"

"*Jah*. But I've known Zilla ever since she moved to Franklin five years ago." She didn't expand on that, apparently content to let him carry the conversation.

"Zilla was quite complimentary about you."

"She had many *gut* things to say about you as well."

This stilted small talk was going nowhere. He finally decided to get down to business. "Since we both know why Zilla brought you here," he said with a self-deprecating smile, "perhaps we should move past the small talk."

Fannie returned his smile. "I do prefer to be direct."

"*Gut*. Then perhaps you should tell me what you are looking for in a marriage."

"Of course." She raised her chin. "First and foremost, I'm not necessarily looking for a love match—I had that with my Thomas. More important to me is to find someone who will be a *gut daed* to my Beth. I know you've raised five *brieder* so I take that as a *gut* sign." She cut him a sideways glance. "But little girls are different. How do you feel about raising a *shteef-dochder*?"

"While I'll admit I don't know anything about raising a *dochder*, I think a little girl would be a welcome addition to our household. If we were to marry, I would do all I could to make sure she would be happy there. As for her being a *shteef-dochder*, I was the *shteef-suh* to a man who set a wonderful *gut* example of what a *shteef-daed* should be."

She smiled. "That does speak well for you. The only other thing I require is that any man I marry be someone I can respect, someone who will respect me, who will allow me to care for our household as I think best. And of course, someone who will provide a sense of security for me and Beth."

"Those are all reasonable, straightforward requests and should be something any *Gotte*-fearing man would give his *fraa* without being asked."

She relaxed slightly. "And what is it you require of a *fraa*?"

Seth waved a hand. "Like you, I want whomever I marry to be someone I can respect and be respected by. She would also need to treat my *brieder* as if they were members of her own *familye*. But I am mainly looking for a helpmeet who is willing to manage many of the responsibilities of our household so I can focus my attention on my other work."

"Those are also reasonable requests." Fannie followed as he changed direction. "Rest assured that I know my duty when it comes to running a household. It will actually be *gut* to be in charge of a home again. And I have no desire to interfere in your work."

Something she'd just said caught his attention. "Do you mind if I ask what your living situation is now?"

"I live with my oldest *bruder* and his *familye*. They have a large home and Beth and I are happy there. But it isn't the same as having one's own home, ain't so?" Then she dropped her gaze. "Forgive me for speaking plainly, but I believe we should be open and honest with each other if we are to make this work. I know I said I wasn't looking for a love match but I would like to have a few more *bopplin* if *Gotte* is willing."

Seth cleared his throat. "I, too, would like to have *kinner* someday."

That won him a soft smile. Then she turned serious again. "What do you see as our next steps?"

Seth paused a moment before answering.

Fannie apparently interpreted his hesitation as rejection. "Don't worry if you've decided an arrangement between us won't work. Beth and I are comfortable and secure with the way things are now and will continue to be so if nothing changes." Her tone and expression were still matter of fact, as if they were discussing the weather.

"I haven't decided any such thing. In fact I haven't decided anything at all. What I was thinking was that we've only had this one short interaction and I haven't even met your *dochder* yet to see how she'll respond to me."

"I preferred to form my own opinion before I introduced you and Beth to each other."

Her caution with her *dochder's* well-being was admirable. "Of course. But I believe we should spend a little more time together while you're here in Sweetbrier Creek before we decide whether we want to take this any further or not."

"Oh." Her brow furrowed. "To be honest from what Zilla told me I expected you to be more decisive."

Her words caught him off guard. She thought him indecisive because he didn't make a life-changing decision based on a fifteen-minute discussion?

"But if you need a little more time," she continued, "then of course you shall have it. I'll be in Sweetbrier Creek for a week."

"*Danke.*" He heard the stiffness in his voice but it didn't seem to disturb her.

She stopped and he paused alongside her. "Now that we've settled that perhaps I should return to the house. I want to check on Beth."

"Of course." He swept a hand toward the house and walked with her part of the way back.

Then they parted ways—she proceeded to the house while he turned toward the barn where a cluster of men were involved in what looked to be an animated discussion.

He had found Fannie to be everything Zilla had promised. She was confident and practical, and didn't care much for small talk. She moved with a deliberate kind of grace that he admired and she was lovely in both face and form. She was plain-spoken and he hadn't noticed much display of emotion in her tone or demeanor during their conversation. The widow seemed to know exactly what she wanted out of life.

Including additional *kinner.*

He had no doubt that his home would run smoothly and efficiently if placed in her hands. He could only assume that her disappointment in his reluctance to make a quick decision meant she'd already made up her own mind to at least pursue the idea of a match.

So why was he hesitating?

The thing was, when she'd asked him what he wanted out of a marriage he'd answered based on his marriage to Dinah. He hadn't really thought it through any further than that. He'd just assumed that since things worked out so well the first time around, that was the kind of *fraa* he needed—and wanted—again. But was that true?

Lately he'd come to appreciate how spontaneity, playfulness and looking at things from a fresh perspective could add a little extra joy and interest to one's daily life.

And somehow he didn't think those were things that would come naturally to Fannie.

When Zilla's friend had talked of not looking for a love match, she'd elaborated, saying it was because she'd already had that with her first *mann*. He, on the other hand, had never experienced that emotion.

He'd never considered that a loss—he'd seen that kind of love between his *mamm* and his *shteef-daed*, a warm, binding, joyous thing. And he'd also seen how it had broken his *shteef-daed* when the object of that love was taken from him. To his sixteen-year-old mind that dependency, that vulnerability, had seemed much too big a price to pay.

But now he looked at people like Fannie and Edna and his *onkel* Samuel. They'd each had loving marriages from all appearances, and they'd each lost their spouse. And while he was sure they mourned their loss they hadn't let it cripple them the way it had his *shteef-daed*. Edna had said once that she'd never once regretted her time with Ivan, even knowing how it would end.

Was he cheating himself by not opening his heart up to the possibility of something more than friendship?

* * *

About fifteen minutes after Phoebe had seen Seth and Fannie start on their walk, she spotted Fannie entering the house, alone. The widow wore the same serene expression she'd had earlier, only breaking into a broad smile when she spotted her *dochder*. Did that mean things had gone well between her and Seth? Or just that she was *gut* at hiding her feelings?

Phoebe stepped out on the front porch——for fresh air of course——and spotted Seth across the yard, speaking with a group of men standing near the barn door.

He appeared relaxed and engaged with the other men in the group. No sign of how things had gone between him and Zilla's friend there either.

Then she reconsidered——that wasn't entirely true. The fact that both Seth and Fannie seemed so unperturbed was telling in and of itself.

And she wasn't sure she liked the story it was telling.

That night Phoebe once again lay awake staring at the darkened ceiling. But this time it was for an entirely different reason.

She couldn't deny it any longer——somehow, in only a few short weeks, she'd fallen in love with Seth Beiler.

Seeing him walk out with Fannie this afternoon had driven home to her just how much she cared for him.

How could she have let this happen? Especially since there was no indication he felt anything other than friendship and perhaps a big-*bruder* sort of protectiveness toward her. Because of course she didn't have the qualities he looked for in a *fraa*. She was nothing like Dinah, the woman he described with such appreciation, and she was nothing like Fannie, this potential *fraa* he had met today.

How was she going to make it through the next few weeks of her stay here and not let her feelings show? Perhaps it was a *gut* thing that she would be going home for a few days at Christmas. It might give her some perspective, some time to think away from the Beilers, away from Seth.

If nothing else, it would give her a sample of how life would be without him once her time here was up.

* * *

Phoebe rose early Monday morning to finish the cleanup from the activities on Sunday. The youth group had stayed late for the singing last night but she didn't begrudge them that—it was *gut* for the young members of the community to have a place to gather together.

And as usual Seth was up ahead of her, making a pot of coffee.

"*Gut matin*," he said with a bit of sleepy gravel in his voice. "I had a feeling you'd be up early today."

She nodded. "There's a lot to be done and I want to get it taken care of before I leave tomorrow."

Seth's smile faltered a moment at that.

Did that mean he was going to miss her, even a little bit?

But he recovered quickly. "Before they head out this morning, I'll get Levi and Daniel to help me move some of the benches around to free up the area around the washer in case you want to do laundry today."

"*Danke*, that will be helpful."

The coffee finished brewing and he poured himself a cup and then to her surprise poured up a second cup. He even remembered to add one sugar and a small dollop of cream before he carried it to her.

"Here," he said as he held it out. "I thought you might need this to help you get going this morning."

"*Danke*." She reached for the cup and her fingers brushed his. Like it had once before, her pulse jumped at the sudden tingling shock the touch evoked. She could tell by the way his eyes widened that he'd felt something too.

Then his lips quirked up. "Sorry. Must be static electricity. Do you have a *gut* hold?"

She nodded and he released the cup and stepped back. He was out the door before she found her tongue.

She had thought that perhaps in the light of day her midnight musings over her feelings for Seth would prove to have been made of nothing more substantial than moonbeams and starlight. But if anything the feelings were stronger today. Perhaps it was a *gut* thing that she would be gone before anything definite would come to pass between Seth and Fannie.

Determined to push those unproductive thoughts away, Phoebe turned to whisking the eggs, using up quite a bit of pent-up energy in the process.

* * *

Seth sat at the head of the breakfast table, enjoying the scrambled eggs. This morning she'd folded in cheese, ham and some finely diced pineapple. It shouldn't have worked but somehow it did.

He was doing his best to pay attention to Daniel as he tried to explain a conversation he'd had with a local farmer about a new grafting technique.

But in truth he found himself distracted by Phoebe. Not that she was doing anything particularly attention getting. It was just that ever since yesterday, when Fannie had asked him what he wanted in a *fraa*, he'd been reevaluating just what his priorities were on that score.

As if reading his mind, Levi turned to him during one of Daniel's pauses. "You haven't mentioned anything yet about how things went with you and Zilla's friend Fannie. Any news to report?"

Seth froze as the whole table went silent and all eyes turned to him. He started to reprimand Levi for asking such a personal question, especially in a manner that blindsided him like this.

But instead he set his fork down and met his *bruder's* gaze. "That's not an appropriate question for you to be asking. But since you *have* asked and the answer impacts everyone at this table in some manner or another then I suppose you deserve a response." He picked up his fork again. "Fannie and I have agreed that we need to spend a little more time together while she's here to get to know each other better before we make a decision." He speared a bit of scrambled egg. "And I expect there to be no more discussion on the subject until I bring it up myself."

He refrained from glancing directly Phoebe's way. What did she think? Did she care about his answer one way or the other?

He'd give a lot to be able to read her mind just for a moment. Then again, perhaps it was better that he not.

After breakfast Seth spent most of the morning cleaning up his workshop and taking care of his tools. Typically he had a few orders trickle in in January as individuals who saw the recipients of his sets asked for sets of their own, but now was the time for maintenance and preparation. And thanks to Phoebe he'd look at preparation in a whole new light.

Yesterday evening as they'd cleared the supper dishes, she'd casually mentioned that he should think about also offering sets in a smaller size. It was an intriguing idea. She had rightly guessed that carving the chess pieces in a smaller size but with the same level of detail would provide a challenge—something that piqued his interest and made him itch to give it a try. He would need to come up with new measurements and patterns for the different components of the chessboard and drawer. Then he'd have to see if he could scale the actual pieces properly and maintain the quality he expected of himself. He couldn't wait to give it a try, and he'd do so, right after Christmas.

Later, as Seth carried his lunch dishes to the sink, Phoebe met his gaze. "We haven't had time to enjoy a game of chess in a while. I thought it might be fun to take time for a match this afternoon, unless you have something else you need to do."

Seth smiled. "I don't have anywhere else to be and I'm not ready to start any new chess sets right now so *jah*, I'd like that."

He retrieved the chess set and placed it on the table. "I want to thank you for the *gut* job you did getting the house ready for the church service. Everything looked *gut* and everyone was well fed." He was babbling, he knew, but for some reason he felt on edge.

"*Danke*, but everyone helped."

"True, but you were the one who came up with the idea and got things started." Then he waved a hand over the board. "Light or dark?"

"Dark."

With a nod he turned the board so that the light-colored pieces were in front of him and quickly made his first move.

Her move was just as quick.

He made his move, then cleared his throat. "You were right about changing up the way I approached creating the chess sets. I couldn't have gotten all of the orders out before Christmas without everyone's help."

"We were all glad to lend a hand." She made her next move after barely giving the board a glance. "I hope you'll continue to use your *brieder's* help when you work on future orders."

He fiddled with his beard while he studied the board. "I know a big reason they worked so hard with me was that I was so far behind schedule, and it means a lot to me that they were willing to bail me out. So, no, I don't intend to shut them out as I did before. But I don't want to make any of them feel obligated to help me on a regular basis if they don't want to."

She countered his move and then placed an elbow on the table and her face in her hand as she changed the subject. "Do you think we should plan a big meal for New Year's Day? Do you normally have *familye* over?"

He liked the way she said "we"—was she even aware she'd done so? "Maybe not for lunch. But a certain amount of snack food—cookies, pies, some savory items—would be *gut* for those who might drop by in the afternoon."

She nodded. "When I get back from Bergamot, I'll plan a menu."

Thinking of her being gone for two and a half days gave Seth a stone-in-his-chest feeling. Hard to believe she'd only been part of this household for three weeks, yet now he could hardly picture their home without her very energetic presence. He contented himself with the knowledge that she would be back in just a few short days.

But perhaps he could give her an early Christmas present in the form of a little extra confidence.

Five moves later, through a series of what he considered cleverly subtle moves, he'd set her up to win. She just had to play her rook and he would be in check, a move later and it would be checkmate. She couldn't help but see the opening he'd left for her.

Phoebe reached for her rook then paused and gave him

a puzzled look. She followed through with the move but then sat back, a brows-down troubled expression on her face. Surely she didn't suspect what he was doing.

He pretended to study the board, stroking his beard contemplatively, then took the bait and captured her rook.

Phoebe sat up straight, two spots of color flaming in her cheeks. "What are you doing?"

The tense passion in her voice surprised him. "What do you mean?"

"Are you *letting* me win?"

He tried to keep his expression blank, but even so, when he remained silent, she shoved her chair back and stood. "How could you? I thought you respected me more than that." And without giving him time to respond, she turned and walked stiffly from the room, toward the *dawdi haus*.

Chapter 33

Phoebe sat on the edge of her bed, kneading her hands in her lap.

How could she have been so wrong about a person? She'd been certain Seth understood her.

If she'd wanted a clear sign that a match between them was not to be, then this was it. A woman like Fannie—a woman he didn't feel he had to treat like a child—would obviously be much better suited.

There was a knot in her chest, coiled so tight she thought any minute it would snap and explode. And a similar knot seemed to be stuck in her throat. And the only thing that could relieve the pressure would be a *gut* cry.

But rather than give in to the urge to curl up in a ball right here on the bed and bawl until she was wrung dry, she stood and smoothed her skirt with hands that were surprisingly steady. She had work to do. The first batch of laundry should be dry enough for her to pull from the line and fold. And then it would be time to get supper started.

Keeping busy would be a very *gut* thing right now.

Phoebe made it through the next several hours without embarrassing herself further, mostly because Seth stayed away from the house most of the afternoon.

She caught Edna staring at her at one point and got the distinct impression her friend knew just what had happened and how it had affected her.

But Edna didn't say anything so Phoebe continued her work in silence.

Just as she was hanging up her dishrag, Phoebe heard someone clearing his throat. She looked up to see Kish and Jesse standing in the kitchen doorway.

"Since you aren't going to be here for the Christmas play," Kish started, "we thought we would give you a little preview, of our parts anyway."

Phoebe clasped her hands in front of her. "That is a wonderful *gut* idea. I'd be honored to get such a preview." She allowed them to lead her into the living room, touched by their willingness to include her in all aspects of their lives.

At least Seth's *brieder* never made her feel small.

Then Kish added, "It was Seth's idea."

She shot a quick glance Seth's way. They hadn't spoken directly to each other since she'd stalked away from their chess game. He smiled back sheepishly, even as he shifted in his seat.

She nodded acknowledgment and took a seat across the room, then turned to smile at the scholars. "I'm ready whenever you are."

"I'm singing a song with four other scholars," Kish announced proudly. He took a deep breath then launched into "Oh Come, All Ye Faithful." He sang four verses before finally ending the piece.

"That was *wunderbaar*! *Danke, danke* for sharing it with me."

After Kish sat down, a wide grin on his face, Jesse stood and moved forward a few steps. "I'll be reciting some verses from the Bible." He cleared his throat, then in a solemn but somewhat shaky voice began to recite from memory the Christmas story, as told in Luke 2:1–20. As he moved further into the passage his voice steadied, grew stronger. By the time he was finished his voice rang with a quiet confidence.

Phoebe clasped her hands together. "Oh, Jesse, that was beautiful." Then she turned to include both boys in her gaze. "*Gotte* was truly honored by what the two of you boys have presented this evening and I'm sure the *familyes* who will attend the program at the schoolhouse will feel that as well."

Then she stood. "I'm going back in the kitchen to bake a big batch of brownies for you to bring for the snack table at the program tomorrow evening."

She also wanted to cook a simple casserole dish they could heat up for supper tomorrow since she wouldn't be here. That meant she'd be up late tonight but she didn't really mind. She wasn't sure she'd get much sleep after all.

* * *

Seth followed Phoebe into the kitchen. They hadn't had an opportunity to talk since their chess game had ended so disastrously and he had a feeling that she'd been deliberately avoiding him.

He'd been floored by her reaction earlier. After all, he'd only been attempting to be nice. He understood why she would be annoyed if she found him out but she'd blown it completely out of proportion. However, when he'd packed up the set to put it away, he'd caught Edna's gaze on him. And the accusation and disappointment in her expression had brought the heat to his neck.

Even so, he still wasn't sure what he'd done that was so wrong—in fact he'd been trying to do her a kindness. But regardless of his intentions, if he'd hurt her feelings, then he supposed he owed her an apology.

But he didn't apologize immediately. "Do you need any help?"

She glanced over her shoulder. "*Danke*, but I think I can manage."

Her tone, while polite, lacked the easy warmth he was used to hearing there. "Phoebe, if the way I handled our chess match today upset you, then I am very sorry."

She had her back to him, and he saw her shoulders stiffen rather than relax. He thought he heard her take a deep breath and then she turned and gave him a smile that didn't quite reach her eyes, eyes that seemed a little too moist. "*Danke* for that apology. And of course I forgive you. Please don't worry any more about it."

Then she turned and went back to work at the counter, effectively shutting him out.

Somehow, despite her words, he didn't feel forgiven.

Phoebe could feel Seth standing behind her as she stirred the brownie batter. But she never looked up and after a while she heard him leave. She supposed she should give him credit for apologizing—he had a *gut* heart for sure and for certain. But it was obvious from the way he'd worded his apology that he had no idea what he'd done and why it had upset her so much.

Which meant he didn't understand her at all.

Could she really continue to remain here knowing she had so misjudged his feelings?

She had a lot to think about before she returned to Bergamot tomorrow.

* * *

Since Tuesday was Christmas Eve there was no school or jobs to go to so breakfast was a bit more of a leisurely affair. Phoebe went all-out, cooking cinnamon pancakes with chunky berry syrup, eggs with bacon pepper jam folded in and diced potatoes with crumbled sausage and cheddar. And all the while her stomach was tied up in knots.

She hadn't managed to get much sleep the night before, which must be the reason for the dull ache at her temples.

When she set the platters on the table the offering was greeted with enthusiastic approval. This genuine appreciation was something else she was going to miss when she returned to Bergamot.

The mood around the table was easy and festive and Phoebe did her best not to dampen it. The mere fact that they didn't have any but the normal farm responsibilities for the day added to the general cheeriness. The two younger boys spoke excitedly about the Christmas program that was only hours away. Mark talked about the plans his *rumspringa* group had to go caroling at the local senior citizens' home. Levi teased her about how boring their meals would be while she was gone. Seth and Daniel discussed whether they wanted to sell some of the fir trees on their land to the *Englisch* for Christmas trees next year.

And Phoebe soaked it all in. This *familye* had given her a gift—pulling her into their fold, allowing her to spread her wings as a homemaker, trusting her to cook and care for them.

She wasn't the same person she'd been when she left home—she only hoped her *eldre* saw the change in her as one for the better.

She certainly did.

After everyone had finished with their meal for the most part, Phoebe called for their attention. "I wanted to thank all of you for welcoming me into your home these past three and a half weeks and making me feel a part of your *familye*. I have truly enjoyed getting to know each and every one of you. I wish that you all will have a very joyous Christmas."

There was a chorus of return wishes. But Seth had leaned back in his chair and his gaze searched her face as if trying to decipher a puzzle. "You said all that as if you don't plan to come back."

She fiddled with her glass. "I haven't made up my mind one way or the other yet. Edna's sling will come off in a week or so and then you won't have need of another housekeeper, ain't so? And I've been away from home for those three and a half weeks. If I did return on Friday as we'd planned, it would only be for a week, ten days at the most." She managed to meet his gaze directly. "So I'll see how much I'm needed at home before I decide anything for sure."

Seth's expression tightened but if she'd expected him to ask her to stay or to say anything at all, she was disappointed. He remained tight-lipped and focused on his milk glass.

The other Beilers, however, were not nearly as reticent. She was immediately bombarded with protests, questions and pleas, some of which threatened to break her heart.

She attempted to respond to a few of them but was secretly relieved when Seth finally instructed his *brieder* to leave her alone. She stood to carry her dishes to the sink. "One way or the other, I will call you, let's say at four on Thursday afternoon with my decision."

Her gaze snagged on Edna's. The disappointment she saw in her friend's gaze drew the heat into her cheeks. But then she lifted her chin and met her gaze head-on. She had to do what was best for her own peace of mind, whether her friend agreed with her choice or not.

By the time the table was cleared and she was ready to tackle the dishes, everyone else had left the kitchen but Edna.

There was a strained silence between them for a few minutes. When Phoebe couldn't stand it any longer, she spoke without turning around. "I truly haven't made up my mind yet, you know. I could very well decide to come back on Friday after all."

"And you could decide not to."

Phoebe didn't bother to argue that point. "I would be leaving shortly anyway."

"My arm is not yet healed."

Phoebe did turn around at that. "I'm sure one of your nieces would be happy to come help you with meals and housecleaning until your sling comes off." She wondered why that hadn't been Edna's choice in the first place.

Edna stood and moved toward the *dawdi haus*. "Perhaps. But one way or the other it will no longer be your problem." And without waiting for a response, she made her exit.

Phoebe finished cleaning the kitchen in solo misery. Why was everyone treating this as if she'd already made up her mind? She just really needed the distance her *familye's* home would provide to think through all of her confusing emotions—that was all.

Her car was scheduled to pick her up at nine o'clock so as soon as the kitchen was cleaned Phoebe went to the *dawdi haus* to gather her things.

When she stepped outside she halted on the threshold, surprise gluing her feet to the porch. All of the Beilers were there to tell her goodbye, their long faces again tearing at her heart. Seth, however, stood apart from the others, his face set in a distant, unreadable expression.

Levi glanced at his older *bruder*, then back to Phoebe. Not wearing that cocky grin for once, he stepped forward to take her bag.

"Did Seth do something to make you want to leave us?" He'd pitched his voice so only she could hear it, but that didn't mask the frustration in his voice.

Phoebe shook herself out of her paralysis and moved forward with him. She chose her words carefully. "Do you think your *bruder* could, or would, try to make me do something I didn't want to do?"

He studied her suspiciously. "Still, this came on all of a sudden. You gave no indication last night that anything was wrong."

"I have my reasons. And I never said anything was wrong, just that I wanted to give my time here some serious thought." Then she briefly touched his arm. "Please, Levi, don't press me on this."

After a moment he nodded. But she saw the look he threw Seth's way.

* * *

Seth watched the car drive away and then headed for his workshop. He had to keep busy, to do something to take his mind off of what had just happened. He'd thought she was happy here, that she might even be willing to extend her stay and help Edna even after her wrist was healed. How could he have been so blindsided?

Time to push thoughts of their fickle housekeeper aside. He'd planned to wait until after the new year to start working on chess sets again but now he felt driven to lose himself in his craft. He went to the stack of boards he used to build the gameboard and drawer, selected what he needed, then measured and cut them.

But no matter how hard he tried to focus, thoughts of Phoebe kept intruding. She'd said she hadn't made up her mind yet but he could see in her eyes that she wasn't planning to come back.

How long had he known she wouldn't be returning after Christmas? Surely she hadn't just suddenly woke up this morning and made that decision. He'd never thought of her as a coward before but the way she'd handled this seemed just that—cowardly. She was running away rather than talking to him about whatever it was that was bothering her.

Seth struck his thumb with his tack hammer. With a growl, he dropped the tool and put the injured digit in his mouth.

Levi picked that very moment to walk into his workshop.

Chapter 34

What do you want?" He glared at his *bruder*, willing him to go away.

But Levi sauntered right up to Seth's worktable and leaned a hip against it. "For someone who's so smart, you sometimes do such *naddish* things."

Seth's glare deepened. "What are you talking about?"

"You should have asked her to come back after Christmas."

He gave an exasperated huff. "You heard her at breakfast—it sounds to me as if she's already decided. I have no right to try to change her mind. And I'm certainly not going to beg."

Levi continued to press. "But do you *want* her to come back?"

"It's what we agreed to at the outset."

"That's not what I asked you."

Seth felt cornered. "*Jah*. Edna is in no shape to take on the role of housekeeper again."

Levi rolled his eyes. "You're so stubborn." Then he met

Seth's gaze again. "Whatever the reason for her leaving, do you think she has any idea how much you'd really like her to return?"

"She should." As soon as he uttered the words he wished them back—he'd all but admitted he wanted her back for more than just her housekeeping skills. And he could tell by the satisfied grin on Levi's face his *bruder* realized what he'd said.

But then he thought about Levi's question and realized he'd never really told her, he'd just assumed she knew. He rubbed the back of his neck. "Anyway, why would it even matter to her?"

"You'll never know if you don't tell her." Levi straightened and gave him a direct look. "I understand there's a phone at her place and I'm sure Edna knows the number."

And with that Levi finally sauntered out of the workroom, leaving Seth to ponder his words and their implications.

Seth went back to work but it was no use. After ruining two chess pieces he was trying to carve he gave up and decided to do some paperwork in his office.

He'd barely settled in when he looked up to see Jesse standing in the door to his office. He set his pen down and leaned back in his chair. "Can I help you with something?" He didn't want to ever again make Jesse feel he was less than any other member of this household.

Jesse moved farther into the room. "When Phoebe left she said she hadn't decided if she'd be back or not. Do you think she's coming back?"

He wished he could say *jah*. But he owed his *bruder* an honest answer. So he chose his words carefully. "That's her decision to make. I guess we'll just have to wait until she makes up her mind."

"Is she mad at us?"

Only at me. "How can you ask that? You know how much Phoebe cares about you—just look at how much she did to make your birthday special." He leaned forward. "But her *familye* and friends are in Bergamot and she was going to leave us soon anyway. So we must be prepared for whatever decision she makes."

Jesse didn't seem happy with that answer. "I wish she could stay here forever." But then he lifted his head and met Seth's gaze. "There's something else I wanted to talk to you about."

Seth waved him to a chair. "I'm listening."

"It's about Phoebe, about why she can't read."

Now the boy really had his attention. "What about her?"

"I talked to teacher Constance about why someone who seems so clever otherwise wouldn't be able to read or write."

Seth frowned. "I'm not sure it's a *gut* thing for you to be talking about Phoebe's business to someone outside the household."

Jesse shifted in his seat. "I know. But I didn't mention any names. And I told Phoebe I did it."

Constance was a perceptive woman. Whether Jesse had mentioned Phoebe's name or not the schoolteacher had likely guessed who he was talking about. But Constance was also discreet and what was done was done.

"So what did your teacher have to say?"

"She said that my friend probably has something called dyslexia. It's a condition you're born with and you can't change it, no more than you can change your eye color or your height. But it also doesn't mean a person is slow-witted. In fact, she said some very intelligent people, people who have created wonderful fine inventions or held important jobs in their communities, have had dyslexia."

"I see."

"She also said that the best way to support a person with dyslexia is to acknowledge her shortcoming but not to treat her with pity or as if she can't handle other aspects of her life."

Seth mentally winced. Is that what he'd done?

Jesse stood. "I just thought you should know."

"*Danke.*"

First Levi and then Jesse. How had they been able to see so clearly what was just now beginning to come clear to him?

* * *

Phoebe hummed as she worked at the stove, determined to focus on what she had here, not what she'd left behind in Sweetbrier Creek. It was Christmas morning and she had decided to get up extra early to cook breakfast for her *familye*.

When she'd arrived home yesterday her *eldre*, *bruder* and Rhoda had all run out to greet her—she'd obviously been missed. But it had quickly become apparent that they expected her to fall into her old familiar role as someone to be coddled.

She was determined to show them this morning just how much she'd changed.

"*Was ist das?*"

Phoebe looked over her shoulder to see her *mamm* standing in the kitchen doorway with a crinkled forehead and a confused expression on her face.

She continued tending to the eggs in the skillet where she had some of her special scramble cooking. "*Gut matin* and *Hallicher Grischtdaag.* As a Christmas gift to you I thought I'd get started with breakfast."

Her *mamm's* expression took on a slightly alarmed look and she crossed the room. "That's a sweet thought but it's not necessary, I don't mind cooking."

"Neither do I." Phoebe kept her tone light but didn't abdicate her place at the stove.

"What's that you're cooking?"

"I hope you don't mind but I'm trying a new recipe I worked on while I was at the Beilers."

"Something Edna taught you?"

"*Nee*. I discovered I like to experiment with recipes."

"Experiment?"

Poor *Mamm*, she was having trouble adjusting to her supposedly slow-witted *dochder's* newfound confidence in the kitchen. "*Jah*. I made a few mistakes along the way, but most of what I came up with made for a *gut* meal. At least the Beilers said they enjoyed them." She turned the burner off and grabbed a large platter to dish the eggs up on.

Mamm held her hand out for the cook spoon. "Here, let me do that."

But Phoebe held on. "*Danke*," she said firmly, "but I can do it. Why don't you have a seat?"

Rhoda entered the kitchen just then. "*Gut matin*." There was a wary, uncertain note in her voice as she looked from one to the other of them.

"*Gut matin*." *Mamm* hadn't moved.

"*Hallicher Grischtdaag*." Phoebe met Rhoda's gaze. "You must help me convince *Mamm* to take a seat while you and I finish preparing breakfast."

Rhoda and *Mamm* shared a glance. But before either of them could speak, Phoebe turned to Rhoda. "My biscuits never turn out as big and fluffy as yours. Would you mind baking some?"

Rhoda seemed pleased by the praise. "Of course."

The two of them worked at the counter and stove, sharing the space harmoniously. With a sigh, *Mamm* finally left them to it and instead contented herself with brewing a pot of coffee. By the time she'd finished, *Daed* was up, closely followed by Paul. Phoebe caught the surprised looks both of them sent her way but neither spoke a word to her.

Once the biscuits were in the oven, Rhoda volunteered to cook the bacon while Phoebe prepared some of the chunky berry syrup the Beilers had enjoyed.

Later, as they passed the platters around, Phoebe explained the dishes she had prepared and was careful to give Rhoda credit for the biscuits and the bacon.

At one point *Daed* leaned back and met her gaze. "You're different than you were before you left us a few weeks ago."

She lifted her chin and smiled with a measure of self-assurance. "*Jah*, I am." Would he agree that it was a positive change?

"I see confidence and maturity in you that I didn't see before."

Phoebe felt a warmth blossom in her chest. "*Danke*."

"*Jah*," *Mamm* agreed, "I see it too."

It was the best Christmas gift they could have given her.

But despite her best effort, as she worked beside *Mamm* and Rhoda to clean the kitchen, her thoughts turned to the Beilers. How had the school program gone last night? Had Seth read the Christmas story from the Bible to them yet?

They were supposed to have Christmas lunch with Hilda and her *familye*. Fannie would be there too, of course. Would Seth take her on another of those walks, just the two of them? Or perhaps Fannie's *dochder* would accompany them so they could get a feel for how it would be to be together as a *familye*.

Were she and Seth getting to know each other better like he'd said they wanted to? Would the two be engaged by the end of the week? After all, they'd both been married before and both knew what they wanted in a spouse. Determining whether or not they suited should be an easy decision for them.

When *Daed* called them together to read the Christmas story from the Bible she felt a sense of relief. This was something to remind her that she was blessed. This was a day to count one's blessings and to give praise and thanksgiving, not to pine over what she could not have.

* * *

Seth rose early Wednesday morning, determined to put on a cheerful front for his *brieder*. It was Christmas after all.

He took over the cooking, fixing scrambled eggs and some baked oatmeal. He also fixed coffee soup. Taking a cue from Phoebe he added a little grated butter and cheese to the eggs and some diced apple, honey and cinnamon to the oatmeal. It came out better than he'd expected and his first thought was to tell Phoebe. A heartbeat later he realized how foolish that was.

Was she cooking breakfast for her *familye* this morning? Were there any of those special *familye* traditions she liked to talk about that her household was celebrating today?

Then he gave his head a mental shake. He was responsible for *this* household, not hers. Time to get the food on the table.

While he took some good-natured ribbing about his food being a poor imitation of Phoebe's, everyone took generous servings and dug in with gusto. The mood around the table was a mix of excitement over it being Christmas and a sober realization that there was an empty seat between him and Levi.

After the kitchen was cleaned, they went to the living room where, as was their tradition, Seth read the Christmas story from the Bible and they had a time of quiet, prayerful contemplation.

Fifteen minutes later Seth cleared his throat. "I think it's time we exchanged gifts." He'd injected as much hearty cheeriness in his voice as he could muster. They'd pulled names so each had one gift to give and one to open. He had pulled Daniel's name and had gotten him a book on the latest techniques on growing and maintaining an orchard. Levi had pulled his name and had gotten him a board game. When Seth raised a brow at the unexpectedness of it, Levi merely grinned and said, "It's to remind you to take time for a little fun in your life, fun you can share with the rest of us."

Unaccountably touched by the gesture, Seth nodded acknowledgment. "*Danke.*"

Looking around the room at the *brieder* who were still examining their gifts, Seth noticed Edna slip from the room. Had they made her feel unwelcome somehow? Or had she had enough of their company?

She returned a short time later, however, and she was pulling a wheeled cart with some wrapped gifts inside. Their *aenti* had gotten them all presents?

She parked the cart in their midst and waited, commanding their attention without saying a word.

When the conversation had quieted she waved to the cart. "Phoebe left these here for you and asked me to pass them out on Christmas morning."

Everyone immediately sat up a little straighter and

exchanged glances. Then Edna began passing the packages out with great ceremony.

Seth watched as each of his *brieder* tore open their gifts. It turned out each contained a unique, beautifully designed origami and cut-paper piece.

Jesse had a wreath. But if you looked closely, you could see that nestled in the leaves of the wreath were six figures holding hands.

Kish had a horseshoe.

Mark had a buggy and horse.

Daniel had a tree, complete with tiny apples nestled in the branches.

He smiled when he saw Levi had a harlequin mask. That was the perfect gift for the *bruder* who rarely showed his true face to anyone.

Seth tugged at the ribbon wrapped around his gift, certain she had done something related to chess—a playing piece perhaps. But when he saw what she had created for him all he could do was stare.

It was a fish dangling from a fishing pole. She'd remembered.

It was perfect. The pole was stuck in the ground with a creel and a cluster of cattails nearby. The detail was amazing. When had she found the time to do all of these? It must have taken her hours.

And he hadn't gotten her anything.

He was a clod.

Chapter 35

The day after Christmas, Seth stood at the counter drinking his first cup of coffee of the morning. It was still dark outside but he could tell from looking out the window that it was snowing.

Edna walked in and without bothering with pleasantries moved to the table. "*Kum*, sit."

He poured a second cup and carried both to the table, setting one in front of her.

"I noticed, ever since you found out that Phoebe can't read you've been overseeing her work more closely."

Direct as usual. "Only when I thought I could be helpful."

"Even though she didn't seem to need that help before you learned of her inability to read?" Before he could respond, she continued. "Phoebe thinks you let her win that chess game on Monday. Did you?"

"*Jah*. But it was just a way to help her feel better about herself."

"Help her feel better, or help you feel better? Because Phoebe has always known who she is and what she is and isn't capable of." Edna leaned forward again. "Let me tell you something about Phoebe. As a preschooler she was a bright, outgoing, confident little girl."

Seth smiled as he got an image of Phoebe as a *kinner*.

"Then she started school and it became clear she was having trouble reading and writing. The teachers tried to work with her, to give her special attention and instruction, but nothing helped. And then people began to treat her differently. Not that anyone was deliberately cruel, mind you, they were only doing what they thought was best for her. They over-explained things to her, slowed down their play as if she couldn't keep up with others around her and gave her only simple chores and tasks to perform. In short, they treated her as if she were slow-witted. And this included her own *familye*."

Edna waved a hand. "The thing is, she was still that same bright, clever girl. But she no longer had any confidence in herself. She became confused and frustrated and tried to make up for it in other ways. She tried to pretend she was right-handed like most of her friends. And she tried to perform tasks faster and better than others to prove she was okay, only to turn clumsy and self-conscious in the process."

Is that why those little accidents she'd had in the early days of her stay had affected her so much?

"Because everyone back in Bergamot knows she can't read or write and has now pigeonholed her that way, I thought a complete change of scene might give her a chance to see if she could stand on her own in a way she was never allowed to at home."

He nodded. "I can see that."

She raised a brow. "Can you? Because as soon as you learned about her inability to read, you began to treat her differently, to treat her as if she was a *kinner* who needed guiding and looking after rather than as the independent woman you'd seen her as before. In other words, just like everyone back in Bergamot."

Seth stiffened. She was being too harsh.

"Oh, perhaps it wasn't quite that bad. She ran the household much as she had before, but you did hover over her more, check on her progress with certain tasks, go over your lists a little too thoroughly."

Had he really been that bad?

She narrowed her eyes. "And did something happen when you took her to town to do the marketing on Friday? She didn't say anything but I could tell something wasn't sitting well with her."

Seth rubbed the back of his neck. "Nothing she should have taken offense at. I did go into the grocery store with her, though, and help her check items off the list."

She raised a brow. "You just checked items off the list?"

"I may have helped grab an item or two." And corrected a few of her selections.

Edna nodded. "I thought as much. After the way she'd handled that first trip to the grocery—her first time shopping alone by the way—you couldn't trust her to take care of it on her own."

"It wasn't that I didn't trust her," he protested. "I just wanted to help."

Edna gave him a challenging look, as if she wasn't sure she believed him. Then she seemed to change the subject. "The summer Phoebe helped me and Ivan get through his illness, she played chess with him to help take his mind off what was happening. She said her *grossdaadi* had taught her the basic moves. She asked Ivan to play to win so that she could learn to be a better player. She told him it made her feel *gut* when someone forgot she was slow and challenged her."

"She's not slow."

"Of course not. But she was sixteen at the time and folks had been treating her as if she were slow most of her life—again, not to be cruel but to be what they considered helpful. She and Ivan formed a special bond over those chess games—she gave him a purpose that he sorely needed, and for that I will be forever grateful. But Ivan gave her something as well. When he learned she could do origami, he asked her to teach him. His hands were weak and shaky but she patiently worked with him. And in those last days, when he couldn't do much of anything at all, he asked her to work on her creations at his bedside because watching her relaxed him. And she went all-out, finding complex patterns and working on them nonstop."

Edna paused for a moment, then continued. "I watched her gain a measure of self-confidence that summer. It didn't last but the seed had been planted."

She stood. "I thought you should know why letting her win that game of chess affected her so strongly."

Seth remained where he was when she'd gone. Had he really treated her so differently after he learned about her challenges with reading and writing? After all, he hadn't interfered with the way she ran the household. Except that he had checked behind her on several occasions.

And perhaps he hadn't been as subtle with the shopping Friday as he thought he had. And he'd read the menu to her with the tone one would use for a little one. He saw the tension he'd sensed in her on that trip to town Friday from a different perspective. How could he have done that to her, made her feel small? No wonder she didn't want to return here.

Then he remembered Levi's words. He'd let her leave without telling her that he wanted her to come back. And more important, how he felt about her.

That was one mistake he could correct.

Chapter 36

Phoebe worked beside *Mamm* and Rhoda in the kitchen. Even though she'd been home for three days, *Mamm* hadn't quite grown accustomed to not hovering over her but she was getting better. It helped that Phoebe herself no longer retreated at the first sign of dismissal.

She'd made the decision yesterday not to return to Sweetbrier Creek. It was probably cowardly of her, but she couldn't bear the thought of having Seth prove one more time that he didn't think she could handle herself like any other adult. She also didn't relish the idea of watching him court another woman, no matter how perfect for him that other woman was.

She'd called yesterday as promised to give him her decision. To her surprise it was Edna who answered the phone. It threw her for a minute—she'd just assumed it would be Seth waiting for her call. But she recovered quickly and let Edna know of her decision. She could tell by Edna's tone that she was disappointed but to her surprise her friend didn't try to change her mind. In the end it actually felt rather anticlimactic.

She finally took herself to task. Of course Seth hadn't been the one to wait for her call. From his reaction when she'd mentioned the possibility of her not returning, his only concern would be the inconvenience of having to find another fill-in housekeeper. His mind had probably already moved on to how quickly he could marry Fannie and remove the need for a housekeeper altogether.

"There's a car coming up the drive," Rhoda said, interrupting Phoebe's gloomy thoughts. She turned to Phoebe. "I thought you'd decided not to go back to Sweetbrier Creek."

"I have. I didn't order a car."

"I don't think anyone did. It looks like there's a passenger. We have a guest coming."

Phoebe's heart leapt. Surely it couldn't be—

Rhoda and *Mamm* quickly slipped into their coats and stepped outside, ready to greet their visitor. Phoebe followed behind more slowly.

As she stepped outside she noticed *Daed* and Paul standing in the doorway of their workshop.

The car pulled to a stop and Seth stepped out holding a large brown paper bag.

His gaze went straight to her face.

For a heartbeat she couldn't speak, couldn't move, couldn't even breathe. Her eyes studied his familiar face hungrily. What was he doing here?

She finally found her tongue and stepped forward. "*Mamm*, Rhoda, this is Seth Beiler, the man whose home I managed while I was away. Seth, this is my *mamm* Verena and my *bruder's* wife Rhoda."

Then, as the men arrived, she continued the introductions.

"And this is my *daed* Joseph and *bruder* Paul." How could her voice come out so coherently when her thoughts were ping-ponging in competition with the dragonflies darting in her stomach.

After the greetings were exchanged her *daed* crossed his arms and drew himself up. "You are most welcome to our home. But may I ask why you're here?"

She wanted to hug her *daed* for asking the question she hadn't been able to form.

"I have some unfinished business that I need to discuss with Phoebe."

What did he mean by "unfinished business"? Was there something she'd left undone? Had he really come all this way on a matter of business?

Daed frowned. "Phoebe told us she's decided not to return to Sweetbrier Creek. If you've come to try to convince her otherwise—"

Seth held up his hands. "I just want to give her something that she left behind and to tell her something I forgot to say before she left."

She'd left something behind?

Mamm stepped in. "Of course. Phoebe, why don't you show Seth that new calf that was born yesterday." She turned back to Seth. "We named her Holly in honor of her being born the day after Christmas."

Phoebe just stood there a moment, her mind frantically trying to think of a way to refuse without appearing rude. It wasn't fair of him to just show up like this without giving her time to prepare. If she was alone with him right now she wasn't sure she could keep her feelings hidden.

Then she realized everyone was watching her and she forced a smile. "Of course." What else could she say?

She turned to Seth. "If you're interested, that is."

Seth gave her an encouraging smile. "I find I'm very interested."

Something about the way he was looking at her stirred up those dragonflies again. "Very well. The barn is this way." She moved forward, not waiting to see if he'd follow.

Seth fell into step beside her.

She waited for him to say something, anything to explain why he was really here. But he remained silent, matching her step for step.

Finally she broke the silence. "How are your *brieder* doing?"

"They are well. They really liked the gifts you left for us. As did I."

Her cheeks pinkened. "I'm so glad."

"But they miss having you there with us."

"I miss them, too, but it's for the best. Did you all enjoy having Christmas luncheon with Hilda and her *familye*?"

"It was *gut*. Very crowded but it's *wunderbaar* to be together for such a special day, ain't so?"

"*Jah*. And is Fannie enjoying her stay in Sweetbrier Creek?"

He cut her a probing look. "She seems to be enjoying her stay, even though we came to the mutual agreement that we won't suit."

Phoebe almost missed a step as something fluttered in her chest. "I know you must be disappointed," she said carefully. "But I'm sure you'll find the right person soon." She ached to add, *If only that could be me*.

"I think you're right. Or at least I hope so."

The cheerful way he said that was painful to hear. She'd prefer not to draw this out. "So why exactly are you here?"

Instead of answering, he handed her the bag. "This is for you."

Was this the item he'd mentioned earlier? "I don't think I left anything behind."

Seth smiled, resisting the urge to tuck that stray wisp of hair at her temple back under her *kapp*. Instead he ushered her into the barn, out of the wind. "Actually I was going to give this to you when you came back to Sweetbrier Creek but since you've decided not to return I figured I'd deliver it in person."

She gave him an uncertain look, then accepted the bag.

While she opened it he continued. "That origami piece you made for me was *wunderbaar*."

"I'm glad you liked it."

Phoebe finally got through the wrapping and lifted out her gift—a hand-carved rosewood box.

She inhaled a delighted breath. "It's beautiful." She used a finger to trace the dragonfly and cattail he'd carved on the lid, a soft smile on her lips. Then she looked up and met his gaze. "You made this?"

"I did the carving, but each of my *brieder* helped." He shrugged. "I thought perhaps you could keep the tools you use for your papercraft in it." His gaze intensified. "Just as you use your origami and scissor work to create things of incredible beauty, I wanted you to have something that in some small way reflects the beauty and spirit you brought into our lives these past few weeks."

Phoebe's eyes shimmered with some strong emotion. "*Danke*, for both the beautiful box and the beautiful words." Then she carefully set her gift on a hay bale and raised a brow. "You said there was something you wanted to tell me?"

So she wasn't ready to completely thaw toward him yet. "First, I need to apologize. I mean *really* apologize."

She crossed her arms. "So you're saying your first apology wasn't real?"

Seemed she wasn't going to make this easy. "Not in the sense that I realized what I'd done to upset you."

"And you think you understand now."

He nodded. "I told myself that by checking after you and going over the lists I'd made for you I was being helpful, that I was doing what I could to make things easier on you. And I thought I was being subtle about it. But I see now that I was being patronizing and I was ignoring your ingenuity. What you deserved was my confidence that you could carry on as you had the first week you were with us and confidence that you would ask for help if and when you needed it."

Her expression softened and she leaned against the stall gate, staring down at the calf. "And you came to this sudden realization on your own."

"I wish I could say *jah* to that. Levi told me I was a fool for letting you leave without telling you how I felt about you. Jesse told me about dyslexia and what he knew of how it works. Then Edna told me about how smothered you'd felt most of your life and how you'd just started to spread your wings in our home."

This time she met his gaze, her eyes wide. "How you felt about me?"

"Ahhh, Phoebe, don't you know? It's why I told Frannie it wouldn't work between us. I don't want a woman who is organized and predictable. I've come to understand that I want someone who's spontaneous and has the ability to surprise me. Who is stubborn enough to challenge me when she sees something amiss in how I deal with *familye* and with work. Who takes an interest in what I do, and not just for the income it provides. Someone who is observant and caring and inventive. Whose food may sometimes go wrong but is never boring, and *jah*, who is a little bit clumsy at times but that's all part of her charm."

"How important is her ability to read and write to you?"

"I'd say it's fairly low on the list. As long as she doesn't let it define her or hold her back."

Her gaze searched his face with a wariness and afraid-to-hope look that almost broke his heart because he knew he was responsible for putting them there.

"Are you sure?" Her voice was almost a whisper.

"Absolutely. I know we met less than a month ago but I feel like I've been waiting for you all my life. You've turned my life all around and upside down and I now find the idea of facing a future without you almost unbearable." He brushed the back of his hand lightly against her cheek. "I love you, Phoebe."

He saw the fire blaze to life in her eyes a heartbeat before she closed them and leaned into his touch. Then she straightened and her gaze searched his face. "Have you really thought this through? I mean, you like to make lists and I'll never be able to read them or write my own. You like to plan things out and I find myself acting as soon as an idea pops into my head. I'll never be very organized or graceful or altogether practical."

"I've never been more sure of anything—or anyone— in my life." He straightened. "But you haven't yet told me how you feel. If I've waited too long, been too much of a blind fool for you to want to have anything further to do with me, say so and I will call the car back, return home and never bother you again, no matter how much that will tear me up inside."

"Don't you dare."

He was taken aback at the unexpectedness of her response. Then he smiled as he realized her meaning.

"I was miserable at the idea of never seeing you and your *brieder* again. But I also couldn't bear to stay and have you look at me as someone who needs to be constantly monitored and who you have to let win a game of chess like you would a little child just learning the basics."

"I am so sorry I made you feel that way. And I would like to spend a lifetime making it up to you. If you'll have me."

Phoebe felt the joy burst inside of her and overflow, coloring the world. He knew all her secrets, all her faults, and he loved her anyway. Was there ever a woman more blessed than her?

"*Jah*, oh Seth, with all my heart *jah*! I love you, Seth Beiler, and it would make me so wonderful happy to be your *fraa*."

He smiled at that. "Even though I don't deserve it, I promise that you will for sure and for certain never have cause to regret giving me this second chance to prove how much I love and trust you."

"Even through all your misguided attempts to 'help' me, you managed to make me feel accepted and needed. You truly listened to my ideas and when you found merit in them you weren't too proud to admit it. You trusted me to run your household in the way that made sense to me, and you put up with my food experiments without complaint. I have never felt more of an equal partner in my life than I have with you."

Seth reached out, his hand gently cupping her cheek, his touch both warm and reassuring. "You've given me hope, Phoebe. Hope for a future I never even knew I wanted— one filled with love, laughter and shared dreams."

Phoebe's breath caught in her throat at the vulnerability

and tenderness in his eyes, and her gaze never wavered from his. "You've shown me that true strength comes not just from being independent, but from allowing others to share in our journey."

With a gentle touch, he pulled her to him, sealing their unspoken promises with a kiss in a commitment to face whatever challenges life may bring, hand in hand.

Epilogue

Two Months Later

Phoebe watched as Seth studied the chessboard between them. They'd been married almost a month now and she still hadn't tired of watching him when he was tackling a problem like he was now—how his rugged features furrowed in concentration, how his denim-blue eyes focused on the board as he leaned forward, and how he absently stroked his thick beard. Every aspect of this man had become etched in her heart.

As if aware of her gaze, he glanced up and caught her staring. A smile tugged at his lips. "Are you growing impatient?"

His grin was infectious but she raised a brow in challenge. "*Nee*, but you do seem to be spending quite a bit of time deciding on your next move. Have your strategies abandoned you?"

He gave her a mock-frown. "Don't think you can distract me with your sweet smiles and challenging tone. I'm still convinced that's what happened yesterday."

The memory of yesterday's victory, her first in their daily chess matches, still gave her a little spurt of pleasure. "I won that game fair and square—if you were distracted it wasn't due to any intent on my part."

His expression softened and he reached across the table to squeeze her hand. "I was only teasing, not trying to take away from your well-deserved win. And don't you know, even when you're not trying, I find you irresistibly beguiling?"

She felt the heat rise in her cheeks but she couldn't resist the urge to roll her eyes. "Now who's trying to distract whom?"

Levi stepped into the kitchen just then and gave them a knowing look when he spotted their joined hands.

Phoebe started to draw her hand away but Seth's reassuring squeeze kept it firmly in place.

"Don't mind me," Levi said, his amusement obvious. "I just thought I'd grab an apple to snack on."

"Did I hear someone mention snacks?" Kish wandered in from the mudroom. It was Saturday so most of the Beilers, with the exception of Mark, were home today.

"We were talking fruit, not cookies," Phoebe answered quickly and smiled at the way his nose immediately wrinkled at that. "But in another hour or so there just might be a pan of warm chocolate chip cookies making an appearance."

Kish's expression immediately brightened.

"You're spoiling them," Seth said drily.

"Them?" She raised a brow. "I seem to recall you sneaking a handful of the last batch I made."

Seth laughed, loving this playful side of his new *fraa*, the way she loved to banter, how she could confidently give as *gut* as she got and how the gold flecks in her coffee-brown eyes sparkled with life when she was happy.

And he wasn't the only one whose life was richer for having her here. Their household had transformed since her arrival. Laughter and love flowed through its corridors, bringing with them a renewed sense of warmth and joy that hadn't been felt since his *mamm's* passing. He saw it in his *brieder's* faces too—the vibrant energy that emanated from Phoebe had been infectious.

And Phoebe had changed and enriched Edna's life as well.

Edna's sling had long since been discarded. But Phoebe, with Seth's blessing, had convinced her to stay on and make the *dawdi haus* her permanent home. Because Edna had such an independent spirit, it had taken a little bit of discussion, but in the end Edna had agreed. It had helped that most of her *familye* resided in Sweetbrier Creek. So now she lived here not as a housekeeper but as a member of the *familye* and that, too, had multiplied the love under this roof.

Jesse stepped inside just then, followed closely by Daniel. "We just set up the badminton net. Who all wants to come play?"

So much for their quiet game of chess. Seth met Phoebe's gaze and saw from the smile teasing her lips she was thinking the same thing. She stood and turned to Jesse. "We're in. Lead the way."

He stood as well and fell into step beside her. As they made their way to the buggy shed he cut her a sideways glance. "I hope you don't mind that we didn't finish our chess match."

"*Nee*. Chess is a game for two and we'll have many more opportunities to play matches in the future. It's important that we balance those times with the times when we can all be together as a *familye*, ain't so?" Then she grinned. "Besides, I'm a very *gut* badminton player."

Seth shook his head in mock-disapproval but gave her hand another squeeze, thinking again how truly blessed he was. Closing himself off from a love like this hadn't been the protection he thought it was, it had been a prison. And his sweet, brave, fierce Phoebe had held the key to set him free.

Phoebe inhaled deeply of the cool, crisp air. Winter hadn't quite released its grasp on the farm yet but there were subtle signs that spring was readying for an appearance. And she couldn't wait to see this place—her home now—in springtime. There were so many new experiences awaiting her that she looked forward to sharing with Seth.

Not that she intended to give up the old comfortable experiences. For one thing, their daily chess matches were too special, too important to her.

But the most important game she had ever played was the one that she and Seth had navigated their way through to get them to where they understood and trusted each other enough to let love in. And in doing so, she had found her perfect match.

About the Author

WINNIE GRIGGS is the multi-published, award-winning author of romances that focus on small towns, big hearts, and amazing grace. Her work has won a number of regional and national awards, including the Romantic Times Reviewers' Choice Award. Winnie grew up in southeast Louisiana in an undeveloped area her friends thought of as the back of beyond. Eventually she found her own Prince Charming, and together they built a storybook happily-ever-after, one that includes four now-grown children who are all happily pursuing adventures of their own.

When not busy writing, she enjoys cooking, browsing estate sales, and solving puzzles. She is also a list maker, a lover of exotic teas, and holds an advanced degree in the art of procrastination.

You can learn more at:
WinnieGriggs.com
X @GriggsWinnie
Facebook.com/WinnieGriggs.Author
Pinterest.com/WDGriggs

Book your next trip to a charming small town—and fall in love—with one of these swoony Forever contemporary romances!

THE SOULMATE PROJECT
by Reese Ryan

Emerie Roberts is tired of waiting for her best friend, Nick, to notice her. When she confesses her feelings at the town's annual New Year's Eve bonfire and he doesn't feel the same, she resolves to stop pining for him and move on. She hatches a seven-step plan to meet her love match and enlists her family and friends—including Nick—to help. So why does he seem hell-bent on sabotaging all her efforts?

HOME ON HOLLYHOCK LANE
by Heather McGovern

Though Dustin Long has been searching for a sense of home since childhood, that's not why he bought Hollyhock. He plans to flip the old miner's cottage and use the money to launch his construction business. And while every reno project comes with unexpected developments, CeCe Shipley beats them all—she's as headstrong as she is gorgeous. But as they collaborate to restore the cottage to its former glory, he realizes they're also building something new together. Could CeCe be the home Dustin's always wanted?

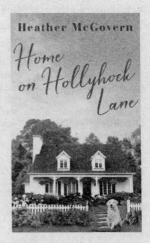

Connect with us at Facebook.com/ReadForeverPub

Discover bonus content and more on
read-forever.com

REUNION IN SUGAR LAKE
by **Marina Adair**

Pediatrician Charlotte Holden knows better than anyone that love leads only to heartbreak. Then sexy Jace McGraw blows back into her small town of Sugar, Georgia, and utters those three words every woman dreads: *We're still married*. The annulment went through years ago— or so she thought. But now Jace offers Charlotte a deal: He'll grant a discreet divorce in exchange for thirty days and nights of marriage. Easy as peach pie. Except this time, he isn't going to let her go without a fight.

FLIRTING WITH ALASKA
by Belle Calhoune

Caleb Stone isn't ready to give up his Hollywood dreams. But after a disastrous run on a reality dating show paints him as an unapologetic player, Caleb needs a little time and space to regroup. Luckily, his hometown of Moose Falls, Alaska, has both, plus a job helping his brothers run Yukon Cider. Even dialed down, Caleb's flirtatious vibes are a hit at work, except for one woman who seems completely, totally, frustratingly immune to his charms—the gorgeous new photographer for Yukon Cider's upcoming ad campaign.

Meet your next favorite book with @ReadForeverPub on TikTok

SUNFLOWER COTTAGE ON HEART LAKE
by Sarah Robinson

Interior designer Amanda Riverswood is thirty-two years old and has never had a boyfriend. So this summer, she's going on a bunch of blind dates. Pro baseball pitcher Dominic Gage was on top of the world—until an injury sent him into retirement. Now, in the small town of Heart Lake, his plan is to sit on his dock not talking to anyone, especially not the cute girl next door. But when they begin to bond over late-night laughter about Amanda's failed dating attempts, will they see that there's more than friendship between them?

SNOWED IN FOR CHRISTMAS
by Jaqueline Snowe

Sorority mom Becca Fairfield has everything she needs to survive the blizzard: hot cocoa, plenty of books…and the memory of a steamy kiss. Only Becca's seriously underestimated this snow-pocalypse. So when Harrison Cooper—next-door neighbor, football coach, and the guy who acted mega-awkward after said kiss—offers her shelter, it only makes sense to accept. They'll just hang out, stay safe, and maybe indulge in a little R-rated cuddling. But are they keeping warm…or playing with fire?

AN AMISH CHRISTMAS MATCH
by Winnie Griggs

Phoebe Kropf knows everyone thinks she's accident-prone rather than an independent Amish woman. So she's determined to prove she's more than her shortcomings when she's asked to provide temporary Christmas help in nearby Sweetbrier Creek. Widower Seth Beiler is in over his head caring for his five motherless *brieder*. But he wasn't expecting a new housekeeper as unconventional—or lovely—as Phoebe. When the holiday season is at an end, will Seth convince her to stay…as part of their *familye*?

CHRISTMAS IN HARMONY HARBOR
by Debbie Mason

Instead of wrapping presents and decking the halls, Evangeline Christmas is worrying about saving her year-round holiday shop from powerful real estate developer Caine Elliot. She's risking everything on an unusual proposition she hopes the wickedly handsome CEO can't refuse. How hard can it be to fulfill three wishes from the Angel Tree in Evie's shop? Caine's certain he'll win and the property will be his by Christmas Eve. But a secret from Caine's childhood is about to threaten their merrily-ever-after.